MAYHEM IN MONTREAL

MAYHEM IN MONTREAL
CASE FILES OF AN URBAN DRUID™ BOOK 1

AUBURN TEMPEST
MICHAEL ANDERLE

This book is a work of fiction. All of the characters, organizations, and events portrayed in this novel are either products of the author's imagination or are used fictitiously. Sometimes both.

Copyright © 2022 LMBPN Publishing
Cover by Fantasy Book Design
Cover copyright © LMBPN Publishing
A Michael Anderle Production

LMBPN Publishing supports the right to free expression and the value of copyright. The purpose of copyright is to encourage writers and artists to produce the creative works that enrich our culture.

The distribution of this book without permission is a theft of the author's intellectual property. If you would like permission to use material from the book (other than for review purposes), please contact support@lmbpn.com. Thank you for your support of the author's rights.

LMBPN Publishing
PMB 196, 2540 South Maryland Pkwy
Las Vegas, NV 89109

Version 1.03, August 2022
eBook ISBN: 979-8-88541-174-5
Print ISBN: 979-8-88541-702-0

THE MAYHEM IN MONTREAL TEAM

Thanks to our Beta Readers:

John Ashmore, Kelly O'Donnell, Rachel Beckford, Jim Caplan, Angela Wood

Thanks to our JIT Team:

Dorothy Lloyd
Diane L. Smith
Deb Mader
Christopher Gilliard
Micky Cocker
Dave Hicks

Editor
SkyFyre Editing Team

AUTHOR NOTE

Welcome to *Mayhem in Montréal,* book one of the Case Files of the Urban Druid, and the second series following the life of Fiona Cumhaill. Michael and I set this book up as an entry point for new readers, but because there are fifteen books prior to this one, some characters, situations, and references might seem confusing.

If you'd like to start at the beginning and grow with Fi as she learns about being a druid, you want *A Gilded Cage,* book one of the Chronicles of an Urban Druid.

If you're game to jump in with both feet, stick with me and I'll try to catch you up as quickly as I can.

Either way,

Happy reading,
Auburn Tempest

THE USUAL SUSPECTS

Clan Cumhaill

Aiden – the oldest of Fi's brothers, druid tank, Toronto police officer, married to Kinu, and father of Jackson, Meg, Ireland, and Carragh

Brendan – Fi's brother, second in the birth order, formerly deceased, given back to the family after the Culling and restricted to living on the mythical Celtic island Emhain Abhlach with Emmet

Bodhmall – Fionn's paternal aunt who raised him and taught him how to be a druid

Calum – Fi's brother, third in the birth order, druid archer, Toronto police officer, and married to Kevin. Together they are foster parents to Bizzy, an otterkie shifter.

Dillan – Fi's brother, fourth in the birth order, druid rogue, Toronto police officer, and in love with Evangeline, Angel of the Choir, formerly a reaper and now a guardian angel

Dionysus – God of Wine and Fertility, Light Weaver, Hunter God, guardian of the mythical Celtic island Emhain Abhlach, and honorary Cumhaill

Emmet – Fi's brother, fifth in the birth order, druid buffer, guardian and committed caretaker of the mythical Celtic island Emhain Abhlach

Fiona – youngest of the six Cumhaill kids, chosen by Fionn to represent the Fianna warriors in a new generation of urban druids, Hunter God, Celtic shaman, guardian of the mythical Celtic island Emhain Abhlach, bonded companion to Bruin and Dart

Fionn a.k.a. Finn MacCool – Hunter God, mythical warrior in Irish mythology, guardian of the mythical Celtic island Emhain Abhlach, ancestor of and mentor to Fi and her family

Kevin – artist, high school sweetheart, and husband to Calum

Lara – Fi's grandmother, nature druid, and the Snow White of the Druid Order

Liam – one of Fi's best friends, now her stepbrother, operator/bartender for Shenanigans

Lugh – Fi's grandfather, druid historian, Keeper of the Shrine, and Elder of the Druid Order

Niall – Fi's father, retired Toronto police officer, married to Shannon and living in Ireland with his parents

Nikon Tsambikos – ancient Greek immortal, Light Weaver, guardian of the mythical Celtic island Emhain Abhlach, and honorary Cumhaill

Shannon – mother of Liam, became the pseudo mother to the Cumhaill kids after her husband and their mother died when they were young. Her husband Mark was Niall's partner and died in the line of duty

Sloan Mackenzie – Fi's soulmate, druid healer, Keeper of the Toronto Shrine, and guardian of the mythical Celtic island Emhain Abhlach

Wallace Mackenzie – Sloan's father, Master Druid Healer, and Elder of the Druid Order, recently separated from Sloan's mother, Janet Mackenzie

Animal Companions

Aurora – Tad's red-tailed kite

Bruinior the Brave (Bruin) a.k.a. Killer Clawbearer – Fiona's mythical battle bear and Bear of native myth and legend

Daisy – Calum's epileptic skunk companion

Dartamont (Dart) – Fiona's Western dragon, involved with Saxa, and oldest brother to twenty-two other dragons

Dax – Lara's badger

Doc Marten (Doc) – Emmet's pine marten followed him home from the Santa Claus Parade

Nyrora (Rory) – Dillan's Koinonos Dragon. Dark purple with gold webbing for her wings, she bonds with him at rest, creating a living tattoo on his skin.

More Greeks

Andromeda Tsambikos – Nikon's younger sister, ancient Greek immortal, Light Weaver, guardian of the mythical Celtic island Emhain Abhlach, and legal counsel for SITFO

Nikon Tsambikos Senior – Nikon's grandfather, ancient Greek immortal, Light Weaver, and guardian of the mythical Celtic island Emhain Abhlach

Politimi Tsambikos – Nikon's younger sister and ancient Greek immortal

The Moon Called

Anyx – lion shifter, Garnet's beta, and mate to Zuzanna

Garnet Grant – lion shifter, Alpha of the Toronto Moon Called, Grand Governor of the Lakeshore Guild of Empowered Ones, Fi's friend, mentor, and boss at SITFO, mated to Myra and father of adopted bear shifter Imari

Myra – ash nymph, Fae Historian, mated to Garnet, owner/operator of Myra's Mystical Emporium, mother of adopted bear shifter Imari.

Thaos – lion shifter, one of Garnet's valued pack enforcers, third in the pack hierarchy

Zuzanna – lion shifter, mate to Anyx, works with SITFO as a member of the Toronto Special Investigations Unit

The Vampires
Benjamin – vampire, companion to Laurel
Xavier – vampire, King of the Toronto Seethes

The Nine Families of the Druid Order
Lugh and Lara Cumhaill – parents of Niall, grandparents of Aiden, Brendan, Calum, Dillan, Emmet, and Fiona

James and Caitrona Dempsey – parents of Brian and Reagan

Evan and Iris Doyle – parents of Ciara

Connor and Kate Flannigan – parents of Erik

Wallace Mackenzie – father of Sloan, ex-husband to Janet

Tad McNiff – recently took his place as a Head of the Nine Families after his father, Riordan, gave himself over to Mingin in a quest for ultimate power

Finley and Elaine O'Malley – parents of Lia

Brian and Gwyneth Perry – parents of Jarrod, Darcy, and Davin

Sean and Maude Scott – parents of Seamus

Friends
Laurel – ghost, companion to Benjamin, Fi's high school friend

Merlin/Pan Dora/ Emrys – druid and wizard of legend, owner of Queens on Queen drag club and the attached soup kitchen, union bonded to the champagne-colored Western dragon, Empress Cazzienth

Patty – Man o' Green, union bonded to Cyteira the Queen of Wyrms, a.k.a. the Wyrm Dragon Queen

Suede Silverbirch – elven representative on Toronto's Lakeshore Guild of Empowered Ones

Zxata – ash nymph, Myra's brother, nymph representative on Toronto's Lakeshore Guild of Empowered Ones

More Hunter Gods

Ahren – Hunter God, shaman, navigates the hunter plane as a golden eagle

Samuel – Hunter God, shaman, navigates the astral plane as an ebony wolf

Quon Shen – Hunter God, shaman, navigates the astral plane as a water dragon

Team Trouble

Brody – wolf shifter/vampire hybrid, new member-in-training for Team Trouble

Dantanion Jann, Dan the djinn, member of Team Trouble

Diesel Demarco – goliath, new member-in-training for Team Trouble

Jenna – siren, new member-in-training for Team Trouble

John Maxwell – Deputy Commissioner of the Royal Canadian Mounted Police, founder of SITFO, the Special Investigations Task Force for Ontario

Iceland Dragons – Free Dragons of Tintagel

Bryvanay – black, majestic, and slightly smaller than Utiss

Cazzienth, Empress of the West (Cazzie) – glistening champagne-colored dragon with gold and burnt orange wings and a strong tail that ends in a treacherous-looking ball-spike

Saxa – a sunshine yellow dragon with dark gold wings and a blunt snout of the same color

Utiss – a massive purple dragon and the dominant male of the Free Dragons of Tintagel

Ireland Dragons

Drakes: Chua

Westerns: Abeloth, Cadmus, Chezzo, Dart, Esym, Kaida, Scarlett, Torrim

Wyrms: Scarlett, +6 we haven't met

Wyverns: 7 we haven't met

Pronunciations

Adelphos – *adelfos* – Greek for "brother" or "my brother"

Cumhaill – *Cool* – Fiona and the family's last name (modern)

mac Cumhaill – *MacCool* – Fiona and the family's last name (traditional)

Mo chroi – *muh chree* – Irish for my heart/my love

Slan! – *slawn* – health be with you

Slainte mhath – *slawn cha va* – cheers, good health

Irish Terms

Arragh – a guttural sound for when something bad happened

Banjaxed – broken, ruined, completely obliterated

Bogger – those who live in the boggy countryside

Bollocks – a man's testicles

Bollix – thrown into disorder, bungled, messed up

Boyo – boy, lad

Cock-crow – close enough that you can hear a cock crow

Craic – gossip, fun, entertainment

Culchie – those who live in the agricultural countryside

Donkey's years – a long time

Dosser – a layabout, lazy person

Eejit – slightly less severe than idiot

Fair whack away – far away

Feck – an exclamation less severe than fuck

Flute – a man's penis

Gammie – injured, not working properly

Hape – a heap

Howeyah/Howaya/Howya – a greeting not necessarily requiring an answer.

Irish – traditional Irish language (Commonly referred to as Irish Gaelic unless you're Irish.)

Knackers – a man's testicles

Mocker – a hex

Och – used to express agreement or disagreement to something said

Shite – less offensive than shit

Gobshite – fool, acting in unwanted behavior

Wee – small

CHAPTER ONE

"Holy crapballs, look at all these people." I stand on the wooden stage usually reserved for live bands on Saturday nights and although I've been in front of audiences at Shenanigans too many times to count, tonight is different.

Sadly, I'm not drunk.

Looking out at the two hundred frustrated Toronto citizens crammed into our family pub, I wish I was.

I wish the world craziness we've been living for three months, two weeks, and four days was all the manifestation of a drunken haze brought on by poor self-control and Redbreast Whiskey.

I wish the Time of the Colliding Realms hadn't changed the world's normal state, and the veil between realms hadn't collapsed.

I wish people could learn to see past tails, horns, and green skin and value a person based on their actions and character without judgment.

Just play nice, people.

Wishes won't turn back time, and Dionysus isn't allowed to fix it, so here we are.

All the wacked and weird previously hidden behind the Faery Glass is now on public display.

Well, not *all* of it.

Teams of empowered folks around the world have agreed to contain the mystery of at least some of the dark and dangerous lurking in the shadows.

Governing bodies and legal authorities have received most of the information but collectively decided the public sector is better off without full disclosure.

In the report Maxwell and I presented to the emergency response committee, we focused on magical creatures like brownies, familiars, and Ostara rabbits. They are cute, with big globe eyes and antennae, and have fur and pretty wings.

People can wrap their heads around that. They can imagine these magical creatures like a weird cat or a mischievous child and not lose their shit.

It's familiar to them and less scary.

We acknowledged the existence of shifters, nixies, pixies, elves, nymphs, and the more benign sects but opted not to mention the species and creatures like djinn, vampires, yeti, and dragons.

We confessed that witches, wizards, and druids are real and can manipulate magic. We left out the part about blood sacrifices, summoning demons, and deciding the alignment of humanity in battles of dark versus light.

The empowered world is best digested in small bites to avoid choking.

No one wants to Heimlich eight billion people.

Who has the time?

After thriving in secrecy for millennia, Pandora's box is open, and the magical black cat is out of the bag with no hope of stuffing the bastard back in.

This is the new world.

Smiling out over the dancefloor, the booths, and the tables beyond, I grip the side of the podium and get this party started. "Hello everyone, I'm Fiona mac Cumhaill, descendant of Fionn mac Cumhaill and the recently appointed fae liaison for Toronto."

"You rock, Fi," Liam shouts from the bar.

I chuckle and wave at my bestie. "Thanks, dude, and thanks again for letting us invade the pub to host our April town hall meeting."

"Pull together and rise above," he says.

"Pull together and rise above," the crowd repeats.

That mantra has gained strength in the past weeks, and I'm so thankful. Extreme situations bring out extreme reactions.

When we're lucky, they are positive.

"Absolutely." I draw a deep breath, the blissful aroma of pub fare and ale calming my nerves. "I welcome you all to one of my favorite places on Earth. Some of you I've met at the past few meetings and some of you are joining us for the first time. Wherever you fit in, I'm glad you're here, and I'll try to answer your questions. First, let's make sure we're all on the same page."

The hopeful gazes reaching up to me from the crowd make my heart ache for them.

"During the Winter Solstice three months ago, a struggle among the empowered sects resulted in the magical screen between realms no longer dividing the human and fae worlds."

I check that everyone is with me, and it seems they are. By now, I'm sure everyone on the planet knows this and is sick of hearing about it.

"The important thing to remember is that it's just the magical screen that fell, not the barrier between worlds. We're not getting invaded by fae monsters or anything like that. For now, it's only prana—the raw magical power of the fae—which is leaking into our world."

"For now?" someone asks.

I shrug. "I'd be lying to you if I said there won't be creatures who cross over into our world. It's early days, and there is no way to know what will happen in the coming months and years."

"Can we put the screen back up?" a woman asks.

"We're trying to figure that out. The best magical minds are working on it. We're hoping, in time, we'll be able to raise the veil again."

"But you don't know?" a man asks.

"No. We're still assessing what is possible. If we can get it up, we will. If not fully maybe partially, or maybe this is our new normal, and we'll have to adapt."

Laughter roars in my mind, and I glance at where Nikon is busting a gut at the side of the stage. *You realize you just told two hundred people if we can't get it up, we're hoping for a partial, right?*

I roll my eyes at the Greek, but it's not just him.

Dionysus and my brothers are snickering too.

Behave. A little maturity in the peanut gallery would be appreciated.

"So, you really don't know anything," a man shouts from the gathering. Frustration hangs thick in the speaker's voice. I don't blame him.

It's frustrating for all of us.

"There are no absolutes right now, no. This is an unprecedented event, and we're trying our best just like everyone else."

"What about the awakenings?" A girl leaning an elbow on the bar asks. "Will they stop?"

Great question. I wish I knew.

With the veil down, the active power of ley lines, fae prana, and source magic have gone haywire. Merlin figures it has amped the ambient energy surrounding us close to eight thousand percent.

As hard as it is for my mental hamster to grab the flailing reins on that, there's no denying it.

The times, they are a-changin'.

People who thought themselves wholly human for their entire lives are finding out they have latent fae DNA that is no longer latent. The sudden triggering of fae traits is causing panic and civil and social unrest.

These "awakenings" are coming fast and furious.

According to Merlin's predictions, if we don't get the veil back up or figure out a way to damper the effect of losing it, there could be as many as one in a hundred affected within a year.

In Toronto, a city with a population of just under three million, that's thirty-thousand people.

That's a huge community for us to police.

"We've got some incredibly gifted empowered folks working on this. Whether or not we successfully restore the veil to its original state, the flood of awakenings will eventually slow."

"When? Once our family and friends all have wings and scales and have turned into freaks?"

I peg the guy that said that with a serious warning look. "The fae aren't freaks—that's your fear and frustration showing. The fae are simply a species of being that possess different physical traits and magical abilities than non-magical humans. We're not here to judge. We're here to become informed so we can dispel fear and build new relationships moving forward."

The guy looks genuinely distraught, but he isn't the only person in the room thinking like that.

"Look, the neighbor you've been shooting the shit with on the driveway for the past eight years isn't a different person if he or she woke up with golden eyes or blue skin. The little girl who plays with your kids at the park isn't a monster because when she gets scared, she shifts into a wolf pup. This is just as scary and unsettling for them. Compassion is the key."

"It's unnatural!" a heckler shouts at the back. "It defies the laws of nature. It's evil!"

I raise my hand to stop the rush of comments. "That kind of

talk is both wrong and counterproductive. My magic comes directly from Mother Nature. There is nothing evil about the goddess of creation."

To prove my point, I hold my palms toward the room and give a little push. Each of the tables is set with a single cut daisy, carnation, or rose. With my intention clear and my connection to nature, I give each centerpiece a boost.

The flowers bloom bigger and brighter.

When I finish, I wait a moment to give people a moment to adjust.

"Magic isn't evil. Evil is evil. That doesn't change no matter how unfamiliar something is to you. The gifts people possess are just that—gifts."

"Says the redhead devil," the heckler shouts. "She's luring you into her web. Don't you see that? Evil comes in many forms."

Uh-huh, there's one in every crowd. "Sir, either open your mind and shut your mouth or leave. Don't let the door hit you on the way out, or even better, let it crack you a good one in the ass."

I wait for the beat it takes for him to get the picture and thankfully, he opts to leave.

When the stained-glass double doors bump shut, I draw a steadying breath and swing my hand across the bar. *"Cleansing Breeze."*

My gentle stirring of the air is like the breath of spring freshening the atmosphere. "Continuing without toxic judgment polluting the room, who else has a question? Ask me anything."

"Will you marry me?" someone yells from the back.

I chuckle. "A proposal from the shadows. Tempting but I must decline. My heart is very taken. Besides, loving me is more trouble than you can imagine."

I gaze at Sloan, and it strikes me—"Oh, I should introduce a few of my family and friends. If your question doesn't get asked or answered while I'm up here, feel free to approach any one of us tonight and we'll try to get you sorted out."

I gesture at my posse standing against the back wall to the right of the stage. "First off, my partner in life and love, Sloan Mackenzie." I point at my guy.

Sloan's got six inches on me, warm brown skin, stunning pale green eyes, and dresses like he came from a photo shoot for *GQ* magazine.

"Sloan is an advanced druid and a scholar. He also has a knack for making me look good. If your question is complicated, convoluted, or perplexing, he's your man."

Sloan chuckles. "Thanks a lot."

"My pleasure, hotness." Next, I gesture at my brothers chuckling in the wings. "You can tell who is from Clan Cumhaill easily enough. These are three of my five brothers. This is Aiden, Dillan, and Calum."

They each raise their hand in turn.

"Each of them is both a druid and a Metro Police Officer, so if you have legal questions or concerns relating to issues on that side of things, they're your guys."

Next, I move to point out the Greeks. "The distinguished gentlemen with the Mediterranean complexions and the sultry smiles are our beloved Greeks. Nikon is the blond and Dionysus is the brunette. They have both lived centuries filled with unique and varied experiences. They are here to help, and I'm sure you'll love them as much as I do."

Turning in the other direction, I find Garnet leaning against the half-wall of the server's station. "Last but certainly not least, the imposing man with the dark hair and even darker scowl is Garnet Grant. He's the boss of the Toronto empowered world and the one you'll find on your doorstep if you color outside the lines."

Garnet arches a disapproving brow, and I grin. It was his idea to make me a liaison.

I gotta be me.

"So, with the introductions out of the way let's get back to questions. If your question is too personal for an open forum and I don't get to you tonight, Liam always has my cards at the bar. Feel free to contact me."

"You look tired, baby girl," Dillan says two hours later. I tip back my tumbler and set the empty glass on the bar. "Why don't you call it a night and have Sloan take you home to bed? Calum and I can stay with the Greeks to ensure everyone gets a chance to ask their question."

I shake that one off and lean sideways to bump shoulders with my brother. "No. If I'm the ambassador to the people, I won't pass the buck for a few extra hours of sleep."

Dillan gives me a sidelong gaze. "I said have Sloan take you home to bed. No one said you had to sleep. Geez, Fi, should I be worried? Are the flames of passion dying? Do I need to have a man-to-man with Irish?"

"Get lost. Why don't you go harass Calum or Aiden about their sex lives?"

He snorts. "Calum is a newlywed and a sex machine, and Aiden has four kids. They've got the Cumhaill mojo flowing. It's you I'm worried about."

"My mojo is just fine, thank you. Now go." Pushing my middle brother away, I chuckle and nod at a woman reluctant to approach.

She has glasses, a kind smile, and is clutching her purse across her front like it's a lifeline.

"Hi, I'm Fiona. Do you have a question for me?"

"I'm Becca, and I did. Or rather, I do." The woman is a quiet talker and anxious.

We're at the front of the bar, so I point toward the door. "Do you want to step outside where it's quieter?"

"Yes, thanks. That sounds good."

I press my finger and thumb under my tongue and let out a shrill whistle. My troop knows the pitch well enough to recognize it as me calling their attention.

When heads turn, I point at the door and flash them five fingers and a thumbs-up.

It's universal sign language for going outside for five minutes. S'all good.

My guys nod from different places in the pub and return to their conversations. "Sorry. They worry. I have a bad habit of getting misplaced by the universe. It's a full-time commitment for them to keep track of me at times."

She follows me out and glances around.

I do the same to ensure there's not someone stalking her or anything.

It's Saturday night in downtown Toronto, so the sidewalks are busy, and there's lots of street traffic. Nothing out of the ordinary triggers my Spidey-senses.

Well, nothing in the dark and dangerous column.

It's impossible for me to be outside and not have a dozen things amp me up. First, there's the way the ambient energy of the city pulses all around us. The veil dropping turned up the power dial of life and now the air prickles at my skin like tiny electric shocks.

It doesn't quite hurt, but it makes me itch.

Then there's the way the air has a pale pink hue and smells like cherry Coke. That's cool, but it's weird when breathing makes you salivate.

The growth of animals is weird too. Toronto now has pigeons the size of roosters and rats the size of pugs. Those I can deal with but don't even get me started on the size of cockroaches and house centipedes.

Nature's wild overgrowth is like we've been cast in a reboot of *Jurassic Park: Life with Prana Powerboost*.

Not that everyone is so affected.

The empowered folks and the awakened are suffering the brunt of the changes. From what we've learned, the more powerful the person, the more sensitive they are to the changes. The non-magical citizens don't notice the air or the tingling.

I gesture beside the door in front of the pub window. A half-dozen lights shine down on the green and gold Shenanigans sign, so we can stand in the pool of light. "So, what can I help you with, Becca?"

"I...uh, I know this is going to sound trivial next to the problems of the world, but I need help, and you said no problem is too big or too small."

"I meant it. What do you need?"

"It's my cat, Tigger. I was wondering...can animals have an awakening because...well, Tigger hasn't been herself the past couple of days."

I pause for a moment, not sure how to answer that. With animals, it's not so much an awakening as a mutation. Except for a few very bizarre cases of animals levitating and spelling their owners, the fur and feathered mammals have been affected by the rapid growth of the prana surge more than having powers unlocked.

But, from what we learned over the past months, people don't like the word 'mutation' associated with their pets.

Look at me thinking before I speak.

Amazeballs.

I meet Becca's concerned gaze and try to offer her reassurance. "In some cases, animals have been greatly affected by the surge in fae power. What happened to Tigger to make you think she's had an awakening?"

"Could you come and see? She's grown rather aggressive, and I can't coax her down from the tree in our complex. My neighbors are understandably upset, but they're threatening terrible things if I don't get her under control."

Sloan and Dillan come out to check on us, and I catch them up to speed.

"Sure, why not?" Dillan pulls out his phone. "I'll let the others know we have a quick errand and we'll be back."

"Thank you so much," Becca says. "Tigger is normally such a good girl. It's all been such an upset."

"Agreed. It absolutely has."

Becca gives us her address. It's not far from a Thai restaurant Sloan and I go to all the time. He *poofs* us there, and we walk the block to her townhouse complex.

Her keys jingle as we approach the locked gate, and we gain access to the shared courtyard at the back of two rows of townhouses.

"This is a nice space." I take in the long strip of green grass with a treed area, gazebo, and backyard barbeque patio.

"Yes, we like it. The thing is there are rules to keep it in good order. Cats and small dogs are allowed, but we're all responsible for our pets."

"That's understandable," Dillan says.

She nods and casts him a sideways glance. "You were one of the police brothers, right?"

"I am, yes."

"Good. I think that's important. Then maybe they'll listen to you."

I'm not sure why she'd need a cop to speak on behalf of her cat getting stuck up a tree, but we're here now, so we'll play this out. "Where was Tigger when you—"

"It's about time you got back!" a man shouts, rounding the gazebo. "That beast of yours is a menace. I'm going to get my rifle and if you haven't got control of her by the time I return—"

"Whoa, hold on there." Dillan switches hats from druid to Metro cop. "You can't threaten people with a gun, and you can't fire a gun at the woman's cat or within the city's boundaries."

"Who are you to tell me what I can and can't do?"

Because of the times we live in, Dillan wears his badge around his neck. He pulls it out from under his shirt and lets it hang against his chest. "Officer Dillan Cumhaill at your service."

That vents some of the man's steam, but he's still fighting mad. As we start walking again, he points toward a cluster of trees. "If you're a cop, I want to file a complaint. That thing pounced out of nowhere and ate my Licorice."

Okay, weird.

I follow his extended finger up to the overlapping foliage of the trees and get nothing back but a deep, throaty growl and the reflective glow of two golden eyes.

Two very large golden eyes.

"Do you have any more licorice, sir? Maybe we can coax Tigger out of the trees if she's a big fan."

The man's jaw drops open. "Licorice was my dog—an adorable, registered, black Pom—and no, I don't have any more for her beast to eat."

Yikes. Oops. Okay, I see the problem.

Dillan looks at me, and his eyes grow wide. I have to look away. I can hear his mind spinning out the black licorice jokes but now is not the time.

"Okay, I think we've got the whole picture. If the two of you will step back with the others, that would be great." I gesture at where a half-dozen people have turned patio chairs and are backyard drinking and taking in the show.

I don't blame them. If this wasn't my shit show to solve, it would be entertaining.

When Sloan, Dillan, and I are left alone, we draw closer to the base of the trees and look up.

"*Faery Fire.*" I raise my hand as a ball of magical blue light burns in my palm and illuminates the scene.

"Fuckety-fuck," Dillan mutters. "Tigger's the size of a tiger."

Yep. Definitely a mutation of growth. Becca's gray tabby is now the size of Shere Khan.

"Well, I doubt one little morsel of black licorice was enough to fill her tummy," I say.

"Maybe someone around here has got a cocker named Cookie or a wiener named, well, Wiener."

I chuckle, assessing how to best tempt Tigger out of the tree and what we'll do once she's under control. "Sloan and I will coax her down. D, you need to call Garnet and ask him if anyone has set up an animal shelter for the mutant mammal misfits of the new world. Tigger is no longer a house cat."

"Okeedokee." My brother pulls out his phone and steps off to make the call.

"Now for our part of the plan. While I coax her down, can you *poof* home and grab the pot roast thawing in the fridge?"

Sloan scowls at me. "Are ye seriously goin' to feed our Sunday dinner to the overgrown kitty?"

"It's better than sacrificing the neighborhood pets."

"Och, I suppose yer right." Sloan *poofs* out, and I take a couple of steps to position myself directly in front of her.

Kneeling on the grass, I connect with the natural world around me, send out my intention, and activate *Animal Friendship* and *Dominate Beast*. "Hey, Tigger. How about you come down from there? Sloan's gone to get you a yummy pot roast to gnaw on. You'd like that, wouldn't you?"

I get a rush of emotions in response.

The big puss is a little disoriented, and a lot annoyed that everyone keeps bothering her. More than both of those, she's hungry. That works in our favor.

Sloan *poofs* back, holding what we intended to be our dinner tomorrow night. He sets it on the grass, and we take a step backward. "Here, kitty, kitty."

I give her some magical reassurance that all will be well, and the giant black and gray tabby makes her way down. With lethal strength and feline agility, she drops out of the tree and pounces on the raw roast.

"Oh, the sacrifices we make for our cause."

Sloan chuckles. "Buck up. There's always pizza."

CHAPTER TWO

The morning after the night before is never fun. Despite last night at Shenanigans being our third town hall meeting, I still didn't learn my lesson. When people in a pub want your time and attention, they buy you a drink. Multiply that by many people and…

"Are you listening to me?"

I blink at the brute sitting across the conference table from me and force a smile. "Of course. You've always been strong and are even stronger with the surge of fae power. You'd be doing us a favor to be part of our team…you have other options you're looking into…oh, yeah, I'm listening. Hanging on every word."

Somehow, that must've been an appropriate answer because the self-proclaimed big strong Bivin launches off into another account of his heroic adventures.

Oy vey.

How I wish I was anywhere but here.

But there's no escaping the math.

Three million people in Toronto. One in a hundred projected awakenings. Thirty thousand empowered citizens in our streets.

Toronto's Team Trouble currently has nine active members:

me and Sloan, three of my brothers, the two Greeks, Tad, and Dan the djinn.

Sure, when things go FUBAR, Garnet and the Moon Called step in and back us up, but Garnet's shifter pride is already busy with Guild enforcement.

They can't take on the daily issues of the street too.

Thirty thousand possible empowered folks divided by the nine of us makes us each responsible for over three thousand Toronto citizens.

That's cray-cray.

And as much as I wish the rest of the family could join in the fun all the time, they are in Ireland and are taking on their own responsibilities.

Therefore, I've been stuck at the Batcave all weekend interviewing potential additions to Toronto's empowered response team.

Going into this, I pictured myself being the Jennifer Lopez on our *American Idol* panel. After four interviews yesterday and six today, I'm Simon Cowell.

Closing the folder in front of me, I lace my fingers and wonder if Bivin will ever stop prattling on or if he's like those swinging silver balls on peoples' desks that keep going and going and going.

Damn, and he would've been good too. At well over six feet tall, strong, and with wings, he'd add a flying component to our team we don't have.

There's no question he has the physical ability to kick ass as part of our team. The problem is his lack of social skills and empathy.

If he showed the slightest potential of being able to get his head out of his ass, I would consider him. He doesn't, so I can't.

"Right. I think we have enough to decide. Thanks so much for tossing your hat in the ring, Bivin. We'll be sure to give your accomplishments consideration."

He nods. "Excellent. When will I start?"

I stretch my neck from side to side, the pop of vertebrae my only relief from this hell. "All candidates start after they get the call and we say they are a good fit."

"So, you think I'm a good fit?"

"No. Sorry. We won't be calling."

His wings flare as he pushes up onto his feet. He pegs me with a haughty glare before glancing at Maxwell. "Are you letting the little girl make the decisions? Aren't you the man who runs this team?"

John Maxwell is a military-fit human with intelligent eyes and an Anderson Cooper vibe that goes beyond his stylish silver hair. Our law enforcement advisor is cool under pressure and cuts to the heart of difficult situations without apology. "Fiona's instincts have never failed us. No, there is no one person who calls the shots. We are a team."

Bivin's brow pinches as if the concept confuses him.

Dionysus makes a face behind our ninth interviewee, and I raise my fingers to warn him off doing something rash. Our resident Greek god is acting the part of our bouncer today and is getting cranky.

I try again to get Bivin to take the hint. "Thanks for coming. We really do appreciate your interest."

The fae leans into his fists. "Tell me why? If you don't want me, fine, but I deserve to know why."

I draw a deep breath and shrug. "If I'm being totally honest, you're not SITFU material. You're aggressive and standoffish. We work with the public. We expect acceptance and tolerance for others."

"I work with the public. I'm a fucking Green Guardian. I'm out on the streets every night."

Ugh...the Green Guardians.

Those vigilante fighters popped up after the veil fell. Now

they're out there making things more difficult for humans and fae to settle into this new world.

I flip the folder open and scan my notes to find his comment. "By your own account, you said, 'I keep empowered assholes in line and let them know the score. I don't care if they're shifters, wizards, or something else. They might think they're tough and at the top of the heap but I'm happy to prove them wrong.' Is that right?"

"Hell yeah. I stand behind that."

"Right, well, that's not the way we think. Our goal is to fix problems, smooth hostilities, and garner trust between the empowered and non-magical communities. We're not trying to hold anyone under our thumbs. We *de*-escalate hostilities and lay our lives on the line to build a stronger cooperative."

Bivin grunts. "Well, when that kumbaya bullshit blows up in your face, you know where I'll be."

"Admiring your big dick?" Dionysus asks.

My laugh bursts free but I cover it by coughing and grabbing my water. "Sorry, spit went down the wrong pipe. Yeah, thanks for coming, Bivin. Dionysus will show you out."

Dionysus walks him out, and when he returns, I hold up my hand to high-five him. "Good one, Tarzan."

"Can we be done with this now?" Dionysus asks. "The new season of *Bridgerton* is waiting, and everyone on the planet has seen it except us. You promised we could do a margarita marathon."

I check my watch and sigh. "Yeah, that was our last one for today. Let's bag it."

I slide the files for the three possible candidates to Maxwell and get up. "Do your thing, Max. If they check out after your vetting, I'll take them out on a few calls, and we'll evaluate them in the field."

Maxwell takes the files and nods. "I'll have these back to you tomorrow. Enjoy the margarita marathon."

Dionysus snaps me home, and I release Bruin the moment my shoes are off and I hang my spring jacket. The magical presence of the mythical spirit bear I carry within me flutters in my chest, and he manifests. The massive grizzly takes form in our open-concept kitchen-slash-living room and shakes out his fur.

"Home sweet home, Bear. Unless something unexpected happens, you're off the clock."

Bruin chuckles, the deep rumble of his voice filling the air between us. He swings his boxy head around to peg me with a look. "Almost everything that happens with you is unexpected, Red."

He's not wrong.

"Point to you, Bear. I'll call if I need you." I grip his wide jaw between my palms and pull his head closer so I can kiss his black nose.

"Done deal. I'll be downstairs with Manx and Daisy. She's spending the night with us, and we're turning on the fireplace and going to tell stories."

"Awesome. Enjoy."

"Rory's down there too," Dillan says, jogging down the stairs. "I think she's been a little homesick for the island. Keep an extra watchful eye on her for me would you, buddy?"

"Will do."

Bruin lumbers off toward the basement steps at the back of the house, and I head for the fridge. "Who's up for grilled cheese?"

"Yummy," Dionysus says. "Do you have any deli ham to add like the last time?"

I check the meat drawer. "Yep. Is that what you're hungry for?"

"Yes, thanks. I'll get started on the margaritas."

While Dionysus and I get started in the kitchen, Dillan pulls up a seat at the breakfast bar. "So, how goes the quest for red shirts? Are you stocked up for our away missions yet?"

I toss the loaf of rye onto the countertop and open the faucet to wash my hands. "I'm trying *not* to have red shirts, thank you very much."

"If it's a numbers game, having red shirts means you come back from the mission."

"It also means I'll be forced to go through the pain of interviewing and vetting again. Hard pass. Been there, got the headache to prove it."

"Another headache, *a ghra?*" Sloan *poofs* into the conversation. "Ye put too much on yer plate, luv. Ye need to take a step back and relax."

I pause the buttering of bread and lean to kiss Sloan. He's a worrier, my guy. My recent appointment as fae liaison is stressing him out. There's nothing to be done about it. Welcome to the new world.

"I'm fine, hotness. No rest for the wicked, amirite?"

He sobers and pauses to get my full attention. "I'm serious, luv. Yer not as much of a machine as ye want to believe. If ye don't start sayin' no and lettin' others carry some of the load, things will get away from ye. People could get hurt."

I hold his gaze to let him know I'm hearing him. "I'm working on not being the be-all-end-all to Toronto, I promise. Now, do you want a grilled cheese?"

He glances at the prep supplies and grins. "Will there be a ham add-in?"

"By Dionysus' request, yes."

He lifts his fist for a bump from the Greek god working the blender. "A man who knows what truly matters in life."

Dillan snorts. "That's ham on a grilled cheese? Forget love and family and the quest for purpose. As long as you've got a slab of Black Forest, our lives are complete?"

Sloan chuckles. "There are different umbrellas of what matters. Not all hold the same weight."

I giggle and start assembling our sandwiches. "Well, for tonight, it's grilled cheese and margaritas while loafing in the basement to binge *Bridgerton*."

Dillan and Sloan look less than thrilled.

"Those not interested need not apply. Tarzan and I have been looking forward to it. Kevin and Calum too."

"Although we're a bit miffed the Duke won't be in this season," Kevin says, coming up our back hall. "He will be sadly missed."

"Yes, that's a definite shame." I gesture at the assembly line of bread, butter, ham, and cheese. "Are you boys eating?"

Calum and his husband, Kevin, each hold up a grocery bag of snacks. "Nope. We ate with Bizzy and dropped her next door for a sleepover with Jackson. We're good until midnight munchies."

At the mention of snacks, Dionysus perks up. "Did you bring those Mick and Nick's I like?"

Kevin chuckles. "Mike and Ike's. Yep, we've got you covered, Greek."

Dionysus grins. "Thank you for remembering."

"That's what family is all about, my man." Calum pats him on the shoulder and pulls down the large margarita glasses, or the *fishbowls* as Emmet used to call them.

Oh, Emmet.

It's crazy how much I miss my goofball brother.

I sigh and turn the burner down on the stovetop.

I realize all the reasons why he's not here with us anymore and understand he's happy living on his self-proclaimed Fantasy Island. Still, we shared a room most of our lives. We were best friends from the time we could share teddy bears. We did everything together, and now he's gone.

Well, he's not gone…he's just not here.

I flip the first two grilled cheeses and smile at the beautiful golden-brown perfection.

At least he has Brendan.

If the two of them can't be with us, at least they're together. That makes things slightly more bearable. The fact that Brenny is with us makes things so much better than this time last year.

I try to keep that in mind.

Clan Cumhaill is once again whole. Gran and Granda, Da and Shannon, Liam, and the six of us. We're all living our best lives and are happy.

That's more important than being nostalgic for the days when Emmet and I were inseparable. Still, no one could ever make me laugh quite like Emmet. No one did as many idiotic things without apology as Em either.

"I think those are ready, *a ghra*." Sloan sets four plates down on the island.

"Oh, goodness, sorry." I scoop the first two sandwiches out of the pan and set them on the plates.

Sloan takes the spatula out of my hand and winks. "It's been a long and trying weekend. Why don't ye take a seat and eat? I'll make the next two."

I laugh. "You're afraid I'll burn yours."

He shakes his head. "I recognize when ye need to be pampered. Sit, luv. I've got ye."

I reach up on my toes and kiss the cook. "Yeah, you do. Thank the goddess for that."

I grab the ketchup bottle from the fridge, round the kitchen island, and am about to climb onto the stool next to Dillan when Nikon snaps in. "Greek, welcome. Do you want a grilled—"

The expression on his face stops me mid-sentence.

"What? What's wrong?" I set my load on the counter and close the distance between us.

He stops me when he throws out his hand. "Don't touch me, Red. I don't know what it'll do to you."

"*Damn*, Greek, the power emanating off you is incredible. What's wrong. What's happening?"

"I don't know...it just builds and I portal. I didn't mean to come here. I felt out of control and thought maybe Irish could help, and here I am."

Sloan moves the frying pan off the heat and jogs over. "Sit before ye fall, Greek. Yer practically vibratin'."

"That's how it feels." Nikon looks at Sloan. Then his gaze roams wildly around the room. "It's like my cells are trying to vibrate free of my body."

The others step closer, and the same look of worry mirrors around the group.

"It's the fae prana surge." I hold my fingers toward him, and the electrical tingle of power rushes over my skin in nasty little bites. "Your heritage power is from source prana. My guess is that it's awakening in your cells the same as the others."

"Only, this isn't the same," Dillan says.

Sloan shakes his head. "No, it's not. Nikon's connection to the source power is stronger than most."

"What about the rest of your family?" Dionysus asks. "If this is happening because of your tie to source prana, what about Andromeda and Papu?"

"And Emmet," I add, cluing in to what he's saying. "He practically has prana flowing in his veins. What is the world's power boost doing to him?"

"Likely not much." Sloan calls on his healing powers to assess Nikon. "The island was already at full power, and after yer brother stopped glowin', he was fine. What happened here over the past months is because the exposure is new to the people within the city."

"Oh, no," Nikon groans. "It's happening again."

My gaze bounces from Nikon to Sloan. "What can we do? I don't want him to portal off to a tropical island somewhere and—"

Magic detonates and pulses out of Nikon like he's the epicenter of a powerful blast.

In the next moment, the seven of us are standing on a beach of pale pink sand with the sun's warmth taking off the chill of the moment and the crashing sound of rocks and surf filling our ears.

"Did someone mention a tropical island?" Kevin chuckles. "Nice one, Fi. I'm glad you didn't say active volcano."

"Or hell," Dillan adds.

Calum smacks him in the chest and scowls. "Let's not add kerosene to the fire, dumbass. The beach is fine, Greek. Think beautiful tropical beaches."

I glance around, and everyone seems to be all right. "Okay, so your portaling has amped up. You didn't touch us, and you've taken us halfway around the world. That's new."

Sloan is studying Nikon and frowning. "Does it ease the buildup of chaos inside ye to portal?"

Nikon considers that for a moment. "It didn't the first time. When I came to your place, I felt just as out of control but yeah, bringing all of you this far did. I feel a bit better."

"Excellent. When you feel the energy starting to overload you, we'll pick another distant location, and we'll rinse and repeat until we've drained you dry." I rush over to stand with him. "I've always wanted to see the Grand Canyon."

"Sedona is breathtaking," Kevin says.

"You can't go wrong with Hawaii," Dillan adds.

"In the meantime, do we have any idea where we are?" Calum glances around. "Not that it matters, but dayam, Greek, you picked us a nice beach."

I breathe in the moment, finding peace for the first time in months. "What do you know, the air here isn't thick and silky, the seagulls aren't the size of eagles, and no sea monsters are breaching the water trying to tentacle us and drag us into the depths."

Dillan chuckles. "Refreshing. It feels like a normal—before the Time of the Colliding Realms—tropical paradise."

Sloan glances at the water, and his frame relaxes a little. "It's likely because there are no direct veins of prana power flowing into the area."

"Then I say we enjoy the moment." Kevin tilts his face to the sky. "I didn't realize there were still places left unaffected by the veil dropping."

"How retro." Calum chuckles.

I raise my face to the sky and revel in the searing heat. "I didn't realize I'm so deprived of vitamin D. Man this sun feels good on my skin."

Dionysus chuckles. "You realize four people in your everyday life can portal, right? Jane, if you want an afternoon on a tropical beach, you need only ask."

"I might do that, but for right now, we need to figure out Nikon's issue." I turn to him and get my focus back on the moment at hand. "Dionysus brought up a good point, Greek."

"About you being a beach bunny?" Nikon asks. "Yeah, I'm all for it. I grew up in the Greek islands. I could use more sun and surf. The scenery is always good at the beach too."

"And the drinks," Dillan says.

I wave to break into the conversation. "Yes, that sounds good but isn't what I meant. No. I'm thinking about whether your family is having similar issues. If the awakening is amping up your portaling ability, maybe it's amping up them as well."

"We should check in on them," Sloan says.

Nikon nods. "Yeah, we definitely should."

"And Emmet too." I look back at Sloan and shrug. "I know he's probably fine, but I won't relax until we know for sure."

Sloan nods. "All right. Back to Toronto to check on Andromeda and Politimi, Greek. Let's see if you can take us all home without contact like you brought us here. Use up that energy."

CHAPTER THREE

As fun as it is bouncing around the globe with friends, I'm relieved when we've confirmed Nikon's family is well and are free to make our way to Emhain Abhlach. The mystical fae island where my brothers live is a direct conduit to source prana and was the first place to be affected by the rise in power.

The jolt in juice when we first gained access to the island lit Emmet up like a hot pink Barbie night light. Eventually he absorbed and adapted to the magic, and when Mother Nature needed a guardian for the island, he stepped in and volunteered as tribute.

After that, we all pledged ourselves as defenders of the island. Now, with the ritual complete and our oaths taken, we can travel straight into the enchanted city instead of passing through all the safeguards to gain entry.

Nikon snaps our group directly into the golden palace, and the moment we take form, we hear Emmet and Brenny laughing and horsing around.

A huge weight dissolves from where it was pressing on my chest, and I hug Sloan's arm. "I love it when you're right. Sorry, as much as I believe in your instincts, I needed to see for myself."

Sloan wraps his arm around the back of my shoulders and squeezes. "I'm glad I was right, *a ghra*. Don't ever think ye need to apologize to me fer wantin' to check in on family."

Reason number eleventeen million why I love Sloan Mackenzie—cuz he just gets me.

"Hello, the house!" Dillan calls. Our little world-traveling group follows the lively banter until we find our brothers standing in the middle of the dead heads room waving their arms around like fools.

Both of them are wearing Oculus masks and are oblivious to the arrival of guests.

"Get the ogre, Em. I've got those fire guys," Brenny shouts, pointing into the air.

"I hate the ogre. It scares the crap outta me when he growls in my face," Emmet says.

"Then kill him before he gets that close."

Dillan holds up a finger, and we let them play on. Dionysus has the same 3D game setup at his loft, and it's tons of fun. Now that Merlin spelled the electronics in the house, Emmet can once again join the twenty-first century and not fry all things electronic.

"Get the archer off my back. I'm taking fire," Emmet shouts, ducking.

Brenny shifts his stance and wildly nocks his imaginary bow. "Got him. Em. You gotta get that ogre. If he gets through the gates, our village will fall."

"I'm trying. He's not an easy one to kill."

"He's half the fucking screen. How can you miss?"

With my phone up, I record this little performance to play back when I'm missing them. It does my heart good to witness this.

They really are okay.

"He's coming, Em," Brenny says.

"I know. I know. I'm trying. Fuck. If Calum were here, he'd be able to arrow this ugly f-ugly into a living porcupine."

"Give it all ye've got, Em," Brenny says in his best *Star Trek* Scotty voice. "Shit, we've got wraiths coming in over the mountain."

Emmet is firing imaginary arrows as fast as he can, and we don't have to see the game screen to know that the ogre Emmet's afraid of is getting closer. "We're not going to make it, Captain."

"You can do it!" Brenny says, a la Rob Schneider.

Emmet continues for a few more shots, then screams and ducks into a ball.

Brendan busts up laughing, pulls his Oculus goggles off, and doubles over. "Oh fuck, Em. It's just as funny every time."

Em drops to the floor and assplants. "Funny for you, maybe. How about you kill the ogre next time? Why does it always have to be me?"

"Where's the fun in me doing it? I don't scream like a girl."

Emmet pulls off his goggles and rolls his eyes when he sees us. "How long have you assholes been standing there?"

"Long enough to know you're getting your asses kicked," Dionysus says. "Would a few more fighters in your party help?"

Brenny sets his goggles and his hand controllers on the table by the wall and comes over to hug me. He, Dillan, Calum, and Emmet look so much alike that there's no mistaking the fact they are brothers. "Hey, baby girl. How's things?"

Aiden and I are the oldest and the youngest and the two that got the red hair, freckles, and blue eyes. Brenny, Calum, Dillan, and Emmet are the middle four, and all have jet black hair and emerald eyes.

I take Brenny's rib-bending hug and don't complain. He's always been a bear hugger, and for over a year I would've given anything to be crushed by his love. "Things are fine. Better now. We needed to check on Emmet and make sure he's not suffering from fae prana overload."

Emmet accepts Dillan's extended hand and rises to his feet. "I'm fine. Why? What's up?"

"Maybe you don't realize it, being isolated here, but the world is whacked right now. With the veil down, there's so much fae magic seeping through the Faery Glass that it's cray-cray."

"At least the physical barrier of the Faery Glass is still there," Sloan says. "If it weren't, our situation would be so much worse."

"What would that look like?" Brendan asks.

I try to think of a way to explain it to him. He's new to all of this and still catching up. "Do you remember the battle on the beach during the Culling? Remember how many portals opened and how the strongest and most aggressive members of the dark fae came through to try to overtake us?"

"Yeah. I remember Dionysus saved you from the freaky twig-headed guy that went after you."

"Yeah, I did," Dionysus says.

I wink at Dionysus. "Yeah, you did."

My brothers give him a round of knuckle bumps for that before I continue. "Well, imagine an entire realm of twig-headed guys, centaurs, giants, and magical beasts all of a sudden being able to step through a portal gate on that side. Then they find themselves in Toronto or Vancouver or anywhere on this side."

"Yeah, that would suck," Brenny agrees.

"It would. Yes, the magic is getting through, but the barrier is keeping everyone on their side of the fence."

"For now," Dillan says.

I roll my eyes. "Don't jinx us, D. Merlin and Sloan are trying to figure out a way to get the veil back up. Have a little faith."

Dillan looks at Sloan and makes a face. "It's been more than three months. Have you had any luck?"

Sloan scratches the back of his neck and sighs. "None to speak of yet, no, but yer sister's right. We can't assume the worst. As long as the fae beasts are staying on their side of the glass, we're still in better shape than we'd be if they weren't."

"Wisdom of the ages." Calum chuckles.

Emmet grins. "As far as your comment about us being oblivious because we're isolated, come see how wrong you are." He waves for us to follow him upstairs and into the Grand Hall. Striding straight through the large banquet room, we step out onto the balcony. "Check it. My city has gone whack-a-doodle too."

It takes a moment for what I see to make sense in my mind. "What is that?"

"It's some kind of fluorescent moss," Brenny says. "It freaked us out the other night. I would've sworn it was growing so fast we could see it moving."

Emmet nods. "We went out to inspect the city the next morning expecting to see that whole section covered in growth. You know, like those tent caterpillar invasions you see on the Nature channel."

Dionysus cringes. "Those are super creepy."

"Right?" Emmet says. "Imagine knowing that's coming your way. I had bad dreams all night about being consumed by moss monsters."

"It wasn't that creepy by the light of day," Brendan says.

"It wasn't?" Sloan asks.

"No. It's a very spongy moss that's only attaching itself to the rooftops."

Sloan tilts his head and considers that for a moment. "It's probably photosensitive as well as bioluminescent. It might seek the sun to absorb during the day and radiate that colorful glow at night. If so, spreading across the rooftops would make sense."

"And it's pretty." I add my two cents. "Hopefully, that means something."

Dillan laughs. "You mean you hope it can't be an invasive killer plant because it's pretty? Do you think that has any bearing on things?"

I stick my tongue out at him. "Maybe."

"Venus flytraps are pretty, but Audrey Two still ate the people in *Little Shop of Horrors*."

"Wow, you're just a ball of dickdom today. When's Eva expected back? You need some divine intervention."

"Which is Fi's delicate way of saying you need to get laid, brother." Calum arches a brow. "She's right. You're cranky AF."

Dillan holds up both middle fingers and twists enough to show them to all of us. "Yo, Nikon, isn't it about time to snap off to the next location? How about we leave these assholes here? I'm thinking Monte Carlo or Ibiza."

Nikon doesn't look like he finds any of this funny. "I think it's getting better. My skin isn't crawling now, although I still feel like I've got too much power."

Dionysus clucks his tongue. "You can never have too much power, my friend, only not enough control."

"No matter how you look at it, it's happening again."

Dionysus holds up a finger and dashes to the rows of liquor on the sideboard hutch. Selecting a large bottle, he grins and jogs back into our little cluster of friends. "Don't worry. I'll replace this. We need something to tide us over on our travels. Be well, Cumhaill Island brothers. Let's go to the zoo next. I want to see giraffes. Ready when you are, Nik—"

We materialize on the hot and dry plains, and I point at the herd of fifteen-foot-tall mammals nibbling on leaves. "Well, you got the giraffe part of the request, but you missed the zoo part, Greek."

I glance around and realize I'm talking to myself. "Greek? Guys? Hello?"

Huh, well, I did not see this coming.

Okay, Nikon is not in control because he's totally left me here on my own.

I pull out my phone and get no love. "No signal. All right. I'm guessing I'm in Africa somewhere, no phone, no food or water… yeah no, I don't like this game."

I scan the wide body of water in the distance and have no intention of heading over. I've watched *National Geographic* enough to know you don't approach an African watering hole unless you want to get snapped up by a hippo or a crocodile.

Which I don't.

I also know giraffes are skittish and kick when frightened. That idea doesn't appeal either.

"It's fine. I'm fine. S'all good." The animals of the savannah take notice of me. I hold up my palms and smile. "I come in peace. I've misplaced my friends. You do you. Look away."

They don't seem impressed with me and go back to their grazing, reaching up to snatch off the top leaves. It's hard to grasp how tall they are. Except for the two young ones.

"Little dudes, you can't reach the leaves. Sad face." The younger giraffes are still ten or twelve feet tall. They just can't reach the tree's foliage. "Let me help."

From where I'm standing in the long, golden grass of the savannah, I crouch and press my hands to the dry ground. Reaching out, I connect with the nature of the area and the vitality of the acacia tree.

Giving it a little druid power boost, I lengthen a couple of the branches hanging over their heads until the leaves are within their reach.

Oblivious to my mealtime intervention, the two plod forward and join the adults grazing quietly beside them.

The movement of me rising to stand draws their attention, but when the curiosity about me dies down, I unzip my hoodie and tie it around my waist.

Man, I said I needed an infusion of vitamin D. I suppose this is the universe's game of "be careful what you wish for."

Taking off a layer helps with the boiling alive issue, but unless I figure out how to get help or get home, being hot will be the least of my worries.

"All right, think, Fi. Garnet lives in Africa. Maybe someone knows him." I snort. Every time I vacation abroad and say I live in Toronto, someone invariably says, "Oh, Toronto. Do you know my friend Greg? He's in Toronto."

Here I am hoping to find Garnet.

"Africa's not that big, is it?" I laugh again, and a couple of the giraffes look over at me. "Well, if nothing else, I amuse myself."

"Jane! We found you." Dionysus throws his arms open and hugs me. "Thank goodness Sloan has you chipped."

I laugh, hug Dionysus back, and accept the bottle of red wine he snagged from Emmet's stash. Tipping it back, I let the fruity explosion of taste quench my thirst. "I'm not chipped. Sloan simply tracks my Claddagh band and finds me when the world misplaces me."

I hold my hand out to Sloan, and he runs a gentle finger over the platinum band that marks us both as taken. "In a lifetime of intellectual triumphs, casting a locator spell on your ring was by far my best idea."

I chuckle and let him have that one. "Your brilliance and foresight know no bounds."

"Oh, yay! Giraffes." Dionysus's attention has squirreled away from me being lost and toward the herd of giraffes now staring at the three of us.

He snaps over to them, and it must be a god thing because he's that close and not spooking them. Raising his hand, he pets the two young ones and talks to them in Greek. The craziest thing is that when they look him in the eye, I'd swear they understand him.

The joy he finds over simple things never ceases to fill my heart.

"Fascinating." Sloan scans our surroundings with a curious expression.

"What's fascinating, hotness?"

"Like the beachfront, the savannah also looks relatively untouched by the chaos of fae overgrowth. The grasses, trees, and animals seem to be carrying on with life as if nothing has gone off-kilter."

I glance around and yep, he's right. "That strengthens our theory that the fae prana is largely being carried from the ley lines through the waterways."

"It does."

"Aren't they the most oddly wonderful creatures?" Dionysus snaps back.

"Well, them and platypuses," I say.

Dionysus makes a crazy grin and chuckles. "Oh, they are totally my fault. Alcohol may have been involved."

I burst out laughing and wave my fingers in a circular gesture. "Do tell. How are platypuses your fault?"

He tilts his head back and forth. "I'm not supposed to say anything, but you are family, and I trust you. You'll keep a secret, right?"

"Absolutely."

Dionysus accepts my assurance and looks at Sloan. "Irish? Are you sworn to secrecy?"

"Discretion is my middle name," he says.

Dionysus frowns. "No wonder you don't like your mother. That's a terrible name."

I laugh, but I'm not one hundred percent sure he's joking. "Tarzan, back to the platypus story."

"Right. One week, early on in the evolution of living things, Mother Nature and I got really drunk and decided to invent some new animals for the land down under. The animals up until then had all been quite sensible, and I challenged her to give at least one continent some creative flair."

"Nailed it. Australia has a lot of unique animals."

"Right, so let's just say we got around to platypuses late in the process and that was when we realized we had to stop because hello…platypus."

I laugh again. "I should've known. Who else could've thought up a duck-billed, beaver-tailed, egg-laying mammal with venomous heel spikes?"

Dionysus makes a face. "I may have gone a bit over the top on that one…and us taking off the safety protocols of creation might've been a bad idea."

My laughter draws the attention of my savannah friends once more. They flick their ears as they chew, grazing lazily and trying to make sense of us.

I wave and introduce them to the new arrivals. "These are my friends I mentioned. Dionysus, this is the herd. Herd, this is Dionysus."

The giraffes watch us for another moment before starting to move away.

I wave again as they put some distance between us. "Okay, have a good one. Don't get eaten."

Sloan chuckles and touches my bare arms. "We better get you out of the sun before you lobster. Your freckles are already coming out."

"Yeah, I didn't know I needed sunscreen to eat my grilled cheese."

Dionysus groans. "Our sad little grilled cheeses are sitting there going cold and waiting to be eaten."

I laugh. "With Bruin, Manx, and Daisy in the house? Dude, those sandwiches are long gone."

"What about our margaritas?" Dionysus asks. The horror on his face is too funny. "Do you think those are gone too?"

I pat his arm. "No. Those are likely still waiting for us

untouched. How about we go home and check?"

Sloan nods and takes my hand. "An excellent idea."

Dionysus snaps Sloan and me home, and the moment we materialize I'm swept up in a hug. Nikon's embrace is tight, and I feel his heart pounding as his energy snaps electrical charges off his skin. "Dammit, Fi, I'm so sorry. Are you all right?"

Nikon's hug is both breath-squishing and shaky. The guy is trembling. I ease back and take his hands in mine. "One hundy percent fine. Dude, is this shaking like a leaf routine because of the prana powerup or because you lost me in transit?"

He closes his eyes. "Much more the second one."

"Then panic no more, Greek. You got the giraffe part of the trip right. I got to stand in the middle of the African savannah to enjoy them. No biggie."

"Dammit, Fi, you could've been seriously lost if Sloan didn't have you chipped."

I roll my eyes. Why does everyone look at it like that? "The point is, I'm here, and I'm fine."

"Your nose got burned," Calum chuckles.

I wrinkle my nose at him and regret it. Yeah, that's going to be sore tomorrow. "Anyhooo, how about them margaritas? With Nikon's new situation, I vote we settle in and have a Drink and Think. That is, if Nikon's able to stay in one place long enough to have a conversation."

"I think I'll be good now. The power surging seems to be over."

"Let's drink to that." Dionysus hands Nikon and me each a large glass.

I sip from the edge of the glass and groan. "I'm so thankful for you, Dionysus. You have leveled up the quality of our drinking more than I can say—and I'm a bartender, so that's saying a lot."

Dionysus raises his glass. "You're welcome. The secret to a great margarita is the juice one-two punch. Freshly squeezed lime juice—not that atrocious bottled stuff you use at Shenanigans—then a splash of fresh OJ. That's right. Fresh-squeezed juice from an actual orange."

I point at the fruit bowl Dionysus raided. "I got those from Emmet's citrus grove down by the city gate. Yes, they're fresh, but I also think them growing on a supercharged power island gives them some oomph too."

"Like when the containers of radioactive fruit and vegetables washed up on the shore of *Gilligan's Island*." Dillan laughs.

"Dude! Classic episode." Calum accepts his and Kevin's drinks. "We should totally stream it while we drink these mutant margaritas."

Dionysus scowls. "There's nothing mutant about my margaritas. I'm the god of good times."

"You absolutely are." I slurp an icy swallow. "Wow, somebody needs to oversee food otherwise we're all going to crash and burn. My stomach is empty, and these are way too good."

"I'll make the pizza run," Nikon says. "It's the least I can do after almost killing you."

I wave away Nikon's self-deprecation. "I've been almost killed enough to know how wrong you are. Now, enough of that, Greek. Positive outlook leads to a positive outcome, amirite?"

Dionysus backs me up with a nod. "Right you are, Jane. Let's keep that in mind. Sure, the world is currently fucked, but we've got good friends, great margaritas, and pizza on the way."

I chuckle. "I think we got outranked by margaritas."

"Rude." Dillan accepts his glass. He takes a long sip from the edge and laughs. "Nah, he's right. Good friends and great margaritas."

I point at the table. "Nikon, sit. I don't want you on a pizza run when your powers are fritzing. We can order old-school and have it delivered."

Nikon curls his fingers into a heart against his chest. "I appreciate you wanting to protect me, Fi."

I snort and take another drink. "Nah. It's the pizza I'm protecting. With the way your night is going, my Hawaiian might end up in Hawaii. Now, everybody sit. What are we going to do about Nikon's power fritzing?"

CHAPTER FOUR

In the aftermath of the Culling, Monday mornings have taken on a new light. No longer are we free to loaf about and make our way into the Batcave before lunch. Now Garnet and Maxwell have a standing team meeting scheduled when they divvy up the tasks that land on Maxwell's desk over the weekend.

Before I go there to do that, it's my task to check in at the bookstore where I work part-time for any emergency additions to our fae awakening watch list.

A warm spring breeze lifts my hair and swings the store sign. It's an old-fashioned painted shingle hanging perpendicular to the building. Suspended over the concrete sidewalk, it pivots on an iron rod.

It *squeaks* and *creaks* as it swings and invites me in.

Myra's Mystical Emporium

Augury, Alchemy, Astrology,

and all Implications of Same

Myra's Mystical Emporium is an enchanted bookstore filled floor-to-rafters with magical tomes, textbooks, and tarot decks. We stock anything anyone might need to find their way in the empowered world.

When Myra first set up shop more than fifty years ago, she enchanted the storefront so only empowered folks could find her store and only if they needed something she offered.

It was how I first found her back in my early days of being a druid. When I returned from Ireland and told my brothers we were druids we were decades behind our peers, and people were already trying to kill us.

Well…me, at least. They were trying to kill me.

We needed to catch up fast on our training, and I had no idea where to start or how to do it. Thank the goddess for Sloan Mackenzie. He found the store, then Myra took me on as a client, an employee, and an apprentice.

I couldn't have been more blessed.

That same enchantment is now calling the citizens of Toronto awakening to their fae power. They need the bookstore, and it draws them like zombies to brains—metaphorically speaking.

They've been coming in droves for weeks, and the two of us have created an intake system to help as many folks as we can, as effectively as we can.

The brass bell over the door rings as I enter. A few voices are talking over one another, but it's nothing like that morning Sloan and I got here in January when we couldn't get inside.

That was the day we realized the veil was down.

That was also the day Merlin gave us a glimpse into the future.

If we don't get ahead of the rise in power levels, the awakenings, the fae race riots, and the hysteria, our future looks much more like a post-apocalyptic horror movie than a fae alternate world.

"Good morning, duck." Myra winks as I make my way to the sales desk on the back wall. "Happy Monday to you and yours."

"Auntie Fi," Imari yells, jumping up from under the sales desk. She runs around to hug me, and I scoop the little monkey up to hug her. "Are you working today? Can we play?"

"Sadly, not today, little bear. I'm off to work with your daddy today."

"Catching bad guys?"

"Yep."

She giggles and taps my nose. "You can be Rudolph guiding the sleigh for Santa."

Myra laughs. "Wow, you really got some sun."

I touch my sunburned nose with the tip of my finger and chuckle. "An unexpected trip to the savannah. Speaking of, can you please send me the coordinates of where Garnet's compound is in Africa? You never know when I might be in the neighborhood and lost."

Myra arches a brow and pegs me with a look. "Do I want to know what you're talking about?"

I wave that away. "It doesn't matter. I'm home and safe now. I realized in my moment of lost and alone that I don't know where the compound is and with my luck, I might need that info again."

The guy standing at the counter shifts, and I realize I've totally interrupted. "I'm sorry. I didn't mean to—oh, Diesel, how are you?"

Diesel Demarco is the living wall who blocked the entrance to the store that day back in January. As big as a barn and as strong as an ox, I likened him to a linebacker. When he admitted his awakening was stirring up sensations of aggression and violence, we had reason to be alarmed.

He proved us all wrong.

We figured out he has goliath ancestors, but so far, no true magical traits have manifested other than strength and the fact that his skin is as tough as armor.

"How are things with you, dude?"

"I've had better days."

I set Imari down and give him my full attention. "Why, what happened?"

Myra frowns. "His boss fired him because of his awakening."

"Seriously? Well, he can't. That was in the first laws Andromeda and Maxwell drew up to protect the innocent going into this."

Diesel lifts one massive shoulder and lets it drop. "Then I suppose my boss didn't get the memo."

"What happened?"

"Nothing really. I went in for my shift at the bank, and the manager met me at the door. He asked for my gun, handed me a box with the contents of my locker, and told me he no longer required my services."

Rude. He's a good guy too.

"Okay then, I'll go with you, and we'll straighten him out. You'll have your job back by your shift tomorrow morning."

He shakes his head. "No. Don't bother. My father always said never to spend time trying to win over people who don't see what I'm worth. I'll find something else."

"Well, that sucks, but you know what they say, when the door slams shut, jimmy the window and don't let them catch you sneaking inside."

Diesel doesn't look like he's following.

"Let me ask you a couple of questions, and it will all make sense. To be a bank security officer, you have to get federally bonded, right?"

"Yeah."

"To get your gun license, you've completed a psych eval?"

"Yeah."

"Are you available to work hard, protect innocents, and be grossly overpaid?"

"Uh…sure."

"Excellent. Then come with me. Bye, ladies. Lurve you lots."

Imari giggles again. "Lurve you more, Auntie Fi."

"Of course, you do. I'm fabulous."

I drive Diesel the four blocks from Myra's bookstore to the building Nikon bought when we needed a home base. "Welcome to the Acropolis." I pull into my parking spot in the front row. "Home to our workout center, art studio, relic shrine, Team Trouble headquarters, and our beloved Greek god."

He glances at me sidelong, and I laugh.

The guy doesn't know what to think of me. Believe it or not, I get that look more often than you'd think.

The door of my truck *creaks* as I swing it open, jump down, and lock things up. "Come on. This is where the magic happens."

The two of us head inside, and I feel ridiculously tiny. I stand an above average five-foot-seven, and he towers over me by almost two feet. "I bet you get asked this all the time but are you a big sports player?"

He glances down at me. "Yes, I do, and yes, I am. Basketball and football."

I bet you rock it too.

A rush of warmth greets us in the lobby, and I point at the deli café across from the elevator bank. "Great corned beef on marbled rye in there. Also, their corn chowder soup is worth the trip."

I hit the elevator and push the button to take us up to the tenth floor. The elevator doesn't move until I pull my pendant from under my shirt and tap the security panel. The gears *click* and *creak* quietly, and we begin our ascent.

"As you know, with the awakenings, there are a lot of people afraid and behaving badly on both sides of the equation. Our team is understaffed, and I'm very particular about who we add to the mix. I think you'd be great and I'm going to nominate you."

"Nominate me? You don't even know me."

I crane my neck to look up to meet his gaze. "Wrong. I have magic in my veins and an enchanted Celtic shield on my back that weighs in on life and hones my skill for evaluating situations. I like you for a spot on our team, and there's no feedback from my shield. That's a good thing."

"You're a very strange woman," he says as we step out of the elevator.

Sloan chuckles and greets us. "She is, but soon enough you'll find it less bothersome and more endearing. After that, you may even begin to see the logic in her crazy ways."

I roll my eyes and lead the way through the first door, scan in, and open things up to access the second door. "Diesel, do you remember Sloan from that day at Myra's bookstore?"

"Of course." He offers Sloan a nod of greeting.

"And Garnet Grant." I gesture at our boss standing in front of the monitor wall with Maxwell and Andromeda.

"Hello, sir," Diesel says. "It's a pleasure."

Garnet extends a hand to him, and they shake. "Staying out of trouble, son? Have you been working on those control exercises we discussed?"

"Every morning and night without fail. Yes. Thank you again."

"I'm glad they're working for you."

Me too. I imagine out-of-control Diesel would be a very dangerous guy. Even more of a reason to have him working with us and on our team.

"This is John Maxwell. He's vetting the team, and he's the one who will investigate your qualifications as a good fit."

Maxwell extends his hand and eyes Diesel up and down. "Besides the obvious physical strengths, what do you think you could add to the team?"

"He's federally bonded as a bank security officer and has his gun license," I say. "He is athletic and strong, *annnd* my instincts say he'll be a kickass addition to the team."

Maxwell blinks at me and chuckles. "Thank you for your input, Fi. Didn't you ask *me* to vet him?"

I wave that away. "Oops, sorry. Okay, why don't you two go into Maxwell's office, and I'll stay out of the conversation."

"An excellent idea," Maxwell says. "The three files from the weekend are there, and our first contestant will be arriving any moment for the morning meeting."

Maxwell gestures toward his office and Diesel follows him.

When the door *clicks* shut, I turn to the others. "Why do I feel like a nervous mother on her boy's first day of school?"

Garnet arches a brow and gives me a look. "To answer that, we'd have to have insight into how your mind works. I'm not getting sucked into that vortex of chaos."

"It's a definite rabbit hole." Sloan chuckles.

"Good morning, all." Calum comes in from the foyer with Dillan. "What's on the agenda today? Has yet another teenage girl turned her boyfriend into a bunny?"

Dillan snorts. "I'm hoping for another horny dog scenario."

Sloan looks around expectantly. "I missed that one."

Dillan chuckles. "We got called to a condo of a new witch who said her husband was nothing but a horny dog. She accidentally turned him into a retriever that wouldn't stop dry humping her leg."

Calum busts up laughing. "I loved that one."

"I'm sorry I missed it," Sloan says.

Calum turns toward us and points his thumb at Maxwell's office behind him. "Who's the Shaquille O'Neal stand-in?"

I grin. "That's Diesel. I brought him in to apply for the team. He's a good guy."

"He's a mammoth," Dillan says.

"Technically, he's a goliath…or at least partly."

"He's really big," Calum says.

"Like really, really fucking big," Dillan agrees.

I frown at them. "Yes, there's no question but try not to be weird. I want him to like us."

The two of them look at one another and laugh.

"You're telling *us* not to be weird?" Dillan asks.

Calum wipes his fingers over his eyes and tries to sober.

"That's the funniest thing you've said in a long time, Fi. Good one."

I leave them to their assholeishness and head back to Garnet standing by the conference table. "Hey, bossman. How are things in our city?"

"Have you ever seen *Planet of the Apes*? I'm thinking of filming a reboot."

I glance up at the screen and sigh. "It's the damned rate of growth. It's like our city is the Play-Doh Fuzzy Pumper Barber Shop."

Garnet glances at me and chuckles. "I got that one. I don't know if that's a good sign for you or a bad sign for me."

"You have a seven-year-old daughter. It's you. But yeah, it's like the pressure of the fae prana is pressing down, and the plants and trees are growing like a throwback to *Jurassic Park*."

"Do you think dinosaurs are a possibility?" Dillan sounds excited about the prospect.

Garnet has scowling down to an art form. He turns his amethyst gaze on my brother and stares. Anyone who wasn't in the inner circle would pause, but Garnet's prickly moments are the norm around here. "Do I think there could be a return of dinosaurs? No. Do I think some other creature might mutate and Godzilla its way through our city? Maybe."

"Can you imagine?" Calum grins.

"A little less enthusiasm on that one, dude." I grab the three folders, sit on the table, and put my feet on my chair. Using my knees as my desk, I open the first folder. "That's our city out there. I don't want it to turn into the set of a B movie."

Garnet points at my chair and growls. "Do you understand how furniture works, Lady Druid?"

"Sorry." I hop down and spin so I'm sitting in my chair. Flipping the folders open, I read the notes Maxwell attached to the top page in each file. "So, all three of our candidates checked out?"

Garnet turns off the wall of screens and sets the controller on the table. "On paper, yes. Take it from me, not everyone who *'could'* be great on the team *'will'* be. Sometimes our line of work doesn't mesh up with expectations. And sometimes there are outliers who you'd never think would fit yet somehow, they do."

"Good morning, *jefe*, Jane, brothers, and Irish." Dionysus appears wearing a royal blue chiton with gold piping and a gold rope belt.

I laugh at the perfect timing and wonder if our Greek was eavesdropping upstairs ready to make his entrance.

"Look, I brought jellies." Dionysus sets down a tray of sugar donuts and a pitcher of orange juice.

"*Noice*, Greek. Thanks." Calum is the first to grab a warm pocket of sugar-jelly bliss and scoops a paper plate under it before he loses any of his powdered sugar. "You're the best."

"That's what she said," Dillan says.

"Oh, *he* said it too." Dionysus laughs and waggles his brow. "At least twice. Dillan, let's not discriminate based on gender."

Calum lifts his donut in a toast. "Well said, Greek."

"Hello all." Tad pushes in from the outer foyer. "Everyone, this is Atlas."

Atlas Grainger, our new trainee, is about Sloan's age, has a slim build, and has a half-elf heritage that he's been aware of since birth. He's not one of the awakened, but the coming out of magic made it possible for him to join society and set his pointed ears free.

"Atlas, this is—och, grand, donuts!" Tad squirrels and changes direction toward the table.

Garnet growls in frustration, and I can't help but laugh. "I'm sorry, big guy. In two years, I've taken all your military efficiency and threat of bodily harm and replaced it with smartasses and jelly donuts."

Our lion king glances down at me and sighs. "You once told me you were here to pull the thorn out of my paw. In truth, you are my life's thorn, but I think I've become a bit of a masochist because I wouldn't know what to do if you weren't here to torment me."

I chuckle and pour myself a glass of juice. Taking a deep gulp, I swallow and glance at Dionysus. "Wow, Tarzan. You've spiked the punch. Are mimosas a good pairing with warm jellies?"

Dionysus chuckles. "Mimosas are a good pairing with anything within brunch hours."

"On a workday?"

Now it's his turn to laugh. "Tell me what day you *don't* work, Jane. Then we can discuss what is and is not a workday."

I lift my glass. "Touché."

Tad lifts his head from ogling the donuts and points at Dionysus's chiton. "What am I missing, Greek? Is it Dress Your Heritage Day and I didn't get the message? I could've worn my kilt, and we could compare knees. What's the occasion?"

"Erotidia."

"What does that mean for those of us who don't speak Greek?"

Dillan says, "More importantly, is it as dirty as it sounds?"

Dionysus makes a sad face. "Disappointingly no. It's the Festival of Eros."

I set my drink down and lick powdered sugar off my fingers. "Why the hell would you celebrate that asshat after what he did to you?"

Dionysus lifts his bare shoulder looking conflicted. "What can I say? A stupid decision can't erase a thousand years of good times."

"He went behind your back with Zeus."

"It's fine, Jane. Eros genuinely believed he was doing the right thing for me by reporting to my father. He was *wrong*, but that's only because he doesn't understand what I found with you and your family."

"And so, you forgive him?"

"Forgiveness is divine, after all." Dionysus holds his palms up toward the heavens. "For gods and immortals, one mistake over an endless lifetime of camaraderie doesn't warrant cutting ties."

I catch the confusion in the new guy's expression. "Atlas, welcome to your first day. Grab a donut, and take a seat. Despite everything you've already been wondering about, the show hasn't started yet."

Maxwell comes out of his office with Diesel behind him. He grins at the platter of sugared pastry and snags himself one. "Welcome to Monday morning, people. I take it everyone has met Atlas and Diesel?"

Cue a round of welcoming nods all around.

"Are we still waiting on Nikon?"

I stride to the table and take my seat with the others. "No. The fae power surge is messing with his portal abilities. The only people we know with experience in portal magic are Patty and the Queen of Wyrms, so Nikon is spending the day in Ireland at the dragon lair."

Maxwell sets his pastry prize on a plate and takes it to the end of the table. "I wish him well with that."

I draw a heavy breath. "Yeah. We all do."

With that hanging in the air, Maxwell swivels his chair toward the group and opens the top file. "All right. It seems that in some parts of the world things are slowing down, and in others, all hell is breaking loose."

"Unfortunately, almost everyone in the 'all hell is breaking loose' crowd seems intent on having a face-to-face with the Toronto fae liaison," Garnet adds.

I shrug. "What can I say? I'm just that lovable."

Maxwell smiles. "Regardless of the reason, you are the woman of the hour, Fi. The trick is deciding how we want to use you as a resource. If we continue to answer every call, the cities with the largest impact won't develop their emergency protocols and become self-sufficient."

That makes sense. "Do you want me to start building replica Team Troubles around the world?"

Garnet nods. "That's what we're thinking. So, going forward, when we dispatch you to a trouble call in another city, we'll have them pair you up with a couple of locals. You can start the process of building response teams in other locations and hopefully they'll get the gist of things and take it from there."

"I like the sound of that," Sloan says.

Calum nods. "Yeah, it would be nice if you weren't in such high demand and could take some real time off."

Yeah. Sloan and I talked about a vacation or some European travel, but the world seems to have other ideas.

"Okay, so what's on the docket today?" I ask.

"Aiden ran into something peculiar this morning on his shift." Garnet gets us started. "We sent Dan to join him, and Tad, you can track him and meet up when we finish here."

"Got it," Tad says.

Garnet takes the top page off the file and glances at it. "Mayor Clarissa Tremblay has requested a visit from Fi. There is mayhem in Montréal. Hostilities are rising between empowered and non-magical folks, and I believe an aspect of that strikes close to home. The mayor is asking that we be discreet."

"Consider it done." I wave away the concern. "Discreet is what I do. There's no—"

I stop as the others dissolve into a fit of snickers.

"What's so funny?"

Calum rubs a hand over his mouth and fights to sober. "Fi, do you honestly think you're the poster child for discretion?"

"Don't you?" I scan the faces around the table and frown. "Okay, obviously you don't, but I'll tell you right now you're wrong. I have walked away from, pretended I didn't see, and never spoken of more moments in your lives than you could realize."

"Because we were drunk for most of them?"

"I couldn't say. I'm too discreet to bring them up."

Dillan chuckles. "Fine. We'll give you that. I think we were thinking more in the 'in your face, redhead, Irish, Taurus' kind of sense."

Calum nods. "Like the time you broke the nose of Liam's roommate in college."

"He grabbed my ass."

"Or the time you stood on the table in the cafeteria at school and rallied a riot over removing poutine from the menu."

"Poutine is a cultural delicacy."

"It's also like a thousand calories, and they were under a new heart-smart mandate from the provincial government."

"I admit, I got fired up about that one."

"If I pay for you to get poutine in Montréal, will you all shut up and let me finish the fucking briefing?"

I meet Garnet's growl with a smile and nod. "Sorry, bossman. Consider the Cumhaill sidebar over. You do you."

He might look like he wants to rip me apart, but he really does lurve me.

Garnet slides the assignment sheet over to me and continues. "Montréal has the highest level of awakenings of anywhere in Canada, and it's straining their municipal system. We need to help them establish a working response structure so they're prepared for events in the future."

I reach for the paper and glance at the details of the case file. "Color me curious. What does this mean—details only to be disclosed in person?"

Dillan snorts and holds up a finger. "I'm gonna go out on a limb and say they'll only disclose the details in person."

I flash him my middle finger and pass the case file sheet down the table to Sloan and Dionysus. "I'm not sure where you've been in Montréal, hotness. Can you get us there or will it be the man in the dress driving the chariot today?"

Dionysus flicks his curls behind his bare shoulder. "Don't be a hater, Jane. You know I look delish."

I laugh and nod. "Like a true god of lust and leisure."

"Excellent. That was what I was aiming for."

Garnet leans forward and takes the second file, opening the front cover. "I planned for Fi, Sloan, Dionysus, and Atlas to take Montréal, and Nikon to take Dillan and Calum to Vegas."

Dillan's expression brightens instantly. "Winner, winner, chicken dinner. Suck it, sista. Looks like you drew the short straw. Sorry, not sorry."

"Vegas baby." Calum meets Dillan for a knuckle bump.

"With Nikon out, we have to revise that plan," Garnet says.

Dillan and Calum both look like he robbed them. "Dude…that was just cruel," Dillan says.

Garnet arches a brow. "I want a person with portal abilities with each team when possible, and with two locations so far, the travel will eat up the wayfarer's power. So, to get around that, Dionysus, you will take Tad, Calum, and Dillan to the Bellagio and come straight back to escort Fi and Sloan to Montréal.

"Atlas and I will meet Dan and Aiden on the local call, and we can all check in later. Then both wayfarers will be at full strength if you need to get out fast."

I take the sheet of paper that details—or rather doesn't detail—my placement for the day and rap my knuckles against the table's surface. "Safe home, everyone."

"Safe home," they repeat.

CHAPTER FIVE

The first thing I notice when Sloan, Dionysus, and I snap to Montréal is that the ambient energy is—believe it or not—exponentially stronger than it is in Toronto. "That explains why they have the highest level of awakenings in all of Canada. Holy hell, I feel like I'm drunk."

Dionysus scans the scenic park setting and tilts his head back to look at the clouds. "Wow. How can anyone focus on being hostile and angry when breathing in makes you feel this buzzy."

"Right?" I draw another deep breath and lift my finger to touch my face. "I can't feel my lips. Wow, this is good stuff."

"Look at the clouds." Dionysus points at the morning sky. "It's like a puppet show."

It is. Instead of random clouds blowing to form shapes in the sky, the clouds over Montréal are animated and performing for the people below.

I gasp as we reach the climax of the story and wince. "Watch out, bunny. There's a wolf behind the tree."

Sloan grabs my hand and removes it from covering my eyes. "All right, *a ghra.* Yer cut off. Ye both are."

I giggle and take his hand, swaying to an invisible beat. "How can I be cut off? Am I supposed to stop breathing?"

"No. Don't do it, Jane." Dionysus wraps his arms around both of us and joins our dance. "Suffocating is highly overrated. Breathing is good."

"*Impenetrable Sphere*," Sloan says. The signature of his druid power washes over me. "*Dispel Magic.*"

As the bubble of his sphere encapsulates us, my head starts to clear. It takes a few minutes, but soon enough, I come down out of the clouds.

Breathing deep to the depths of my lungs, I get nothing but oxygen and more clarity. "First, you're a total buzzkill, Mackenzie. Truly. That was the best high I've ever experienced, and you killed it. Second, what the hell was that? And third, why weren't you buzzed too?"

Sloan scans the park setting in the historic stone buildings beyond. "Do ye remember in the early days when yer grove was suckin' up all the ambient magic?"

"You mean when the entire empowered community of Toronto wanted to kill me and my family...yes, I vaguely recall that."

"Well, we found out the Laurentian River System has major ley lines and deposits more water into the system than any other waterway in Canada. If the tropical beach and the savannah experienced less of an alteration, it makes sense that the opposite would be happening in a hot spot like this."

I blink at him in wonder. "Kudos to you for remembering that. I vaguely remember us saying we'd need to take a trip to Quebec to tap into the St. Lawrence Seaway but yeah, good on you."

"Remembering mind-boggling facts is what Irish does," Dionysus says. "Well, that and looking sexy as fuck in those ripped black jeans of his."

I give Dionysus a high-five for that one. "True story. So, back to the last question. Why weren't you affected by the loopy air? And why isn't everyone in Montréal prana shitfaced?"

Sloan shakes his head. "It's not that I wasn't affected. I felt the kick of the power but nowhere near as strongly. I'd bet the stronger the natural affinity of the person, the stronger the effect. Yer both incredibly powerful and therefore, it hit the two of ye hard."

I laugh and wave that away. "I'm okay, but not even in the same league as Dionysus."

"Maybe not in overall power, but where his power source comes from the Greek pantheon, yers comes from the fae realm. I think that tips the scale yer way."

I glance at Dionysus. "What do you think about the bigger they are, the harder they fall theory, Tarzan?"

"Sure. I try not to argue with Sloan. He's a thinker."

"That he is. A quick thinker too. Sealing us in an impenetrable sphere was a solid idea. It doesn't bode well for us outside the sphere, but whatevs. I guess I'm the girl in the bubble."

Sloan chuckles. "I don't think we have to resort to that. Now that we realize what will happen if yer bombarded, cast a spell to protect yerself from magical influence."

"Okay, but I'm still wondering what's happening to the empowered people of Montréal. Do you think they're all super high and prana drunk?"

Dionysus chuckles. "Montréal is a well-known party stop. They have great clubs here and a fantastically fun and free vibe. Would anyone notice?"

Sloan arches a brow. "I think they would, yes. More likely, the people who live here were able to absorb and adapt over time. The three of us snapped here and got blasted with the full effect all at once."

"Like the frog in the pot," I say.

Sloan nods. "Exactly."

"Why is the frog in the pot?" Dionysus asks. "Is it a French frogs' legs thing because those are delish."

I shake my head. "No. It's the theory that if you toss a frog into a pot of boiling water, he'll hop out but if you put him into a pot of room temperature water and bring the water up to a boil, he won't hop out and will boil."

"That's barbaric." Dionysus scowls. "Who's boiling frogs alive and why? That's just wrong."

"It's an analogy, sweetie. I don't think any actual frogs died in the making of the theory."

"Well good. That was a horrible story."

"Oh, look. What lovely architecture." Sloan changes the subject. He's smiling across the road at a beautiful five-story, gray brick building with an intricate copper roof.

I giggle. "Leave it to my guy. The world has gone to hell, we're getting drunk from breathing, and Sloan's mesmerized by a centuries-old Gothic city hall."

Dionysus shakes his head. "The architectural style is Second Empire."

"The patina on the copper is lovely," Sloan says. "Although, I would've expected a slate roof for a building of the style and era."

I have no idea about that, and honestly, I don't care.

I clap once to get everyone's attention. "That concludes the art appreciation portion of our visit. How about we go find the mayor? I'm curious about the details she has yet to reveal."

"I hope it's something like her having an *Alice in Wonderland* moment," Dionysus says. "She ate the cookie and grew as big as the room."

"Easy-peasy, then we only have to find the bottle marked 'Drink Me' and we're all set."

"Except nothing is ever easy for us," Sloan says.

"May I help you?" A metrosexual guy in slacks and a vest meets and greets us the moment we step inside the public entrance of the Montréal City Hall. The space is bright and impressive, and the entire area is beige and cream marble.

I pull out my SITFU badge and hold it open for him to see. "I'm Fiona Cumhaill, fae liaison of Toronto. Mayor Tremblay requested a visit from my team."

He lifts a leather case and flips back the front cover to expose a tablet. "Yes, perfect. Can each of you sign in at reception? Then I'll take you up."

The three of us do as asked and follow him through the foyer to the base of an amazing old-fashioned elevator. Instead of a standard steel box, it's made from iron and glass and rises through the center of the building so we can see into the atrium.

As we step inside, he closes the iron accordion door, and I scan our surroundings. "This is a lovely old building. I never used to be interested in architecture, and I'm certainly no expert, but I get the sense that this building is special."

Our escort, Marcel, smiles at the atrium beyond. "It is. It's considered one of the best examples of the Second Empire style in Canada. Also, it was the first city hall in the country to have been constructed solely for municipal administration."

Huh, that's less cool than I thought.

Sloan's gaze narrows, and he holds up a finger. "Forgive me, but was there an extensive remodel? The interior doesn't match the era of the exterior."

"A discerning eye for detail, sir. You are correct."

I chuckle. "He usually is."

Marcel nods. "Yes, the original building opened in 1878 but was gutted by fire in 1922, leaving only the outer wall. The architect commissioned for the reconstruction built an entirely new, self-supporting steel structure inside the shell of the ruins. The new building was modeled after the city hall of the French city of Tours and opened in 1926."

I glance around, wondering how Sloan can look so enraptured with Marcel's account.

The building burned and they rebuilt it.

It's enough to know it's a nice old building.

Thankfully, the elevator bumps to a stop on the fifth floor, and the lesson in historical architecture ends.

Marcel opens the accordion gate to let us out. "This way please."

We follow our escort away from the elevator and along the iron rail that overlooks the atrium below. Our steps fall silently on the industrial carpet as we make our way through the outer lobby of the mayoral offices.

When we get to where we're going, Marcel stops inside the door. "May I introduce Her Worship, Mayor Tremblay."

A distinguished brunette woman wearing a navy pantsuit and heels rounds her desk. "Miss Cumhaill, thank you for coming all this way. I appreciate it more than you know."

She extends a hand to me, and I accept her welcome. "It's our pleasure to help. What can we do for you?"

"We'll get to that. First. I'll need you to sign a very simple non-disclosure agreement."

"An NDA? Seriously?"

The warmth in her smile cools considerably. "Yes. I am serious, Miss Cumhaill."

I wave away the formality. "I'm Fiona…or Fi if you like. Sorry, you caught me off-guard. Of course, if you need us to sign something, we can do that. Can you give Dionysus a copy? He'll zip to Toronto and have our in-house council read it quickly."

Marcel goes to the desk outside the door and comes back with a piece of paper.

Dionysus accepts it and snaps out.

Mayor Tremblay stares at the spot where Dionysus disappeared and frowns. "What exactly is he?"

"He's not a what. He's a who," I correct her.

The mayor draws a deep breath and exhales. "Of course, he is. My apologies. I'm afraid there's been so much thrust upon us so quickly that I haven't adapted as well as I would like. I aim to do better."

"Apology accepted. To answer your question, he's Dionysus. *The* Dionysus of Greek myth and legend. God of Wine and Fertility."

"Thus, the toga," she says.

I chuckle. "He doesn't normally dress like that, but today is a Greek holiday, and he's honoring a friend."

Dionysus snaps back and gives us a nod. "Andromeda signs off. We're good to go ahead."

"Thanks, Greek. Much appreciated."

We take turns signing our agreement to keep things confidential and wait.

The mayor dismisses Marcel, closes the door, and stalls out.

I offer her as much reassurance as I can with a smile. "This is the part when you explain why we're here, Madame Mayor?"

"Yes, of course, it's just...I have both an official reason for bringing you here and an unofficial one."

"All right, where would you like to begin?"

She considers that for a moment and returns to her desk to offer me a file folder. "I've been tracking the reports of awakenings, civilian violence, and police response calls to domestic situations, and I am both alarmed and concerned for the people of Montréal."

"How so?" I accept the folder and flip it open.

"We seem to be experiencing a more pronounced occurrence of awakenings than other cities of our size, yet no one is offering any explanations as to why. Also, regardless of why it's happening, we need measures in place to deal with the fallout, yet my counterparts don't seem to be making any measurable effort."

I hear the frustration in her voice, and I sympathize. It's hard to rule in times of chaos and hardship. "The first part of your concern is something we have a theory about, but I can't help you on the second."

Sloan and I take the next ten minutes to explain the ley lines and how the St. Lawrence Seaway is the merging point of an incredible number of tributaries now actively carrying fae energy to the area.

"It's only our theory based on what we knew prior to this, but it's sound," Sloan says.

Mayor Tremblay nods. "At least you have a theory. That's more than I've managed to scrape together over the past months. I feel like I'm the only one looking around and seeing what is happening in our streets."

I finish scanning the report. "I don't understand this. Is your police force not putting together a team to educate citizens and reach out to those affected?"

"I've been trying to organize, but I'm getting no support from the police. Chief Monet keeps telling me he has no resources to spare on social programs because the force is overwhelmed by the increased calls for his officers."

"I get that, but it's a chicken and the egg scenario. If you take time to soothe the conflict, maybe there won't be so many conflicts to respond to."

"Which is why I called you. I'm getting nowhere here and thought having your team evaluate our situation to give us some starting points might give us the kick in the pants we need."

"We'll do our best. Did Maxwell mention to you on the phone that we'd like to mentor local officers so they can, in the future, become fae liaison officers themselves?"

"I asked Chief Monet to appoint a team or at least ask for volunteers, but I think he ignored my request completely because the friends I have in the local PD knew nothing about it."

"All right, so we start there. We'll help you put together a team and branch out."

"Chief Monet won't like that."

I shrug. "I'm not trying to step on anyone's toes, but I've got federal support behind me that trumps whatever issue a municipal police chief might have against the empowered citizens in your city."

Mayor Tremblay arches a brow. "I admire your conviction, Miss Cumhaill but be aware that they will see you as a young, female, English-speaking, Toronto girl with opinions. There are a lot of boy's club Frenchmen here who won't take kindly to you telling them how to run this city."

I shrug again. "I have no intention of telling people how to run their city. Honestly, I don't. I'm also not afraid of stubborn, alpha cops who think themselves better than the citizens they work for. I grew up with my entire family on the job. I'm not new to the culture."

She takes that into consideration and nods. "All right. Where do we start?"

"The first thing we need is an audience with your cops. We need to get our call for liaison duty through the channels. Montréal can't be much different from Toronto. We started with the cops who experienced awakenings themselves or who have close family and friends who did. They are the ones most invested in the outcome of calming the waters."

"That was my thinking too. The problem is, Police Chief Monet has been so vocal in his condemnation of the fae not belonging in our city or on our force that everyone is afraid to step up and admit they have fae genes."

I'm starting to dislike this guy.

I look at Sloan and shrug. "What do you think? Where do we start?"

Sloan has that glimmer in his eyes that says he's piecing together a brilliant plan. "Madam Mayor, can you call an audience with the local officers to introduce Fiona's arrival?"

"I can, but again, I want to caution you about side-stepping Chief Monet. He's not a man to underestimate, and when he realizes I'm moving ahead without his consent, he won't be happy."

Sloan shakes his head, a sly smile curling his lips. "If things work out as I believe they will, by the end of yer address, I'll have the names we need to put on yer list and yer chief won't be any the wiser."

I grin, excited to hear his plan. "Yay, you."

CHAPTER SIX

As it turns out, our audience with the police force is less of an address to introduce our arrival and what's working in Toronto and more of a response call to a protest and potential riot outside the building.

"How many are you expecting?" I ask Marcel after he informs us of the hostile groups expected to take position outside.

"Hundreds on both sides. Some idiot posted a TikTok challenge to draw attention to the protest, and now it's gone viral."

"Is there a time and place where it prompts these folks to converge?" Sloan asks.

"Noon, in the park behind the building."

Sloan lifts his wrist and checks his watch. "All right, that gives us just over an hour before we need to be on high alert."

I glance back at Mayor Tremblay standing behind her desk. "Your police chief said he couldn't afford to send you anyone because of how busy his officers are, responding to calls. This incident might work in our favor."

Sloan nods. "It does, and my idea still stands. Fiona can assess the crowd, and I will assess the potential power and disciplines of the officers who respond."

"You can do that?" Marcel asks.

"Aye, it's part of my abilities. With the briefest touch, I can read the magical strengths of those with fae power."

I smile. "It's how we first met."

Mind you, I mistook him for a mugger, and we ended up in an all-out brawl behind Shenanigans, but that's another story altogether.

"Then we wait and prepare," the mayor says. "Marcel, inform the staff of what's going on and encourage all non-essential staff to leave and work from home if their jobs allow. Is David in yet?"

Marcel flips the cover of his tablet open and nods. "Yes, Deputy Mayor Olivier is here. He is in his office on a call until eleven forty-five."

"Fine, don't disturb him, but send him a message to let him know what's happening."

"Yes, ma'am." Marcel excuses himself and closes the door as he leaves.

When it's only us in the room, she swallows. "Now to the personal matter I mentioned."

Right. I almost forgot.

The mayor moves to the far wall to open a second door that leads to an adjoining room. "*Ma belle*, come meet some new friends, will you?"

"*Oui, Maman*," a little voice says.

A moment later a dark-haired girl of about six comes out of the adjoining room, and I see the mayor's concerns immediately.

"She's got horns," she says, her voice strangled.

"She sure does." Dionysus grins. "And what beautiful horns they are."

The man melts my heart. Seriously. How could anyone have hated and ridiculed him? Even after centuries of people trying to end him because of who he was born to, he has so much love and acceptance to give.

Taking a few steps closer to the girl, I sit on my knees and hold my hand out to see if she'll come to me. "What's your name, sweetie?"

"Bella." She reaches out to shake my hand without hesitation.

"Hello, Bella, I'm Fi, and these are my friends, Sloan and Dionysus."

"Do you really like my horns?" She's staring at Dionysus as she lifts her hand to run a tentative stroke over them.

"I do. Very much. You remind me of a rain nymph princess I used to know. She had pretty horns too."

I study the brown and beige ram horns that come out of the front of her skull and curl back to hang freely by her ears. They are delicate and ribbed. Between them, on the crest of her forehead, sits what looks like a birthmark of a crescent moon.

I run a gentle finger over her forehead and my skin tingles as I touch the crescent on her brow.

"What am I?" she asks. "Do you know?"

"Of course, I do, silly. You're a beautiful and smart little girl."

"I have horns. I didn't use to, but I do now."

"I know exactly how that feels." I unzip my jacket and set it on the floor next to me. "Do you want to see something I have that I didn't until fae magic touched my life?"

"Okay."

I turn my back to her and pull my shirt up so she can see my Fianna shield.

"That's pretty. Is it a tree?"

"It is. It's the tree of life." I let my shirt drop and face her once more. "One day, before I knew I was special, I felt a little funny. When I tried to figure out what was making me feel weird, there it was…a tree of life covering my back."

"Really?" the mayor asks. "That's not a tattoo? You seem to have many."

I glance at the Celtic runes and knotwork Pan Dora, and later Merlin inked onto my skin. There is an ouroboros band on my left bicep that the Queen of Dragons gave me as a portal link to her lair. Last but certainly not least, there's the inked form of my enchanted spear, Birga, resting on the inside of my right forearm.

"No. These are mastered spells, portals, and weapons here for me to draw on in battle. The tree was the first. It manifested there right before I learned about my druid powers and my heritage. Its arrival left me stunned, confused, and burning for answers."

"That's exactly how I feel," the mayor says, panic sharp in her gaze. "Bella is adopted, so I don't have any way to get those answers."

I step in close with Dionysus and Sloan. "Any initial thoughts on the origin of her awakening?"

Sloan looks perplexed. "Nothing that wouldn't be a guess and even then, it's not a perfect fit."

The mayor lets out a pained sound. "You don't know? I thought for sure you'd have answers."

I pull out my phone and offer her a reassuring smile. "I know exactly the person to help us if you'll permit me to call in a friend."

Mayor Tremblay stiffens, and I shake my head. "No one here will do or say anything to harm your daughter. Beautiful Bella is one of us. She's special and has an empowered heritage. You can trust us to keep her safe."

I think she hears the truth in my words because she relents. "All right."

I call up Myra's number and hit send.

"Miss me already, duck?"

"Always, you know that. Hey, if I send Dionysus to you, can he portal you and Imari to Montréal for half an hour? I've got a little girl here who's had her awakening, and she and her mom have questions I think you'd be the best at answering."

"Oh, lovely. I'll put out the gone to lunch sign and be ready in a snap."

"Thanks, girlfriend. 'Kay. See you in a few." Glancing back, I meet Dionysus's gaze. "Two for a pickup at the bookstore, if you will."

Dionysus winks at me. "Be right back."

When he's gone, I explain to the mayor and her daughter. "My friend Myra is an ash nymph. She adopted a little girl about the same age as you. Her name is Imari, and she's special too."

"Does she have horns?"

I shake my head. "No. She can turn into a bear."

"Can I do that?"

I shrug. "I don't know yet, sweetie. My friend Myra will be able to tell us more. She's a Fae Historian and knows more about fae races than anyone else I know."

Mayor Tremblay seems to be losing steam. "Do you think she'll be able to help us?"

"I absolutely do. She might not know immediately, but we'll keep searching until we find the answers you need. I promise we won't quit until we know Bella's heritage and what it means going forward."

Dionysus snaps back a moment later with my two favorite ladies.

I greet Myra and wonder what the mayor and her daughter see when they look at her. No doubt, the Bohemian patterned bell-bottoms, and the electric blue hair cropped on a severe angle from shaved short on one side of her head and hanging to her shoulder on the other.

Like most nymphs, she is tall and beautiful with vertically slit eyes, but her designation as an ash nymph means her skin is pale, almost silver, and is cracked with darker tones beneath. The effect reminds me of the bark of a birch tree.

It's unusual but lovely.

I gesture at the mayor and her daughter. "Myra and Imari, this is Mayor Tremblay and her daughter, Bella."

"It's wonderful to meet you." Myra is her usual warm and wonderful self. She clutches the mayor's hand in hers, then turns to the little girl. "Oh, Miss Bella, what a pretty dress you're wearing. It's lovely."

Bella smiles, her attention locked on Imari. "Can you really turn into a bear?"

"Sometimes. Mostly when I'm scared."

"I hide under my covers when I'm scared."

Imari chuckles. "I do that too."

"I wish I could turn into a bear."

"My daddy says when I'm bigger, I'll be able to do it whenever I want to."

"That's cool. Do you want to color?"

"Sure."

Imari and Bella shuffle off to the other room, and I move our conversation so I have a line of sight on them. Garnet would never forgive me if I involved his daughter in a case and lost track of her. Especially when I know there is trouble on the horizon.

Sometimes life is a balancing act.

"Thanks for coming," I say to Myra. "Might you know what Bella is?"

Sloan joins us and leans in. "I thought she might have faun genes, but with only the horns and not the legs of that race I wasn't sure."

Myra nods. "That was my first thought too. There are a few other fae races that have horns, but her skin is pale and soft, so I don't think she's a tiefling and satyr isn't right either."

Dionysus shakes his head. "No. I've known a lot of satyrs in my existence, and I don't think that's right."

"Then I'd guess she's part faun." Myra smiles at the mayor. "Fiona mentioned you adopted her. Do you have access to any of her birth information?"

"No. That was the first thing I did when her horns appeared, but there's nothing they can tell me. She was abandoned anonymously at an orphanage and put into their care after being checked out by the staff doctor and the police. They had no reason to believe she was anything but one hundred percent human. How is everyone suddenly turning fae?"

Sloan shakes his head. "No one is *turning* fae, Madam Mayor."

She waves his words away. "Please call me Clarissa. You're here at my request and helping me when you have no reason. There's no need to be so formal."

Sloan nods. "Very well, Clarissa. What people don't understand about the awakenings is that they are just that—an awakening of what already exists within. Dozens of fae and empowered races have lived hidden in this world for centuries. There have been mixed marriages and liaisons and a crossover of species all along."

The mayor runs rough fingers through her hair. "I can't wrap my head around that…and to be clear, I'm not naïve enough to think we know all of it. Obviously, there is more. Your office is much too careful with the information to believe everything is out in the open."

I shrug. "The world has enough to deal with as it is. There's no need to overwhelm everyone and cause a panic. I'm sure, in the end, it'll all become public knowledge. For right now, it's best not to open the flood gates and drown everyone."

She meets my gaze, and I can see she's warring with herself about whether to be a mayor at this moment or a mother.

I gesture at the girls giggling and drawing pictures on printer paper on the mayor's coffee table in the seating area. "Your daughter appeared wholly human until recently, but the truth is, the genetic building blocks that tie back to a faun community—or whatever race she might be—were already there."

"It's showing itself because the veil dropped," she says.

I nod. "There must've been an element of the veil that blocked or suppressed fae traits. They were part of your daughter, but they were latent and non-dominant."

"And now they aren't."

"Exactly. She's the same little girl she was last week and last year, except now a trait of her heritage has shown itself."

"What happens if the barrier between worlds is reinstated? Will the horns be reversible?"

I look at Sloan and Myra for the answer to that one.

Both of them shake their head.

Sloan rubs a hand over his mouth and smiles at them playing happily. "Liken it to a sapling tree growing a new branch. Once it sprouts and grows, there's no reversal. It's now part of the beauty that makes up the tree."

Point to Sloan Mackenzie for that one.

That's a lovely way to put it.

The mayor takes that in stride. "You're sure she's healthy? She won't change more? She's not in any pain?"

Myra fields that one. "You can always have a fae healer look at her—human doctors won't even begin to know what they're looking at—but from what I see, she's a happy, healthy, well-adjusted little girl."

"So, it's as simple as that, is it?"

I catch Myra's wince, and my skin tightens. "It's the crescent, isn't it? You're wondering what, if anything, that means, aren't you?"

Myra meets my gaze, and I read the worry in her eyes. "There are many legends about crescent-born fae, but from what I remember, they all died out a long time ago. I don't know what it means that Bella bears the symbol now. Is it part of her buried heritage or is there another meaning we're not aware of yet?"

The mayor's brow pinches. "Why does it have to mean anything? Can't it be a birthmark?"

"Was she born with the mark?" Sloan asks.

The mayor shakes her head. "No. It didn't appear until her awakening."

"Then I think that's your answer." Myra lays a gentle hand on the woman's arm. "The fae universe has plans for your daughter and for now, we don't know what those plans are."

The shattering of glass brings my attention to the growing hostilities building outside. "Madam Mayor, do you have somewhere safe for your daughter to go? If things go south here, I don't want her caught up in the tensions of fae hatred."

The mayor shakes her head. "I adopted Isabella because I was alone in the world. There's no one."

"Let me take her." Myra steps forward. "She can spend the afternoon in the bookstore with Imari and me. It'll be fun for them, and I swear she'll be safe."

I nod. "It's a great idea. I know you don't know us yet, but we'd never let anything happen to innocents. Myra's bookstore is enchanted, and only fae who need to be there can access it. It's a quiet, magical place, like something out of Harry Potter."

The mayor considers that for a moment and nods. "All right. I'm sure Bella would enjoy that...but I have your word you'll watch over her and keep her safe?"

Myra presses her hand against her chest. "From one mother to another, I swear it."

Clarissa nods. "Very well, please take the girls somewhere safe."

I gesture for Dionysus to join us as the mayor and Myra step away to speak to the girls. "Three to beam back to the bookstore, Tarzan. Please deliver them and come back as soon as you can. I have a feeling tension is ramping up outside, and we'll need to get out there."

"BRB. Whatever you need, I'm there for you, Jane."

CHAPTER SEVEN

It doesn't take long before Dionysus is back and we're ready to face the hostilities of the world outside. I take a quick trip to the bathroom to pee, splash some water on my face and get into the headspace to tackle the next hurdle. Sloan's right. Being on high alert and getting pulled in every direction is wearing on me.

I dry my hands and meet my gaze in the mirror.

"Whatevs. There will be time enough to laze about when we're dead." I think about my brother Brendan and chuckle. "Maybe not even then."

After tossing my paper towel, I turn the door handle and go out to join the others. "All right. Is everyone set?"

I'm not worried about Sloan, but I check in with Dionysus. "You're with me, Tarzan. While Sloan takes the magical temperature of the police officers outside, we'll work on calming everyone and keeping things friendly. Oh, and I suppose we should spell ourselves against the effects of the ambient levels in the air."

Sloan joins us. "I've been thinkin' about that. If we alter the purpose of *Impenetrable Sphere* so it's less of a beach ball of shieldin' and more of an aura of protection, we could reduce the density of the ambient magic so we don't get overloaded outside."

I look at him and chuckle. "When you say *we could* I'm super-duper hoping you mean *you could* because that was way over my paygrade, hotness."

He rolls his eyes. "Aye, of course. If ye think the idea has merit, I'll take care of things."

I curl my fingers into the shape of a heart and press them against my chest. "I heart you hard, Mackenzie."

Dionysus presses a hand flat against the belt of his chiton and bows. "I have faith in you, Irish. Hey, if it doesn't work, that'll be fun too."

I laugh. The ambient high was fun but now is not the time. "All right. Now I need to figure out how to communicate my point to the people out there."

"Here, let me help make that happen." Dionysus steps in and touches my throat with gentle fingers. I feel the pulse of his magic the moment his skin touches mine.

When he steps back, I brush my fingers over the warmth his touch left behind and swallow. "What did you do?"

"Mayor Clarissa said the people might not like you because you don't speak their language. Now, whatever language the people in the crowd speak, that's what they'll hear. Your words will connect with everyone who hears them. In turn, you'll understand what's said around you so you can answer appropriately."

"You put a universal translator spell on my throat?"

"Just a little one," he says, looking worried. "Was that wrong?"

"No. S'all good. That was a great idea. It'll help."

Dionysus stands straighter and pushes back his broad shoulders. "Nailed it."

"Yeah, you did."

Sloan comes back to his idea about shielding us in ambient free aura bubbles, and Dionysus and I let him do his thing. He's confident it should work and honestly, I believe in him enough not to question it.

With that taken care of, the four of us glance at one another, and Mayor Tremblay gestures at the outer office. "Shall we?"

I nod and take the lead, ensuring she isn't exposed to undue hostility. "Here we go."

The ride back down the elevator isn't nearly as relaxing as the ride up. When we got here two hours ago, the day was all about promise and the hope that maybe my team could step in and teach a few officials how to make the world a better place.

No such luck.

Then again, given the choice of my life being easy or hard, the fae universe always seems to lean toward hard. Well, if not hard, then at least convolutedly not easy.

The scene at the back of the Montréal City Hall stands in stark contrast to how things looked at the front a couple of hours ago when we arrived.

There is a large, grassy green space that runs the length of the city block and people holding signs, waving slogans, and shouting at passing civilians have completely overrun it.

I take a moment to draw in a couple of deep breaths and move around in my anti-ambient aura. Yeah, I think I'm good. "Sloan Mackenzie earns a hero cookie."

"I thought we award greatness with Oh Henry! bars," Dionysus says.

"We award pranks, and jaw-dropping life twists with Oh Henry! bars. We award greatness with whatever strikes our fancy."

"Ooo, if we're speaking of striking our fancies. I'd love to reward him with—"

I laugh and shake my head. "Stay on topic, Tarzan. This is a park riot, not an orgy. Let's keep it PG."

"Make love not war. Isn't that a human thing?"

"It is, but this crowd doesn't seem inclined to kiss and make up at the moment."

Sloan points and brings our attention to the four vans parked in the lot on the park's north end. They have network logos painted on the side and camera crews getting their systems ready.

I blink as the crews start to work the crowd. "News trucks already. Wow, they're on the ball."

Mayor Tremblay sighs. "I know they say any attention can be good attention, but honestly, I've come to believe that's not true. I wish our media could start focusing on stories that would unite instead of divide."

"Preach."

As we descend the stairs, several of the police officers taping off the back steps of the building turn to greet our arrival.

"Madam Mayor." A plain-clothed officer in his forties joins us. He looks good in a pair of jeans and a blazer, has a crooked nose that's been broken one too many times, and possesses a wariness in his eyes that says he's been through some shit but survived. "I don't suppose you'd consider staying inside until this protest nonsense is over?"

She tugs her light jacket closer to her neck and shakes her head. "I'm afraid not, Rene. What's happening in the city is affecting all of us. It's important the citizens see me right there with them."

"How did I know you were going to say that?" He makes eyes at her before extending his hand to me. "You're the Lady Druid from Toronto, right?"

I accept his welcome and shake. "Fiona Cumhaill, and these are my partners in crime, Sloan Mackenzie and Dionysus."

"Rene Michaud," he says. "Thank you for coming to help sort

out our mess. It's like the world went crazy on us and we can't seem to get it back to normal."

I shake my head. "That's your first mistake. The objective can't be to fix it back to how it was. The only thing we can do is strive for a peaceful new normal."

He draws a deep breath and sighs. "Wouldn't it be nice if we could go back?"

Sloan fields that one. "Maybe, but wishing it will not make it so, Monsieur Michaud. The awakening you've experienced is just that, an awakening of what has always been within."

Rene glares at Sloan. Then in a flash, the emotion is gone. He forces a laugh and waves between them. "I'm not sure what you're implying, Mr. Mackenzie, but I wasn't referring to myself."

"Of course, ye were, although perhaps not entirely."

"I'm not fae. I'm only a detective in Major Crimes who's trying to hold his city together."

Sloan flashes him a knowing smile. "And I'm an empowered druid who reads not only levels of fae power but also recent memories. Pardon the invasion, but we're here to help Mayor Tremblay, and she needs officers like you."

Before he has a chance to answer, the mayor grasps his wrist. "Rene, please, Sloan is right. If you have fae genes coming to life, you're exactly the man I'm looking for to help me put together a response team."

He glances over his shoulders and leans closer to her. "If Chief Monet or any of his lackeys find out, I won't be an officer long enough to help anyone do anything. The chief has made it damn clear fae freaks don't belong on his force."

I chuff. "Then Chief Monet is in for a rude awakening himself because it's a complete violation to fire anyone affected by the activation of fae genes. It was one of the first laws we put into place at the federal and municipal levels. It can't happen."

He shrugs. "You're assuming he'd come right out and say it. No, mark my words. If you make my situation public knowledge,

I'll be gone inside six months, and it'll be for some trumped-up bullshit like insubordination, conduct unbecoming, or failure to log in evidence."

A group of protestors marching down the road round the corner and come shouting into earshot. The crowd already gathered in the park grows more riled up, and it's not hard to see where this is heading.

"How about we table this discussion for the time being?" I say. "Mayor, maybe he's right, and you should wait this out inside."

"Not going to happen," she says.

Rene mumbles something in French that makes no sense to me, even understanding the words. Quebecois sayings can be truly bizarre.

He's singing me the apple.

Boss of toilets.

Born to be a bun.

Like I said...bizarre.

Turning away from our conversation, Rene lets loose a sharp whistle and raises a hand toward a brunette standing at the side of a car parked on the north end of the green space.

When she turns to see what he wants, he pats his chest and points at the mayor. She nods and circles to the car's trunk.

"If you insist on being out here, at the very least, you'll have a vest on."

I nod. "That's fair. It keeps you here yet safe."

Mayor Clarissa concedes. "That's fine, as long as I'm here and can have my say once things get started."

I don't suppose there's any other answer that will win her over. While Rene works out the logistics of the mayor getting a vest, I step aside to speak to Dionysus. "Whatever happens, keep an eye on the mayor. Sloan will be working the crowd control cops, and I'll be busy assessing the crowd. I need you to keep her safety as your priority."

"Not a problem. I'll wrap her in cotton and coat her in varnish?"

"That sounds sticky and weird."

"It's not. Cotton to keep her safe and varnish because that hardens for protection."

I chuckle. "I get the idea."

The crowd of dozens has tripled with the arrival of the marching and shouting crowd, and I'm disappointed to see how truly riled up they are. Sure, we've had a couple of people in Toronto spout off, but for the most part, the citizens have taken things pretty well.

As the tensions grow more pronounced, I abandon my position on the steps of the building to get into the thick of things with the protestors. The composition of the crowd is about seventy-percent non-magicals and thirty percent empowered.

"Make the fae go away! Make the fae go away!"

The mantra is short-sighted and rude. I suppose protest mantras are never sweet and sunshiny but still.

I head over to the douche canoe with the megaphone. The guy is a Viking-type blond with loose curls and two-day scruff. He's got his hand fisted in the air and is provoking the crowd with all he's got.

When I get up to him, I grab the megaphone and pull it away from his mouth. "Dude, isn't it bad enough you're spouting off hate without blasting it out at a hundred and twenty decibels?"

He continues to pump his hand and shout as if I'm not even there.

Leaning into his line of vision, I wave my hand. "Yoo-hoo, Ragnar, are you with me?"

"Make the fae go away!"

No, he's not with me.

What the hell? My shield tingles against my back, and I take a closer look at the most obnoxiously vocal crowd members. A bearded lumberjack guy. A woman with scraggly white hair wearing a patchwork coat. A college frat boy in a hoodie.

"*Detect Magic*." I cast my powers over them in a broad reach to see what I get back. My shield ramps up from a tingle to a niggle, and I frown.

It's not fae magic, but it's not normal either.

Someone or something is controlling these people somehow.

Jogging over to find Sloan, I grip his hand and tug him a few steps away to speak to him privately. "I think the troublemakers here have been compelled or bespelled somehow. I don't think this hostility is natural."

Sloan frowns. "Stay here. Let me have a look. Who specifically?"

I point out the half-dozen people I'm referring to, and he moves through the crowd. To keep the attention away from him, I bring the megaphone I swiped to my lips and decide to address the people.

"Good morning, everyone. I'm Fiona Cumhaill, fae liaison of Toronto, and I'm glad to be here with you today so we can open a dialogue and get to the heart of what's bothering you."

My intro doesn't even put a dent into the shouting.

"In Toronto, we've been hosting monthly town hall meetings at a local pub so everyone who has questions or concerns regarding the awakenings can access a forum and engage in a peaceful conversation. Let's try that here. Let's take the shouting down a notch and address some of your concerns."

There's no reaction from the crowd. It's more than them ignoring me. I don't think I'm even registering on their wavelength.

I drop the megaphone from my mouth and catch up with Sloan. "I might as well be invisible and mute. What the hell is going on?"

"I'd say almost ninety percent of the people here are being

compelled. They don't see ye or hear ye, luv. They're lost in their compulsion."

"Well, *that's* not good."

"Och, that's an understatement. Ye must ask yerself, what's to be gained by coercing hundreds of people toward anger and righteous judgment?"

I don't need to ask myself. The foreboding of what's to come is electric in the air. "Someone wants a riot."

He nods and frowns at the rising tensions around us. "If we don't act quickly, they're going to get it."

With no idea what else to do, I pull out my phone, call Garnet, and give him the quickest version of the story I can think of. "We're standing in the center of a race war bomb about to detonate."

"Give me two minutes to pull together a team and get there. Behind the city hall, you said?"

"Yeah. You wouldn't happen to know of a way to break a mass coercion, would you?"

"No, but I'll bring Dan. Maybe he might."

"Okay, I'll try Merlin and see if he has any ideas." Hanging up, I find Merlin's contact next and press send.

"Hey, girlfriend. What's new with you?"

"Hey, sorry, no time. How do I break a mass coercion spell in a public forum?"

"What kind of coercion?"

"No idea. I've got three or four hundred protestors programmed to go off at any moment." I check the time on my phone and curse. "I'm guessing they're set to riot at noon. You've got four minutes. Go."

"Fuck, Fi." I hear his breath pick up as he runs through his loft apartment over his club. "Best guess on the cause. Do they look drugged, possessed, spelled, or compelled?"

I take another moment to study the people around me and frown. "I'd say spelled or compelled."

"You don't know?"

"Sorry."

"Uh..." I hear him scrambling through papers on the other end of the line. "Who's on your team today?"

"Sloan and Dionysus are here with me, and Garnet, Dan the djinn, and our new elf trainee on the way."

"Uh..."

I check the phone again and frown. "Less than two minutes."

"Fuckfuckfuckfuck...okay, knock them out. It's the only thing I can think of. Have Dionysus—"

"—no, he can't do the god save."

"Right, but he can bring Emmet to you. Dan has the psychic power to pull someone's cognitive plug and knock them out but not enough juice to do it to hundreds of people at once. Emmet's a buffer and supercharged from living on the island. Have Emmet boost Dan."

"Got it. Thanks." I hang up, and thankfully Dionysus is close by and listening. "Emmet, please. As fast as you can."

I turn to search the crowd and see Garnet and his team rushing in from the sidelines. "Sloan, I need to get to Dan, now!"

Sloan's head turns from where he's standing fifty feet away. He *poofs* to get me, and we *poof* almost instantly and wind up standing directly in front of Dan.

"Dan, I need you to knock out everyone in this crowd who is mind-altered. Merlin says you can pull their plugs and Emmet will give you the power boost you need to do it."

As if on cue, Dionysus snaps my brother into the mix. He's only wearing boxers and crazy pink sunglasses, but that's beside the point. "Em, boost Dan, now!"

Emmet raises his palms toward Dan and runs to close the distance.

He's not close enough.

Shit. He's not going to make it.

A shockwave of power detonates from our djinn, and my heart stops. The moment hangs in the air, then...

The crowd of protestors drops like marionettes with their strings cut.

They did it.

I pat my racing heart and study the field of the fallen. Not everyone hit the grass. Right, Sloan said around ninety percent of the crowd was altered.

Those who weren't are still standing.

Some fae are looking around as if wondering what happened. A couple of humans are doing the same thing. And about two dozen are neither fae nor human and staring at me like I just ruined all their fun.

My shield ignites, and the urgency of the warning leaves no time to consider what the danger is.

"Incoming! This ain't over, people."

CHAPTER EIGHT

"*Tough as Bark.*" As my protective armor activates and the inking fretwork covers my skin in an almost impenetrable layer, I call Birga to my palm. "Bruin, we need you, buddy."

I release my bear and take a beat to assess whatever is about to rain down on us. "Dionysus, snap the mayor out of here. Take her to Myra's shop and get back here as quickly as you can."

A dozen attackers are racing toward the mayor, Rene, and the brunette cop from the car. As they close in, I see their dropped fangs and raised clawed fingers.

"Fucking vampires." I race to block their access as Dionysus grabs the mayor by the wrist and snaps out.

The moment they disappear my focus shifts.

"*Bestial Strength.*" I call on the power to match a vampire's attack and get ready for anything.

"Game on, assholes."

I'm not sure why they wanted a riot or what they intended to do, but it's obvious within a few racing heartbeats they didn't expect to run into opposition.

As our crew and Garnet's team take up arms against the

invading force, I notice a man standing in the distance. The guy is a long and lean silver fox wearing a snazzy pressed suit and a silk pocket square.

If I'd walked past him on the street, I'd think he was a CEO on the way to the boardroom. He seems wholly out of place standing in the shadows watching a bloodbath in motion.

A dismembered head spins through the air spraying blood as Bruin gets his groove on.

Sloan and Dan shift into position with him to battle.

Atlas looks a little lost, but it's his first battle. I suppose that's to be expected.

Emmet has fashioned a staff out of a tree branch and is giving it a workout despite his lack of clothes.

Garnet and his men are fighting, pushing the opposing force away from the downed innocents.

As the boys dig in, I lose track of the CEO for a moment. Twisting this way and that, I see several vampires have evaded us and made it into the building.

"There's no one there, assholes," I shout, gripping Birga in my palm as I give chase. There are, but not many. Mayor Clarissa sent home all non-essential personnel, but I'm not sure who that leaves inside.

By the time I get to the back steps, Dionysus snaps back. "Where's the fire, Jane?"

"Inside. I think they might've planned the riot to create a diversion."

"Subterfuge. I love it." He falls in behind me.

It's crazy inside, and if we're supposed to decipher who's after what, it will take some doing. *Bruin? I need you and some backup inside. It's bedlam in here.*

On our way, Red.

The elevator's movement brings my attention to the CEO guy arriving on the top floor and heading toward the mayor's offices.

"There!" I point. "Get me up there, Tarzan."

"As you wish."

We snap from the main floor of the atrium into the mayor's office, and I catch the man in the suit by surprise. He's only swung the door open and stepped inside, and he seems genuinely startled to find us there standing in front of him.

"Who and what are you?" he growls, studying me.

"I'm the thorn in your side, the spoiler of plans, the itch you can never quite scratch. Whatever you came here to do, pack it in, and I'll pretend you got lost in the chaos and let you leave."

He chuckles. "*Let me*, will you? I think you'll find I can take care of myself."

Two vampires race in behind him, and he gestures toward us. "Have your fun, boys. Don't let me stop you."

His men rush forward, and I'm about to meet their attack when Bruin materializes and rears on his back feet. My mythical battle bear has his armor activated and is in full Killer Claw-bearer mode.

Not one to ruin his fun, I let him take on the battle.

A powerful swipe of his claws sends one head sailing through the air. It lands on the expensive area rug with a hollow *thunk*. Then he engages the second.

The rage CEO pegs me with warms my innies.

I shrug. "I think you'll find that we too can take care of ourselves. So, can I give Mayor Tremblay a message for you?" Another hollow *thunk* and the battle is well and truly won. "Last chance. Either accept you've lost and give up or join your minions in a game of detachable noggin."

His gaze narrows and the promise of violence is palpable. "Do you have any idea who you're talking to, little girl?"

"The Vampire King of the Quebec seethes?"

"And yet you look me in the eye and joke about killing members of my kind?"

I shrug. "It's a kill or be killed world, Your Highness. You and your boys came here stewing for bloodshed. That's what you got. Just not the way you planned. Tough noogies. Sucks to be you."

He glances from me to Dionysus and Bruin. "You'll regret what you've done here today. Mark my words. You made a grave error. Vampire enemies are not to be taken lightly."

Dionysus chuckles. "Okeedoodle, thanks for letting us know."

I gesture toward the sitting room where the mayor's daughter was playing. "Now, if you're opting to keep your ears above your shoulders, take a seat. We've got to call this in to the locals. I have a feeling we've got some 'splainin' to do."

He slides a hand into the pocket of his slacks and my shield ramps up for an inspired second wave. Several explosions detonate downstairs. The building shakes on its foundation and the screaming begins.

Vampire King's mouth curls in an eerie smile. "You didn't think this invasion was only to scare people, did you?"

"Well, I did until you said *that*."

Another explosion goes off, and the vamp boss becomes a blur of a fancy suit as he races off.

"We've got a runner."

Bruin ghosts out in his spirit form and Sloan, Dionysus, and I race through the mayor's receiving room and toward the atrium. "Shit. Is he dead?"

Sloan kneels to check on Marcel.

The mayor's aide is slumped on the floor beside his desk. I can't tell by looking if he's gone or only out cold.

Sloan frowns as he straightens and shakes his head. "There's nothing to be done for him, I'm afraid. His neck is broken."

The screaming downstairs hasn't stopped and my focus shifts from the dead to the living. "How many vamps have we got down there?"

Dionysus runs to the rail and looks down at the floors below. "A dozen at least."

Damn it.

"Okay, everyone, take a floor," Sloan says.

"I call ground." Running at a clip, I vault over the rail and let gravity take hold. *"Diminish Descent."*

The speed of my rapid return to the ground floor has my shirt fluttering and my hair flying free in the air behind me. I scan each floor briefly as I fall, taking in the damage from the explosions.

Despite the way the building shook while the blasts were going off, the damage doesn't seem to be structural.

Looks like the building will survive once again.

Spotting my target below, I grip Birga and get ready to engage.

Two vampires have a woman pinned against the elevator and are non-con feeding on her. Preparing to land, I slow my descent even more, ready my weapon, and cushion my fall.

The first vamp's neck is no match for Birga's jagged, marble spear tip, but the second guy wrapped himself around his victim, and I can't risk hurting her.

With a spin of my spear, I crack him in the lower back with the blunt end of Birga's staff. That gets his attention. When he drops the woman and she slumps to the marble floor, there's enough space between him and me to follow through with my attack.

"Taking what isn't offered is a criminal offense, dude. Not to mention very rude."

The vampire is still in a state of heightened frenzy from feeding. His eyes are glowing scarlet, and his fangs have extended like something you'd see in a horror flick.

"Who the fuck are you?"

"I'm the girl who's not going to let you get away with feeding on an innocent human."

The guy doesn't offer me a response—well, he does, but it's not a verbal one. He lunges at me with fangs and claws bared, and

I shift back a couple of steps to put some distance between him and his victim.

I swipe Birga through the air, keeping him at a distance for the moment. It won't last long.

Thankfully, by the groaning and her weak attempts to crawl away, the woman he was feeding on isn't dead. There's enough of that going around without adding to the body count.

The blood-thirsty vamp smiles at me, eyeing my throat. "You chose the wrong time to assert yourself, kitten. If you don't want me feeding on her, I'll have to find another tasty morsel to satisfy my hunger."

"Then, by all means, try to chow down."

He grabs a metal rod from the debris of one of the explosions, and the two of us go at it.

When I first claimed Birga as my weapon, I worried that with her age, she might not be as strong as some of the more modern weapons we come up against. I thought the wood of her staff might be brittle or that a smooth spear tip might be better than the jagged marble.

Doubting her was foolish.

Birga rules.

The one thing about fighting against vampires is that, for the most part, they aren't tactically amazing opponents. They are uber strong and virtually indestructible, and they rely on those two truths to win battles.

Neither of those works against me or mine.

Druids can call strength from the world around us. With the prana power in such a surge here, my cells burst with energy. Also, between Sloan and Merlin cracking the whip, we've been training hard every day for over a year.

I allow my opponent a couple of test hits to gauge his ability and quickly end things with a brutal swipe under his left ear.

It strikes me then. I'm stronger because of the surge in the world's power, but the vampires aren't. They don't use magic.

Therefore most of the empowered world is leveling up around them and leaving them in the dust.

Aw, sad face. Too bad.

As yet another noggin rolls, I straighten, taking in my surroundings. Sloan has made his way down to the ground floor and is finishing with his opponent.

When he ends his battle, he joins me and helps get the woman off the floor and seated on the retaining wall of a planter.

"So, I take it we've cleared the decks." I glance around at the aftermath.

"Seems so, although more than a few cut their losses and got away."

"Big bossman included?"

He nods. "With the building secured, we need Dionysus to bring back the mayor. We've made one hell of a mess, and I don't want to be held responsible for it."

"Good point. Do you see him?"

Sloan looks around and shakes his head. "No. I'll go find him. Are you ladies good here?"

"We'll be fine," I say, leaning closer to whisper. "But maybe you could ease the horror of vampires feeding on her?"

He winks at me and turns to the woman, who is still in a half-daze. "Do ye mind if I examine ye fer a moment, miss? Just look right into my eyes. Aye, that's it."

The woman lets out a feminine sigh, and I'm not sure if it's an aftereffect of her ordeal, the relief of him wiping away the trauma of her being fed upon, or simply falling into Sloan's beautiful, pale green gaze.

I don't blame her a bit if it's the latter.

A moment later, Sloan squeezes her wrist where he was monitoring her pulse and stands to straighten. "All right. I'll find Dionysus. Call if ye need me."

"Will do, hotness."

While the woman catches her breath, I pull out my phone and

send a quick text. My phone buzzes in my hand and sings the lyrics...*I'm gonna do bad things to you.* I chuckle as TruBlood's theme song announces Xavier's response.

> **The *King* of Montréal is Gabriel Lauden. He is a pompous ass, but his people are loyal and ruthless—especially his right hand, Vincent.**
>
> **I haven't had the pleasure of meeting him.**
>
> **Count yourself lucky. Don't let Lauden's expensive suit fool you, Fiona. He's lethal when vexed. Don't make an enemy out of him.**

I glide my thumbs over the screen.

> **Oops. Too late.**
>
> **Of course, it is. Use my name if you need to. I don't know that it'll save you, but it might give him pause long enough for you to figure out how to survive.**
>
> **I'll try not to name drop, but thnx.**

Next, I head back outside to find Garnet. We need to expand cleanup and make friends with the local PD.
Man. Things did not go as smoothly as we hoped.
Not by a long shot.

It takes only ten minutes for Garnet's shifters to flash away all the expired vampires and locate the heads that belonged to them.

Then, once that's taken care of, Dan wakes the unwitting protestors group by group, and we clear them from the park.

"Thanks for the assist, Em." I hug my brother before Dionysus snaps him back to Fantasy Island. "Sorry we caught you with your pants down."

He laughs. "They weren't down. They simply weren't on. It's laundry day. They weren't dry."

I laugh and shake my head. "How is it you can prance around in your boxers all day? Isn't Sarah there, helping you debunk and wake up the city? Shouldn't you have pants on for her modesty at the very least? She's a white witch."

Emmet rolls his eyes. "Boxers aren't nearly as risqué as you're making them out to be and yes, Sarah's around. Although, she picked a house down the hill a bit from the palace and is making it her own."

"That's awesome."

He nods. "Actually, it is. I'm glad to have had the chance to smooth out some of the rough edges with her and patch up our friendship."

"That's all it is? Friendship?"

"For now. I moved really fast with Ciara, and I don't regret it, but the aftermath has been hard on my heart."

I know how gentle Emmet's heart is and it kills me that he's been hurting. "I know it has, Em, and I'm sorry. Have you heard from her?"

"Oh, yeah, now that Merlin fixed me so I don't kill electronics, we talk on the phone a couple of times a week. It didn't end because we didn't love each other. We still really care and enjoy one another."

"I know, and I think it's great that you both love each other enough to want the best for the other."

"We do."

"What about waking the city? How is that going? Has there been any progress?"

He shakes his head. "No. Not really. Sarah and I are trying. She's come up with a dozen great ideas, and I've been boosting her, but there's something blocking us. It's like the city is a temperamental teenager and doesn't want to wake up."

"Hitting the snooze button on you, is it?"

"Yeah, it is."

"After things settle down, maybe Sloan and I can stay with you guys for a bit, and we'll see if we can come up with something to entice your city awake."

"That would be great. We'd love to have you."

A gust of wind *whooshes* in the front doors of the city hall as a portly man in uniform breezes in looking angry. He gives Emmet's current state of boxer beauty a glare but no more attention than that is wasted as he storms past us and heads toward the elevator.

Yikes. "Okay, I think that's my cue. Thank you. Love you. Give Brenny my love too."

Emmet hugs me, and I call Dionysus over. "One big brother to return to his palace, please."

Emmet meets Sloan and me with a knuckle bump, and he snaps out with the Greek.

"We need to get upstairs." I lace my fingers with Sloan's. I gauge the rise of the elevator and feel the urgency of the situation building. "Straight into the mayor's office, please. I sense another battle about to break out."

CHAPTER NINE

Garnet has spent the past hour with the mayor and her team, trying to locate and treat the staff on all five floors. Thankfully, many of them had taken her up on the suggestion to evacuate and work from home, but sadly that didn't include everyone. Rene and his partner from Major Crimes have been busy handling those killed from the police side of things.

"We'll find him, Madam Mayor." Rene flips his notebook shut and steps back. "I'm sure there was an oversight during the evacuations, and his name got missed on a list somewhere."

"Who's missing?" I ask Garnet quietly, gauging the tension in the room.

He leans closer and whispers, "Deputy Mayor Olivier, but as Detective Michaud said, with the chaos and commotion, it's likely he was simply treated and taken to hospital and his name missed on a list."

"Okay good." I move to the next problem on the list. "I'm sorry to interrupt, but a portly, bald man in a suit is coming up on the elevator. By the haughty indignance he's oozing, I'm guessing maybe your chief of police?"

"That would be him." Mayor Tremblay draws a deep breath

and moves to stand behind her desk. I take it from her reaction that she and the police chief have gone rounds and she needs to shield herself a bit when facing him.

I'm not surprised. I've heard Da and the boys tell many stories about how the police chiefs over the years have clashed with the mayors of Toronto.

Anyway, I'm glad I was able to give the mayor a moment to prepare because by the look of her, she needed it. Yes, it's been a stressful time, but this attack happened in her personal space and impacted people she knew and considered friends.

Hell, someone killed her assistant in the next room.

The woman has every right to be affected.

The door to the outer office is open, so the police chief doesn't need to slow down. He storms in like a juggernaut, glares around the room without taking much notice of anyone, and sets his sights on the mayor. "What an absolute debacle, Clarissa. You have made piss-poor decisions before, but I will see you ousted from office for this."

Mayor Tremblay presses her palms onto the surface of her desk and leans forward. "Oh? What have I done now, Thomas? What part of today's attack are you going to try to pin on me?"

He gestures out the window and curses. *"Tabarnak de câlisse,* these people you brought into my city attacked hundreds of our citizens! Cast spells on them! Almost killed them! What were you thinking?"

I'm about to speak up, but Garnet gives me a firm head shake.

Fine. I know. Not my circus. Not my monkeys.

Mayor Tremblay meets him with a level gaze. "These people I brought to *our* city were the solution to what went wrong today, not the problem. Now, if you calm down and hear me out, I'll explain what happened."

"I know what happened. It's all over the news. This redhead child commanded her people to take down hundreds of peaceful protestors on the back steps of this building."

"You should be thanking her, Thomas. Those protestors were compelled by vampires and about to start a riot. The entire protest was a ploy by an empowered faction to stir up trouble and increase the fear and disquiet in our city. Thanks to Fiona's quick thinking that didn't happen."

Police Chief Monet turns his anger on me. "Vampires? That's your excuse for your actions?"

I lift my chin. "I don't need an excuse, Chief. That's what happened. I know you received a complete briefing package because I helped put them together. You've already been informed vampires are real."

He shakes his bald head. "Gaslighting tactics. There are no such beasts in my city."

"Oh, I assure you, there are. Would you care to see the proof?" Without waiting for an answer, I look at Garnet. He lowers his chin and gives me the okay.

Dionysus, can you grab one of the heads from the discard pile, please?

Dionysus snaps out and back a second later dangling a severed head, his fingers gripping the black curls of a vampire. With the scarlet red eyes and the dropped fangs, and the venom lances exposed, there's no way to look at that head and deny what's obvious.

"Chief Monet, this is a vampire." I watch his expression during the big reveal. I've been through this a few times now. People are generally shocked and appalled when they realize vampires are real.

Chief Monet isn't.

"Their leader is Gabriel Lauden," the mayor says.

He scoffs. "That's slanderous. Repeat that, and I'll have you charged and arrested right now."

"No one is above the law," Clarissa says. "Isn't that right, Chief?"

He rakes her with a scathing glare. "Fine. What could make you say that?"

"He was here. Fiona spoke to him. He broke into my office during the attack."

He laughs and waves that away. "That man sits on half a dozen boards with you. Did you consider that perhaps he saw the commotion and rushed here to check on you? And look, the man braves an ugly, bloody battle to get to your office to ensure your well-being and you accuse him of being not only a monster but the king of monsters. Shame on you, Clarissa."

Mayor Tremblay exhales. "I'm beginning to wonder if you're interested in truth and justice, Thomas. What's gotten into you? I'm accustomed to you being a bully, but you've never been naïve."

Thomas Monet flicks his hand at the mayor. "Gabriel Lauden is one of the city's praised philanthropists. He runs charity drives and work placement programs for the underprivileged. Hell, there is a wing of the hospital named after him."

"That wouldn't happen to be a hematology lab, would it?" I ask.

My question is partly a joke and partly curiosity, but by their reactions... Ha! Nailed it!

"No one said you could speak," Monet snaps.

I wave that away. "I've never needed an engraved invitation. Listen, Lauden running a blood lab is a good thing. It's more than convenient. Maybe he's like the King of the Toronto seethes and tries not to let his minions feed on the general public."

Clarissa blinks at me. "Should I be happy that vampires use blood from the blood bank to feed?"

"The empowered world is sometimes about picking the lesser of two evils. For all the vampires juice boxing from a lab, you've got that many fewer feeding on late-night clubbers staggering home."

"Are you making light of this, Miss Cumhaill?" Chief Monet snaps. "You think tarnishing the name of a great man is funny?"

"Not at all, Chief. The secret of successfully policing the empowered world is not to look too closely at it with the moral microscope of humanity. If you do, you'll never survive. You have to make accommodations for needs, motives, and actions to be outside the scope of what you feel comfortable with. Sometimes, the only way to deal with that is to laugh."

Mayor Clarissa runs her fingers over her forehead. "I wish we could turn back time four months and live in a world where my biggest worry was opposition parties jockeying for my job."

I totally get that. "Sadly, that decision wasn't ours, and we're the ones left cleaning up the mess."

"Technically, they are the ones cleaning up the mess." Dionysus points at Garnet's team in the outer office. "Let's take a moment to be thankful for the working class because I really wouldn't want to have to do that."

Chief Monet throws Dionysus a dirty look.

"He really did mean that as a compliment," I say.

I'm not sure if he's buying that. Doesn't matter. His phone rings, and he steps toward the window to answer it in private.

While we have a moment of reprieve from hostility, I turn my attention back to the mayor. "Speaking of taking a moment for those who work for us, I'm sorry about your assistant."

She glances up at the ceiling and blinks. "Marcel was a wonderful young man. He just started dating a new boyfriend and was so optimistic about the coming months. Losing him is senseless. It breaks my heart."

"I think that was their intention," Garnet says, coming in to join us. "In more than one city around the world, the vampires are causing trouble within the political structures of society."

This is the first I'm hearing of this, so I perk up to pay attention.

"You see, there was a natural hierarchy of power for centuries.

Vampires were always near the pinnacle until now. However, the recent glut of fae energy is changing the dynamics."

That goes back to what I was thinking earlier.

Clarissa doesn't seem to be following, so I help her out. "Vampires don't have magic. Their power comes from strength, speed, and near immortality."

Garnet nods. "The other aggressive and dominant races like hobgoblins, shifters, wizards, and witches are gaining power by the day."

"Knowing how arrogant vampires can be, they don't want to get pushed out of their spot near the top."

Garnet checks his watch and sighs. "I can't say for certain what your Mister Lauden wanted here today, but if I were to guess, I'd say it might no longer be solely the parties of opposition gunning for your job."

I step back, perching my butt on the edge of the hutch against the wall. "Can you imagine a vampire running for office? How would that play out?"

Garnet arches a brow. "I don't suppose Gabriel Lauden intends to run, Fi. If I'm right, he's following in the pattern of the other cities. He simply thought to take the position by removing the obstacles in his way."

Clarissa shakes her head. "What do I do?"

"You let the authorities handle things," Chief Monet says, returning to the conversation. "The Montréal authorities, not these otherworld killers who think vigilante justice is acceptable in our streets."

My jaw falls slack. I really want to tell this putz where he can shove his vigilante justice when Garnet beats me to it.

He stands to his full height and presses his broad shoulders back. "Well, Chief, you might choose to think of us as otherworld vigilantes, but I assure you, we live by and respect human laws."

"Forgive me if I find that hard to swallow, Grant. The bloodshed today in this building and out in that park proves differently."

Garnet arches an ebony brow. "You know who I am. Should I be flattered?"

"Hardly. I've had a long-standing friendship with many of the leaders in Toronto, and they told me exactly what I can expect from you being a liaison in my city. It seems they were right."

I hold up a finger. "Technically, I'm the liaison. I only called him after I realized the crowd was enthralled and about to riot."

The chief's venomous ire turns my way. "Shut your mouth. Children are supposed to be seen and not heard."

Before he says anything, Garnet's growl rumbles deep in my chest. His eyes flip from purple to the gold of his beast, and the hair on my arms stands on end.

I've seen Garnet face off with and take down men ten times as dangerous as Chief Monet, so this might be all for a show of power.

Unless it's truly about the man insulting me.

Aww...if it is, how sweet for him to get riled up on my behalf. Such a grumpy puss.

The advance of Garnet's lion releases a strength of magic into the air that even a non-magical human can sense. Maybe Chief Monet truly does know what Garnet is capable of because his bravado has drained from his rosy, round cheeks.

"Say what you will about me, Chief. I've earned every ounce of negative press, but Miss Cumhaill is to be treated with respect. She does nothing but give to the world and try her best. You would do well not to pass judgment on her, or there will be a great many powerful people lining up to take issue with you."

Yep. It was about me.

He lurves you, Jane, Dionysus says into my mind. *You're in his pride, family, like Andromeda, Maxwell, and me.*

I love that Tarzan includes himself in Garnet's pride. Truth be told, the alpha lion would argue, but when push comes to shove, he's a "no man left behind" kind of leader. Dionysus is mine, and therefore he is Garnet's too.

Chief Monet seems to have at least enough self-preservation to offer me a more pleasant glance before steeling himself to speak with Garnet. "My point, Mr. Grant, is that I won't tolerate the kind of underhanded dealings you're known for in Toronto in my city. That extends to include any adversaries, employees, or envoys you might deploy."

Oh, that would be me.

Garnet meets the man's gaze and lowers his chin. "When members of the empowered community misbehave, my envoys aim to defuse the situation and handle it without violence or with minimal force the same as your officers. *But,* on the occasions when someone from our community truly means to do damage, putting them down is the *only* way to handle things."

Monet shakes his shiny, bald head. "Even if the world is going crazy, the laws of this land apply to all citizens, not just the ones who belong here. If your people are in my city, there will be no putting anyone down. If there is, I will charge them with murder."

Garnet's grin is polite, but his growl holds all the hostility and judgment the situation demands. "You'll find out soon enough how ineffective and naïve that stance is. Your need to flex your muscles will get good people killed, but we'll play your game. No one from my team will kill until you deem it necessary. Let me just say upfront the blood is on your hands."

CHAPTER TEN

When the bald bully storms off to speak to Officer Rene and his partner, Mayor Tremblay sinks into her office chair and shakes her head. "No matter what Chief Monet said, I have no qualms about how your group handled the incident outside."

"I appreciate that. Thank you, Mayor." Garnet nods, then gets beckoned over to speak to one of his team members. "Excuse me, ladies."

When it's just us girls, I move to one of the two guest chairs opposite her desk and take a load off. "Despite what the chief implied, killing isn't our goal. It's an unfortunate by-product of surviving an attack from the most violent species of the empowered races."

She swallows and glances around the room to ensure our conversation is still our own. "I've heard from several of my staff about how you and your team rescued them from terrifying situations. It might not be the politically correct stance, but I'm glad you took those vampires off the board."

"My concerns going forward are about the vampires we *didn't* put down. If Gabriel Lauden was brazen enough to break into this office, whether to access something or do you harm, I have a hard time believing he'll leave and forget about it."

"I'm inclined to agree. Gabriel is known for being a ruthless businessman. I doubt his empowered dealings would be any different."

"Which is why I think you should consider Bella staying with friends or family for a few days. As horrible as it is, children are powerful leverage when bad men want an advantage."

Clarissa frowns. "I wish that were an option. As I mentioned before, Bella and I are basically alone in this world. There's no one I trust with her, which is why she comes to work with me on days she's not in school. With the awakening of her fae trait, I don't even know if she'll be going back to school. Kids can be so cruel."

"That's true. Would you like me to ask Myra if she can keep Bella for a day or two with her and Imari?"

Clarissa presses a hand to her forehead and rubs her brow. "We don't even know them. They don't know me. It's all so much."

"I know, but I give you my word Bella would be safe and well cared for. My niece and nephew stay with them for play dates and sleepovers all the time. It might even help Bella come to terms with the changes she's experiencing. My nephew, Jackson, just got his wayfarer gift as well. They'd have things in common."

"I don't know. Do you think they would mind? Taking care of another person's child for an unknown time seems like too much to ask."

"Consider it done," Garnet says, coming back to join us. "Sorry for interrupting, ladies, but if I heard correctly, you have nowhere for your little girl to be safe while we work out this vampire business?"

Of course, he heard correctly. He's got the heightened senses of a Moon Called predator. "That's right. Would you and Myra mind?"

"*Oh*, you're Myra's husband?" Clarissa asks.

"Her mate, yes. With Moon Called, or what you would call shifters, we use the term mate."

"And you adopted Imari?"

I grin. "His lion was lost to that little girl the first time he saw her. If I were in your shoes, there's no one I would trust my child with more."

Mayor Clarissa seems to be calming down about the idea. "You don't think your family will mind?"

Garnet's expression loses its severity, and the mayor gets a rare glimpse of Garnet, the friend, mate, and father. "It would be our pleasure to host your daughter. Honestly, Imari loves to have friends for sleepovers. And just so you know, we live in a secure compound in the African savannah. We have a lovely home with an oasis pool and plenty of things to entertain little girls."

"In fact," Dionysus says, "I'm taking Imari's unicorn there this afternoon. I'm sure Bella will have fun with Contessa McSparkles."

That's news to me. "Is Contessa ready to go back to the compound?"

"For a visit, yes. She misses her girl and says she'd like to spend some time with her. Although, she made me promise to ask that she not have to dance for you."

Garnet nods. "You have my word. The unicorn doesn't need to dance, and your daughter can stay as long as it takes to ensure it's safe to return home."

Who says Garnet Grant is unreasonable?

Clarissa exhales a long breath. "Thank you."

Garnet slides his hands into the pockets of his slacks and shakes his head. "It's our pleasure. You are welcome to come and check on her whenever and as often as you need to."

"To Africa?" she asks.

He nods. "If you let Fiona know you'd like to come, she can have Dionysus bring you."

I meet the confusion in her gaze. "The idea of magic and portaling anywhere can be a lot at first, but not all things about the empowered world are bad. We've got great things too."

"I'm sure that's true. Actually, I need that to be true. If Bella is to join your world, I need for there to be wonder and joy."

"I promise you, there are. Now, if you'd like to go home to pack a bag for your little girl, we can take it to her, and you can explain to her yourself why she's staying with friends for a few days."

Clarissa draws a deep breath. "Why are you doing all this for me?"

I meet her gaze and shrug. "Because you asked for help and it's within my power to give."

"It's what she does," Dionysus says, joining us. "Fi and her family gather lost souls and give them safe harbor when they need it most. It's a Cumhaill thing."

I chuckle. "Dionysus, will you please escort Clarissa to her home and then take her to Garnet's compound to speak to her daughter?"

"Not a problem. Do you think we could stop by my loft and get Contessa McSparkles?"

"Only if you portal to Africa and not ride Contessa. I think Mayor Clarissa has had enough excitement for today without flying on a pegasus." I look at the mayor and think about that for a moment. "Unless I'm wrong and you want to fly on his winged unicorn?"

Clarissa blinks at me. "I'm not completely sure if that's a serious question, but if it is, portaling will be quite enough, thank you."

Dionysus nods. "Be back in a flash. Don't miss me too much."

"Impossible. Now go and be careful with the lady mayor, please, and thank you."

The two of them snap out, and I meet Garnet's gaze and giggle. "Yes, he marches to his own drum, but he means well."

"He's got the power of an atomic bomb and the maturity of a teenager."

"All the more reason to guide him through his transition into humanity. Seriously, he's good people. He's loyal and brave, and he's a hell of a lot more mature than he lets on. He's simply enjoying the freedom to be himself that was denied him for his entire existence."

Garnet nods. "If you say so."

"I do. If the world were to close in on us, there's a millennia-old superpower behind that façade of irreverence. He's just trying out something new."

The two of us exit the private sitting room and return to the mayor's office. Sloan is speaking to the dark-haired cop that came with Officer Rene Michaud this morning. The woman is about my age, wearing jeans and a black leather trench. Maybe I'm crazy, but she's got a wicked *Underworld*, Kate Beckinsale vibe going on.

When Sloan sees me, he smiles and waves me over. "Fiona Cumhaill, meet Officer Juliette Gagne."

"Jules, please. Everyone calls me Jules."

I go over and shake her hand. "I'm sorry. We've been skirting around in the same circles for hours and never got a chance to meet. I should have made an effort to say hello before now."

"No, don't apologize. It's been a day."

"It certainly has."

Sloan slides a gentle hand to the small of my back and smiles down at me. "It seems Chief Monet has decided the Toronto liaison will now have a Montréal liaison for as long as we're in town."

I grin at the woman. "Wow. You drew the short straw. Sorry about that."

"No need to worry. The straw isn't that short."

I chuckle. "You don't have to pretend to like it. I've heard my brothers complain about how much they hate it when babysitting gigs pull them off the street."

"Your brothers are on the job?"

I nod. "All five brothers and my dad at one time."

Her ebony brows arch high. "Wow, that's a serious commitment to law enforcement. In my family, it's just me, but my dad was a fireman for most of my life."

"Same circles, different bars after shift."

"True enough." She laughs, and her expression is open and genuine. "Your husband caught me up on things. Vampires and politics and you being leashed by Chief Monet."

"That pretty much sums things up."

Her radio squelches as someone shouts something I don't quite catch. Juliette pulls the walkie out of the pocket of her trench and turns away to listen.

I take a moment to address my guy. "My husband, eh? Are we going with the title now?"

Sloan chuckles. "I said no such thing. Could it be that she's a detective and we're wearing matching bands on our left fingers?"

"I suppose that could be it. Or maybe she's intuitive and senses the heated passion and attraction burning off us in waves."

Sloan arches a brow. "Are ye makin' fun?"

I step against his chest and tilt my head back to reach for his kiss. "Only a little. The passion and attraction are there, but we hide it like pros."

He chuckles against my lips. "She says as she kisses him in the middle of a crime scene."

I step back and feign offense. "So surly and serious. If they only knew the other side of Sloan Mackenzie."

He pegs me with a look. "The whole point of bein' professional is that no one knows what goes on in private lives. The fact that we know is enough."

Jules slides the police radio back into her pocket and rejoins the conversation. "Sorry about that."

I chuckle, the heat warming my cheeks nothing I could hide even if I tried. "No apology necessary. Is there a problem?"

"Possibly. There have been three calls into dispatch about wolves on the island...which is weird because there aren't wolves there. Fox, deer, and beavers, sure, but I jog through the national park all the time, and I've never seen wolves."

Sloan frowns. "Well, land animals don't usually migrate onto an island."

"Not unless they know how to paddle a boat," I say.

"Difficult without thumbs," Sloan counters.

"True story. So, do you want to check it out?"

Jules waves that away. "Dispatch sent a car. I'm sure it's kids drinking and not knowing the difference between a silver fox and his bigger cousin. No. Rene and I are your shadows. Go ahead and do what you need to do to handle whatever this was."

I chuckle. "Thanks. Yeah, as soon as our friend returns from a personal errand, we can—"

Jules's radio goes off again, and this time it's the cops screaming for backup. Before Dionysus' translator spell, I wouldn't have had a clue what they were saying, but now I don't miss a frantic word.

"The wolves are killing us..."

Jules looks torn.

There's no time for that. "Look, I get it. Something dangerous is happening in your city, and you're stuck babysitting, but we're druids. We can talk down and contain animals. Take us with you, and we'll help."

"Yeah? You can talk to animals?"

"For reals."

"Good enough. Let's do it." She jogs to the outer office, and we find her partner. "Rene, we need to get over to the island."

He steps away from where he's taking a statement from one of the municipal employees and nods. "Not a problem. I'm still in the lot at the park's north end."

As we rush toward the door, I glance back at Atlas. "Dionysus will be back any moment. Wait for him, and the two of you join us at…" I look at Jules for her to fill in the info.

"Boucherville National Park. It's the forested island southeast of here."

Atlas nods. "We'll be there as soon as he arrives."

"Thanks. Good luck."

Sloan *poofs* the four of us out to the small parking lot at the park's north end. We materialize at Rene's patrol car, and he unlocks things so we can get gone.

"Can't you magic us to Boucherville?" Jules asks, glancing at Sloan. "Our men are being attacked. Why bring us here when they're hurt?"

Sloan jogs around the back bumper of the cruiser to get into the back seat. "Apologies. I can't portal to anywhere I haven't been before. I've only been to Montréal one other time, and someone brought me to a meeting in the commerce district. I've never been to your national park."

The four of us get in and buckle up.

"It's like a personal GPS system," I explain. "If he's never been there, he doesn't have the internal coordinates to *poof* there."

Jules turns in her seat as Rene hits the lights and we tear off, weaving through traffic. "Remind me to give you an extensive tour of the city when we finish. It seems dumb not to give you what you need to use that power to our advantage."

Exactly right. Smart girl.

It takes very little time to get down to the waterfront where the bridge spans the St. Lawrence River and stretches over to Boucherville Island and the national park within.

"So, you've never had wolf attacks in the park before?" I shut the door behind me, and the four of us run against the flow of panicked citizens.

"Not at the park, in the city, or anywhere through the Laurentians. At least, not that I know of."

I glance at Sloan and elaborate. "The Laurentians is a vast natural area of Quebec about an hour north of the city that extends into the Laurentian mountain range."

"There's never been trouble with wolves?"

"I'm not a wildlife officer, but I don't think so."

The deeper we get into the wooded area, the more panicked and injured the citizens are who are fleeing. We pass a male jogger, wincing as he hobble-runs despite an injured ankle. Then we come upon a couple covered in blood. They look like they're about to drop.

"I'll catch up." Sloan drops back to help.

"Watch your ass, hotness."

He winks. "I'd rather watch yers. Now, off ye go."

I chuckle and keep moving, picking up speed now that I hear the vicious snarls of beasts.

Jules is still glancing back as Sloan pulls the couple to the side and starts assessing their injuries. "Is he a doctor too?"

"His father is a Master Druid Healer, and he has a strong aptitude for magical healing as well."

"Handy guy."

"Very." The three of us continue to close the distance and my shield flares to life. "Be aware that my magical warning system just went off. This isn't only about wolves."

Rene pegs me with a gaze. "What does that mean? Those looked like wounds from animal attacks."

"Maybe, but my shield has never been wrong." I call my body armor forward on the fly, and my skin hardens beneath the intricate depiction of branches, roots, and leaves.

"Whoa, what the hell is that?" Jules asks.

"My armor comes straight from the tree of life. It's a lot to look at but has saved my life a hundred times."

"It's cool…magic is still kind of crazy to me."

"Okay, stay behind me until we know what we're dealing with."

"Not bloody likely," Rene chuffs.

I slow down as we close in on the noise of feral beasts and turn to give Rene and Jules a clear look at me. "I have magical armor and can speak with and gain control over wild animals. You don't. There's no sense getting your throat ripped out over jurisdictional pride."

"She's got my vote," Jules says to Rene, chuckling. "Go ahead and Dr. Doolittle the shit out of this."

I laugh, liking this girl more and more. "Sounds good. Stay behind me and look badass in that coat. I lurve your boots by the way."

"Thanks. Let's try not to ruin them."

"I'll try my best." I call Birga to my hand, and their eyes widen. "Magic, amirite?"

"Go you."

I laugh and get us going. "Remember to stay behind me as much as you can and if I release an eight-foot battle bear, don't shoot him. He's on our side."

"Gotcha, I won't shoot him," Jules says. "Although I can't promise I won't pee my pants."

"Understandable. It's kinda been a Depends day all around. No fault. No foul."

I move deeper into the forest, following the soulful wails of wolves and the crunching of bones. The hair on the nape of my neck stands on end. Jules swears there have never been wolves on this island, and I am inclined to agree with her.

If she jogs here on the regular, she'd know.

"How is it so dark in here? It can't be much past noon, yet it's like the dead of night."

Jules shrugs. "I'm only along for the ride. Magic, I guess? You know more than me."

"Yeah, but what kind of magic?"

Dionysus and Atlas flash in with Garnet and half a dozen of his men.

"What do we know?" Garnet scans the area and takes in the lay of the land. "Why the fuck is it so dark here?"

"We were just discussing that." I don't have much to report, but I give him what I can. "We nearly got trampled by citizens making a run for it. Sloan's helping a particularly chewed-up couple."

Another round of baleful cries sounds off.

Garnet twists to face the direction from which it's coming. "That howling doesn't sound like any pack of wolves I've ever come up against...natural or Moon Called."

I frown at the bizarre darkness, straining to hear the approach of any four-footed predators. "Agreed. The real problem is that the concentration of fae magic here is three or four times what it was in the city proper and twice what it was in the parking lot."

"What do you think that means, Jane?"

"I think there's a fae realm breach occurring in this forest. The last time I felt my skin crawl with this kind of power was on the beach of Emmet's Island when all those portals to the fae realm opened."

Garnet curses. "You think there's an open portal somewhere here?"

"I do. Either someone opened it and let the wolves through, or it opened spontaneously, and the wolves came through on their own. Whichever way it played out, those wolves aren't from around here."

"They aren't wolves," Atlas says, glaring into the forest's darkness. "They're grom."

I release my fae sight and the world shifts from the diminished color of human eyes to the strange night vision Mother Nature gifted me with. "What the hell are grom?"

"They're cunning, malevolent creatures from the fae realm

that resemble wolves but more closely align with hyenas. They have longer front legs than back and goblins and hobgoblins have used them for centuries as beasts of burden and mounts."

"Are they self-aware or beasts?" Garnet frowns at the forest around us. "The police chief was very clear about us not killing people in his city."

"They're evil beasts that delight in hunting and feeding on creatures weaker than themselves. They'll gnaw your arms off your body for the fun of it."

"Well done, Atlas. Contributing on your first day." I glance back at Jules and Rene. "The empowered world is kill or be killed. Despite what your chief says, if you want to survive, you fight to the death."

"Monster fae hyena wolves." Jules pulls her sidearm from her shoulder holster. "I'm good with not having my arms gnawed off."

I catch a blur of movement advancing in the trees and adjust my stance to ready for the attack. "Get ready people because all hell is about to break loose."

The grunts and snorts of the beasts make it easy to track the approach. Then the grom are upon us.

CHAPTER ELEVEN

The forest around us erupts in a battle of force and fangs. Our group spreads out and creates a defensive circle. While them being wolves is probably the closest explanation in our animal kingdom, Atlas is right. They are very definitely not of the *Canis lupus* family.

Broad, muscled shoulders taper down toward slender hips and a long tail. Unlike true wolves, these creatures have blunt snouts and elongated canines.

"Wow, these things are fucking ugly," one of Garnet's men says.

"Or as my brothers say it, super f-ugly."

That's all the time we have for conversation before the battle goes next level and we've got more important things to deal with than commenting on the enemy.

I release Bruin, and the two of us work our section of the forest. "There are so many of them," I call, trying to create a break in the action long enough to focus.

"*Beast Bond.*" Activating my powers, I push out my intention and try to connect with the beasts. The chaos that comes back at me is like nothing I've come up against before. The aggression isn't new, but the strength of number is a first.

"They share a hive mind connection. One I could do, but dozens are too much for me to influence or control."

"We need to shut the portal opening," Dionysus shouts. He's battling old-school with a sword in each of his hands and a smile on his face.

"Can you do it, Tarzan?"

"Am I capable? Yes. Am I allowed? No. Sorry, Jane. I can't swoop in and fix this for you."

I understand that Dionysus walks a fine line, but I really wish the pantheon laws of gods didn't bind him. "Then what do we do?"

Garnet has shifted into his animal form, and so have his men. The battle ratchets to a new level of primal as beasts roar and claws swipe through the air.

"Make sure you only fire on the groms," I shout to Jules and Rene. "The other wolves, bears, and lions are on our side."

"*Tabarnak de câlisse*," Rene snaps, firing his gun in one hand and swinging a large stick with the other. "The world's gone mad."

Dionysus is swinging his swords around in his toga, looking like he's having the time of his life. When he catches me watching, he waggles his brows. "If only we knew someone with mad portal skills. Maybe someone working to manage a sudden boost to his portal magic."

My mouth falls open. "Nikon? Nikon's the answer?"

"What's that you say?" Dionysus widens his eyes as he feigns surprise. "You think you should contact Nikky? That's a fabulous idea, Jane. Inspired wisdom."

I laugh, swinging Birga to gain a bit of breathing room. Unfortunately, I can't text and fight. Distracted battling against otherworld beasts is even more deadly than distracted driving.

Go figure.

Sloan *poofs* in and joins the fray. "What did I miss?"

I toss him Birga. "Take my girl for a sec and cover me. I need to phone a friend."

"Impenetrable Sphere." When my magic bubble of protection forms around me, I pull my phone out of my pocket and call up my contacts list.

Selecting Nikon is the work of a moment. Connecting the call takes a little longer.

Garnet's lion throws the carcass of a dead grom out of his way, and it hits my protective bubble. The impact knocks me staggering a couple of feet, but no damage done…well, other than to the aesthetic of my sphere.

My bubble of protection is now dripping forest green, goopy blood.

Gross.

The call goes through, then Nikon is on the line. "Hey, Red. How's things? Do you miss me?"

His teasing charm is such a juxtaposition to the gore and violence surrounding me that I have to laugh. "Miss you so much. If you're in control of your faculties, I need you to snap to the Boucherville National Park in Montréal. Beasts from the fae realm are attacking us, and I hope you might be able to close the portal allowing them passage."

"How am I doing that?"

"With your newfound portal awesomeness, the support of good friends, and a little luck?"

"Fi, I love that you have so much faith in me—"

"Because you're awesome."

"True, but I've barely got a handle on not transporting entire rooms of people with me when I go places. Have you forgotten I lost you yesterday?"

Bruin rears up on his back legs with a lung-vibrating roar.

"Shit. Are you guys actively in trouble?"

I chuckle. "Did you miss the part about beasts from the fae realm attacking us?"

"Sorry, I didn't realize you meant...never mind. All right. We're coming. Patty, look up Boucherville National Park in Montréal. Get me a Google Earth map."

"See you soon, Greek." Hanging up, I pocket my phone and drop the bubble of my protection. "Nikon is on his way."

Sloan makes a super sexy swipe left on the beast he's fighting, and I take a brief moment to admire my guy in action.

He really is breathtaking.

He spins to give me back my spear and catches me staring. Tossing me Birga, he chuckles. "Although I appreciate that sparkle in your eye, this isn't the time for ogling and daydreaming, *a ghra*."

I suppose not.

With Birga singing happily in my palm, I jump back into action, recognizing a truth people don't often consider. When a battle occurs in close quarters, bodies pile up, and tripping over them makes fighting more difficult.

"Sloan, I need you," Jules shouts from across the warzone. She fires her gun point-blank at the head of the grom coming at her and swings a broad branch to beat the beast away. When the mangy beast of matted fur falls to the ground with a heavy *thump*, I see the problem.

Rene is down and looking bad.

"*Poof* them back to the city hall." I shift to cover Atlas as two more grom come at us. "There are still medical teams there to tend to him."

Sloan *poofs* over to them and *poofs* out.

At the same moment, Nikon snaps in with Patty.

"Welcome to the fun, boys," I say.

"Feckin' grom." Patty scowls at the scene. Our Man o' Green has come prepared with his weapons vest on, a battle-ax in hand,

and his mindset locked. "Where these beasts draw blood, their masters are never far away."

I never considered that. "I figured they were wild and stumbled upon a portal breaching the worlds."

"Not feckin' likely." Patty sheaths his ax before pulling out a couple of shuriken. Pink hearts, yellow moons, orange stars, and green clovers fly through the air and lodge into the thick hides of our opponents.

"The leprechaun is right." Atlas doubles over to prop his palms on his knees as he draws a breath. "Grom are domesticated beasts. For there to be this many on the attack, they have either united to destroy their masters or are here with them and set loose on the human world."

Neither of those bodes well for us.

"Ye can refer to me as Patty or the Man o' Green," Patty snaps, "but if ye call me the L-word again, I'll rip yer wee elven clovers from yer body and feed them to these beasts."

I make a face at Atlas before he gets any ideas about talking back. "Just go with Patty in the future, please, and all will be forgotten."

"Uh...yeah, I didn't realize...sorry."

Patty has already moved on, and whatever hostility he's feeling over the slight, he's taking out on the beasts.

"Where are they all coming from?" Nikon looks stunned.

"That's what we need to find out," I say.

"And soon because I'm getting blood all over my good chiton," Dionysus says.

Nikon looks at him and snaps his fingers. "Shit. It's Erotidia. I totally forgot."

I wave that away and point at where the forest grows darker. "Let's end this, and the two of you can clean up and pay your tribute to a dickwad god that doesn't deserve either of you."

Nikon arches a brow. "All righty, then. How about we focus on the invasion of our realm?"

Dionysus grins. "A splendid idea, *adelphos*. Let's."

"We're off to try to close the portal," I announce to anyone who wants to know.

"On your six, luv," Sloan says, returning from his rescue of Rene. Jules is still with him, and I can only imagine she refused to be left behind. "Lead the way."

Leaving Bruin, Atlas, Garnet, and his team to continue the battle, I lead the six of us—Nikon, Dionysus, Patty, me, Sloan, and Jules—into the darkness to find the open portal gate.

It's not hard to find the path to where we need to be. The grom left dead bodies and bloody animal carcasses to mark it.

"*Faery Fire*." Sloan creates a ball of blue flame in his palm and reaches over to touch the branch clutched in Jules's hand. "It won't burn you, but it will help you see."

"Thanks." Jules grins at the blue flame residing at the end of her club. She meets my gaze, and her grin widens. "Very handy guy. You should keep him."

"That's the plan." I step over the upper half of a devoured deer and push toward the rush of fae power building ahead of us. "Do you guys feel that?"

Nikon winces. "The electrical snakes racing over every inch of my flesh? Yes, I feel them. They're giving off sparks and shocks and making my bones vibrate."

"Oh, sweetie, I'm sorry."

"We went over this all day." Patty tosses a yellow moon into the air above his head and snaps his stubby fingers. What is ordinarily a weapon hangs in the air over his head and gives off the magical glow equivalent to a light bulb. "Yer either in control or yer not, Greek. Yer the conduit of the power, but if yer not its master, it will run amok."

Discomfort is plain in Nikon's expression. I make a mental

note to take him to Shenanigans for many drinks later. "You've got this, Greek. I believe in you. You rock my socks, Tsambikos."

Nikon looks at me and chuckles. "Believe it or not, having a cheerleader helps. Although, it would help even more if you were in a short skirt and shaking your pom-poms."

I laugh. "Nice try. I've never been the girl on the sidelines. I was the girl running the field and getting penalties for slashing."

"Can we keep our heads in the game, kids?" Patty asks.

Nikon shrugs. "Just distracting myself from the fact that I don't have any idea how to close a portal to another realm."

"We have to find the thing first." Patty raises his arm, and a shillelagh appears in his hand. I hope it's not the cursed one his ex-wife gave him that we snatched from over a witch's bar in Dublin.

The last thing we need is bad juju.

Our band of battlers follows my wee friend, and we make our way through the wilds of the forest. After a few minutes of tromping, he stops, and we're looking at a colorful, swirling vortex ahead.

"Yeah no, I don't know shit about what to do with that." Nikon glares at the portal.

"Then it's a good thing I'm here, isn't it?" Patty says. "With my knowledge and yer power, we'll get ye there, lad."

"I appreciate that, but—"

My shield flares for the third time today, and I groan and search our surroundings. "Incoming!"

The portal gate ahead of us bursts to life, and the energy in the air snaps with magic. "Hobgoblins," Atlas says, racing past us to intercept. It takes a moment for me to catch up on that one. Where did he come from? Wow, the elf can book it when he's inspired.

He's also right.

A band of maybe ten hobgoblins steps out of the portal and stops, blocking us from doing what we need to do. The raiders look like characters from one of my brother's role-playing modules. They're decked out in leather chest plates and shoulder guards, and their weapon belts hang heavy with axes and swords.

Hobgoblins aren't as humanoid as many of the fae races living among our citizens on this side of the Faery Glass. They have animalistic faces with wide and flat noses and ears extending off the side of their heads in four-inch points. The hair color of their race is ebony black, and they each keep it slicked back and tied at varying lengths.

No. They would never be mistaken for a human but they glamor to compensate. Or at least they did until the secrecy of the veil dropped.

"What the hell are they?" Jules asks, her eyes wide.

"Those are hobgoblins," Garnet joins us.

"I thought they were little, dumb, and green."

"That's a goblin. Hobgoblins are their larger, smarter, and much more vicious cousins."

"Oh goody. I take it from their expressions that they aren't amicable?"

"Nope." I shift to widen my stance and get ready to engage. *Bruin, we've got a bunch of hobgoblins here. If you're able to join the party, I'm extending an invite.*

Comin', Red.

Our battle party digs in, ready to fight.

The leader charges forward, tossing a black sphere into the air. Out of nowhere, a grom barrels out of the trees and leaps into the air. It closes its maw around the sphere as if we're playing a game of catch and runs straight at us.

"What the fuck is that orb?" I ask, my shield exploding into a DEFCON warning like you read about. "Take cover!"

The words are still stinging my tongue when an explosion goes off, and the world erupts in a wave of hot energy. Thrown through the air, I hit the wide trunk of a tree with my side and crumple to the ground.

My bell is seriously rung.

Forget seeing stars or little Tweety Birds. I've got black spots and a swirling forest coming up to smack me in the face.

"What the fuck?" Nikon groans, lying prone in the scrub not far from me.

"Is everyone all right?" Garnet pushes up from the ground. "Let's hear it."

"I'm good." My voice sounds tinny and distant to my ears.

"Aye, I'll live," Sloan says beside me.

It goes like that for a moment, and in the end, we've all checked in…except Atlas.

"Oh, shit." With my gaze locked on the tangled mess of elf, I push up to my knees and crawl toward his body. "Nonono, this isn't good. Hotness, we need some magical healing here."

Garnet gets to me first and frowns. "He needs more than that. Dracus, take him straight to the emergency operating room in the Guild building."

"On it." One of the shifters he brought with him hurries in and flashes out.

I'm left with blood on my hands and a ringing in my ears that has nothing to do with living through the detonation of a bomb.

"Where'd the hobgoblins go?" Patty asks.

I sit back on my heels and scan the devastation of our group. "No idea."

"Back to the fae realm, do you think?" Jules asks.

"The human says with hope thick in her voice." Nikon coughs.

I wave away his teasing with a sloppy hand. "It's a nice thought, but I wouldn't bet on it, no."

Jules looks at the point where the hobgoblins disappeared and back at us. "Okay, so vampires are real, and those hobgoblins are lethal. Please tell me these are some of the worst your empowered world has to offer because honestly, their pet wolves have been bad enough."

I release Birga as Bruin materializes beside me and looks around the empty section of forest. "The hobgoblin horde bugged out, buddy. Sorry."

He swings his massive, round head toward me and chuffs. "Och, weel, that's disappointing."

I chuckle at his glum expression and return my attention to Jules. "Vampires and hobgoblins are some of the worst but by no means the very worst."

"Surprisingly, this does not cheer me up."

"Can you imagine fighting them without being able to kill them? Chief Monet has no idea what he's done by tying our hands."

She runs her fingers through her dark hair and exhales. "I understand that, but surely you believe in policing the fae society over dropping people on sight."

I push up to my feet and check my balance before letting go of the tree I'm using to prop myself up. "Of course, if we're dealing with one of the races that makes that possible."

"Hello, ladies?" Sloan says, waving a hand between us. "Can we get back to the point of our story?"

I blink up at him and scan the swirling iridescent air where he's pointing.

"Right. Closing the portal."

Garnet nods. "Regardless of who and what came through, our first order of business is to cut off further realm-to-realm migration."

Patty pushes off the tree he's using to prop himself upright, and he and Nikon face the portal. "All right, lad. Let me walk ye through the instructions of closing this thing."

Sloan steps in behind me and wraps his arms around my shoulders. "We need to pour Nikon many drinks tonight. He's been squeezed through the wringer."

I chuckle. "I thought the same thing about twenty minutes ago. Great minds think alike, hotness."

"And fools seldom differ."

"All righty, folks." Patty jogs back to stand with us. "If all goes well, that portal will be closed in ten minutes, tops."

I glance down and meet his gaze. "And if it doesn't go well?"

"Och, well, let's not tempt the Fates. Everythin' will be grand, I'm sure."

Only…he really doesn't sound sure.

CHAPTER TWELVE

"A druid, a Greek immortal, and a Man o' Green walk into a bar." I chuckle but find nothing funny about any of this. "Damn, I wish this was a bar."

"Me too, Red." Nikon glares at the swirling energy vortex right in front of us. "Or if not a bar, maybe Dionysus's loft or a backyard bonfire at your grandparents or a weekend at the vineyard with Papu, or—"

"Yeah, we get it, Greek. Anywhere but here." I pat his back and yank my stinging hand away from his skin. The energy from the portal is snapping off him like electrical barbs nipping anything they contact. "You can do this, Greek. Just follow Patty's lead and be the awesome you that we all love."

"Follow my lead, lad." Patty raises his shillelagh in front of us. "Our magic is different, but if luck is with us, the two systems shouldn't react too much when combined."

"What if luck *isn't* with us?" He stares wide-eyed at the vortex of energy in front of us. "Patty? What happens if our powers don't mix?"

Patty makes a face at me behind Nikon's back and pats his

hip. "Och, nothin' to worry about, lad. I'm sure it'll be fine. Just, whatever ye do, don't get sucked through."

Nikon's head turns with a look of horror that would make me burst out laughing if the poor guy wasn't about to melt into a puddle of panic. "What happens if I get sucked into the vortex?"

"Nothing," I say, taking control of that one. "Nothing will happen because you've got this. You're Nikon-freaking-Tsambikos, and you're a fae prana immortal. You've been to The Cistern. You've survived the worst Hecate threw at you. And you've got Patty, Dionysus, Sloan, and me here to help you through this."

Patty looks up at me and frowns. "This isn't a prize-winning fight, and he's not Rocky Balboa."

Seriously? He's dissing me when he doesn't know what a power mix between their two magic systems might do? I'd call him on that if it wouldn't make things worse for Nikon.

"Palms up and connect with the energy, lad." Patty moves forward. "Feet firmly planted. Sift through the energy of the opening. You should find a seam on this side of the energy and one on the other. The hardest part will be stretching your connection to close the seam on the fae realm side."

"How do I close it?" Nikon asks.

"It's magic, son. Imagine yourself pinching it shut like a freezer bag or pulling a tab and zipping it shut or if yer handy with a needle and thread, have at it. Whatever the workaround you settle on, own it, and envision it happening."

Nikon lifts his hand and clenches his thumb to his first finger as if he's closing his fingers around a zipper tab. "Fuck. It's so much worse when I engage with it. I feel like I'm going to break apart."

I fight the urge to start quoting Scotty and shouting *Star Trek* favorites. "We're breakin' apart, Captain!"

I'll give myself a maturity point for that later.

Right now, I'm too worried about my friend. "We're here with you, Greek. We love you and believe in you."

Sloan has his hands up, and I feel the signature of his healing energy washing over Nikon.

Great thinking, hotness.

"Something's happening." Nikon's voice comes out strangled. "I don't like it."

"Hold yer course, lad," Patty shouts, pointing his shillelagh at the vortex.

Magical energy arcs out from the swirling chaos of colors, snaking to the tip of Patty's outstretched staff and over to zap Nikon. The bite of the shocks is getting worse. I grab the hair whipping my face and take a couple of steps back.

"I'm going to come apart," Nikon shouts.

"I've got ye, Greek," Sloan says.

But then...

A blast of energy explodes, and Jules, Sloan, and I are pushed back behind a wall of power.

"What the frickety-frack?"

A duplicate of Nikon has appeared in the opening of the vortex, and as I look from one to another, I can't tell them apart.

"Greek, are you okay?" I shout over the whistle and whine of the energy storm. "Is that you?"

"Yes...no...I don't know."

"See if you can get him to close the other zipper," I suggest. "He can close the fae side, and you can work on this one."

"Okay. I'll try." Nikon's pained expression cleaves my heart.

"Maybe we should stop. We can find another way to get this done."

"Too late now, Red," Nikon says, his skin glowing with the kaleidoscope colors of the power fluctuations. "In for a penny in for a pound."

I hate this.

With my heart pounding in my chest, I rush to where

Dionysus stands looking anxious. "Please don't let him die. I'll take the heat from the pantheon if I have to but don't let this kill him, Tarzan."

Dionysus hugs me tight against his chest, and I close my eyes. "I promise, it won't come to that. It's almost over."

As the words leave his lips, the world goes silent, and the sudden noise loss is incredibly unnerving. I ease back from Dionysus and rush to where Nikon has fallen to his knees.

Other than his skin still glowing with color, he looks whole. "Nikon. Look at me. Are you all right?"

He meets my gaze, and I've never been so glad to stare into his beautiful eyes. With a trembling hand, he reaches up and wipes my tears off my cheek with his thumb. "Mischief Managed."

"To the man of the hour." I hold up my tumbler of Redbreast Whiskey a few hours later, and even though it's not my first, I still haven't stopped shaking. For me to be in danger doesn't bother me. When the people I love suffer, it shakes me to my core. "I thank the goddess every day you're in our life, Greek. You're smart and funny and kind…and today you are definitely a hero."

"A rainbow inspiration." Dillan chuckles. "Available for children's parties, light show events, and holiday festivities."

Poor Nikon. The wildly shifting kaleidoscope colors our immortal Greek suffered through when engaged with the portal gate hasn't stopped.

His normally warm, Mediterranean skin tone is cycling through the colors of the rainbow about every thirty minutes. Currently, he's a lovely teal color that looks great with his eyes and blond hair.

"Why couldn't we drink at home?" Nikon frowns at us.

I wave away his concern. "No one noticed. Besides, the magic of the world is out. There's no reason you should hide away just because you're playing the part of a lava lamp tonight."

"True story." Calum lays his arm across Nikon's back and hugs him to his side. "Besides, people love lava lamps. They're mesmerizing."

Nikon meets Calum's compliment with a shrug and a scowl. "Thank you?"

"Och, chin up, lad." Patty empties his ale. "It's just a wee bit of magical oil and water. Fae immortality and Man o' Green dragon longevity don't seem to mix well. Odds are ye'll be over it by mornin'."

"And if I'm not?"

Patty chuckles and shrugs. "Then ye'll be that much more interestin' to the ladies. Tell me, Greek, is yer willy wand a rainbow glowstick too?"

The table bursts out laughing, and Nikon raises both fists and flashes us a middle-fingered salute. "You assholes will never know."

"Never say never." Kevin grins. "What if Calum and I think you deserve the full hero treatment tonight? Would you let a little tie-dye drama deny you your due?"

Nikon snorts. "You want to see if my cock glows, don't you?"

Kevin and Calum shrug. "Maybe," both of them say in unison.

"Hey, aren't I the Greek of celebration tonight?" Eros snaps in next to our tables and crashes our party.

Dionysus shifts over on the long bench and pours a glass for our late arrival. "I was wondering how long you'd be able to resist. Blessed Erotidia, *adelphos*."

Eros accepts the glass, but before he slides in to take a seat, he meets my gaze. "Am I welcome at your table, Lady Druid?"

It never fails to piss me off that the sultry voice of the god of love resonates deep inside me and makes me want things I don't want. I know it's not real and a side effect of his station, but my attraction to him is unwelcome.

I meet the gaze of the tall, Mediterranean man with shoulder-length ebony hair and swirling silver eyes, and I lift my chin. "Hello, Eros."

He offers me a sexy smile. "When last we met, you formed an unflattering opinion of me and shared some rather strong words."

"Which you deserved."

"Perhaps, but your frame of understanding is based solely on your interpretation of who and what I am."

"Uh-huh. Isn't that pretty much the very definition of an opinion?"

"Of course, but your opinion is based on knowing me a few months and having a handful of encounters. Isn't it possible Dionysus and Nikon might know me better after a lifetime shared?"

"It's possible, but actions matter. You intentionally went behind Dionysus's back, betrayed his trust, and tattled to his daddy about something you don't understand. You hurt him. That is not the act of a friend."

Eros has the good sense to sober. He offers me a genuine moment without all his usual brash and sassy. "I truly regret the pain I caused my friend. In truth, you can only shoot an arrow by drawing it back first. When life drags you backward, it is about to launch you next. If we focus and keep our trajectory true, our friendship can soar forward from here."

I hear the wisdom in the metaphor, but I'm not sure Eros deserves to soar forward with Dionysus and Nikon. Then again, I suppose it's not my place to make that decision for them.

"Fine. You're welcome to join us and celebrate Nikon saving the day. I'm willing to give you another chance, but you need to re-evaluate your definition of friendship. Actions matter."

Nikon slides his arm across my back and squeezes my shoulder. Pressing a chaste kiss to my temple, he gives me a side hug.

"We lurve you too, Red. Thanks for being our guard dog. Or, in our case, our chimera."

I envision the ferocious, fire-breathing monstrosity that possesses the body and head of a lion with the head of a goat protruding from its back and a serpent for a tail.

My last encounter with one of those beasts was when we were sucked back in time during the Challenge of Trials to set Nikon free from Hecate's control.

I didn't almost die for his freedom simply to bind him to my will.

"I'm sorry if I get overly protective. If you boys think Eros is worth your friendship, I respect you both enough to leave it at that."

Dillan raises his beer. "One small step for Fiona Cumhaill. One large step for Greeks everywhere."

I flash my brother my middle finger and swig back the last of my whiskey. "If you need me, I'll be at the bar."

"Barkeep, I'll have another." I push up onto the stool at the end of the bar and set my empty glass on the pitted wooden surface.

Liam smiles from where he's finishing an order assembly and comes down to join me. "Hey, Fi. Are you okay, baby girl? You look rough."

"Charmer."

He chuckles, grabbing the bottle of Redbreast Whiskey and setting it on the bar between us.

The beauty of having a family-run Irish pub is not only having somewhere to hang out when the day has been too much but also having an ever full glass.

"I'm serious, Fi. You look bagged. I'm here for you if you want to vent."

I sigh and meet his gaze. "Do you ever miss the blissful pleasure of you and me hanging out behind the bar tearing up the night with our *Cocktail* routine?"

He chuckles and pegs me with a loving smile. "Every damned day. We had a good run, but yeah, I miss it."

It both hurts and helps to hear that. "I heart you hard. You know that right?"

He holds out his hands and glances down his muscle-hugging shirt and sexy ripped jeans. "How could you not? I'm fucking fabulous."

"No argument."

He grabs a bar towel and a sadness I'm getting used to sneaks into his ice-blue eyes.

My heart aches for him. "Is Kady still mad?"

"I think mad would be a thousand times better than where she is."

"I'm sorry. Is there anything I can do to help?"

"Can you turn back time and give me a heads-up that the fae and empowered worlds will be outed and that all the hiding of truths and smudging of lines I'd been doing would come out and hit me in the face?"

"If I could, you know I totally would. Sadly, the outing of the empowered world was beyond my control."

He finishes with the wipe down and hangs the cloth over the side of the sink. "Yeah, well, when you ended up on the front page of the papers as the spokesperson for the empowered races of Toronto, it left quite a bit of egg on my face. Not only did *I* lie to her, but we all lied to her every night and day for a year and a half."

I finish the shot he poured me and grab the bottle to refill. "Do you think she'll cool down?"

He shrugs. "I honestly don't know. We were in an amazing place, and she got blindsided. I hope she comes back, but she's feeling really betrayed...and rightfully so."

"I'll call and try to talk to her. Maybe if I let some of the egg hit my face, it might make her feel a bit better."

He sighs. "You can try, but I'm not sure it'll help."

"Well, it can't hurt. You deserve to be happy. I never wanted to tank your life by becoming a druid, and who are we kidding? I got you kidnapped and shot. I'll be damned if I break you up from your girl too."

"Well, I wish you well because I miss her like crazy. Honestly, when the fae and empowered shit hit the fan, I was jazzed. I thought I could finally tell her what's been going on and get it off my chest."

"But you didn't get the chance?"

"No. The world blew up and stole my thunder."

"She'll cool down." Dillan steps in to join the conversation. "Kady's got the fire of the Irish in her, but she loves you. The two of you were building something real. She'll come back to that."

Liam extends his arm, and the two of them knuckle bump. "Thanks, D. I know it hurt you to give her up."

Dillan shrugs. "I wanted more for her than being in constant danger. You were the better choice for her right from the start."

"That means a lot. Thanks."

That's my brother. Dillan is a broody cranky pants and can be a royal pain in the ass, but anyone who knows him knows his heart is solid gold. He's hot-tempered, no question, but he lives by a gentleman's code in all things that matter.

He wanted more for Kady than he thought he could give her, so despite being thoroughly captivated by her, he set her free.

All's well that ends well.

If he wasn't open to a new romance, he never would have found his beloved angel. Evangeline.

"Okay, enough brooding." I reach forward to flip two more glasses. I pour each of us a shot and push one toward Liam and the other to Dillan. "We're healthy and live lives filled with friends and good fortunes. Put out into the world that which you wish to receive."

"Thank you, Confucius." Dillan lifts his glass. "Namaste."

Liam tosses back the shot and bangs the tumbler's base down on the bar. "Fi's right. We can't sit around on a night like this and moan about life. We've got too many things going right to dwell on the few things going wrong."

"That's the spirit." I like the uptick in energy. "We're blessed and have true happiness in our sights."

Dillan tosses back his head as he empties his dram. When he sets the glass down, his expression is practically glowing. "Out of the mouths of sisters."

I follow his line of sight to the curvaceous blonde beauty that is his angel. Evangeline is cutting through the crowd, making a beeline straight for us.

Dillan is gone without a backward glance as the world melts away for both of them.

"That's the last we'll see of Dillan for the next few days." I giggle and refill my glass, then Liam's.

Liam watches the two come together on the dancefloor and *clinks* his glass with mine. "To the return of lovers too long away. *Slainte Mhath.*"

I lift my glass to meet his toast. "*Slainte Mhath.*"

CHAPTER THIRTEEN

Tuesday morning comes earlier than I expect, and I wake to the brush of the back of Sloan's finger against my cheek. "Sorry to disturb yer snore-fest, luv, but Garnet called, and we're to meet him in Montréal in an hour."

I groan and pull the covers over my head. "Didn't I put out the 'Do Not Disturb' sign last night?"

"I can't speak to that, but if ye did, he ignored it."

I close my eyes, trying to recapture the dream that is fading away. I can't quite remember what it was about, but it involved Sloan, a lot of skin-on-skin, and lying on a beach somewhere.

"Are ye awake, *a ghra?* Can I leave ye and trust that ye'll get up and get ready?"

I chuckle at the nagging doubt in his tone and flip the covers down to meet his gaze. "Yes, Da. I'm up."

He stands, leans over me, and gives me a gentle kiss. "All right. I'll be in the kitchen fixin' ye somethin' to fill yer tummy. Don't be long."

As he moves to step away, another thought strikes. "Hey, hotness? Did Garnet say anything about how Atlas is doing?"

The answer in his expression daggers me. "I'm sorry, luv. His injuries were too severe fer Garnet's team to mend. They weren't able to get him back."

"Oh no." That hits me right in the feels, and I ache for the loss of a good guy who wanted to do good things. "That's so sad."

Sloan nods. "It is at that."

My heart hurts as he crosses our room and heads toward the door. "I heart you, Sloan Mackenzie."

He glances over his shoulder and winks. "I heart you right back, Fiona Cumhaill."

Taking a beat to thank Atlas for his dedication to the good fight, I send up a prayer to Lady Divinity to watch out for him.

With that taken care of, I untangle my feet from the depths of our sheets and slide my legs through the slit in the draped curtains. The last thing I feel like doing is abandoning my sacred place to go back out into the crazy world so soon.

I pat the mattress. "I miss you already, King Henry. Save my spot."

Manx lets out a wide yawn where he's curled up in a ball at the end of the bed. He shakes his head and the black tufts coming off his ears flick in the air. When he stretches, his long gray-gold fur twitches and settles back in place. "I don't suppose ye need me to come today, do ye?"

I hear the sadness behind his words, and it hurts to know he feels left out. "Of course, puss. If you want to come, you're welcome. The fae and empowered worlds are out of the bag. There's no reason you can't join us on our adventures going forward."

"Aye, ye think?"

"Sure do. Check with Sloan and fly the idea past him, but I don't see why he'd object. Animal companions are best utilized in companionship." I drop to my feet and pad across the master bedroom floor toward my dresser. "If he asks, you can tell him I'm up and headed into the shower."

"Will do. And Red…thanks."

I drop my silk skivvies where they lay in my drawer and backtrack to hug our boy. "You don't have to thank me, sweetie. I'm happy to have you with us. If I had my choice in the matter, I'd have Dart with us too."

"Dragons haven't been outed in the great new world of the empowered."

"No. Not yet. But who knows, in another year someone might get sick of life being settled down and calm and decide to stir things up again."

"Let's hope not. This has been quite enough chaos for one lifetime."

"That it has, buddy. That it has."

Manx heads downstairs and I release Bruin. It was late last night when we got home, and my grizzly bear mythical companion was sound asleep after his big day of battling vampires and grom.

"Buddy, go ahead and spend a few minutes outside stretching your legs. Once I'm showered and dressed, Garnet expects us in Montréal."

"Again? Wasn't our visit about the mayor not knowing what to do about her daughter now that the child sprouted horns?"

"It started that way, but with the vampire attack and the hobgoblins arriving and buggering off to who knows where it looks like our presence is required again."

"All right. I'll go have a quick bath in the river, say hello to some of my girls, and be back in fifteen minutes."

"Wow, you're the bear. Several girls and back in fifteen?"

The long, low rumble of his amusement fills the bedroom. "I said I'll say *hello* to my girls, nothing more. Mind out of the gutter, Red."

I laugh. "Sorry. I know how much of a stud you are and realize you haven't gotten out much lately."

Bruin grunts. "I'll have you know I never concern myself worryin' about yer sexual conquests."

I laugh harder and return to grabbing my clean clothes for the day. "Point taken. Moving forward, I will strike all liaisons with your forest paramours from my mind. Carry on."

He dematerializes and ghosts out with a *whoosh* of a breeze and a flutter of my hair.

What a crazy life I live.

I'm still chuckling about Bruin when I get downstairs and sit at the breakfast bar in front of a plate of blueberry pancakes with banana slices on top. "You're much too good to me. You know that right?"

Sloan pours me a glass of juice and slides it to my place setting. "I may have been told that on more than one occasion."

I chuckle, finish chewing, and swallow. "Rude. By whom?"

He points at me and chuckles. "Every time yer drunk or hexed or loopy for one reason or another, ye always tell me I'm too good to ye."

"Then it must be true."

He sips from his mug and shakes his head. "What ye forget is that I find great purpose and pride in bein' good to ye. Growin' up with my parents and seein' how yer grandparents treated one another, there was no doubt in my mind which of the two relationships I wanted fer myself."

I reach across the island and sigh. "Do you know what I think?"

"Rarely if ever, no."

I chuckle and give him that one. "I think we should make it official."

"Make what official?" There's not an ounce of teasing in his voice. He truly doesn't have a clue what I'm suggesting.

Hilarious.

I set my juice glass down and dry my hands off on my jeans. "Sloan Mackenzie, love of my life, partner in crime, straight man to my wisecracks, I think we should tie the knot."

He sets his mug down on the counter. His eyebrows arch so

high they might be trying to escape his forehead. "Yer serious. Are ye askin' me to marry ye?"

The shock in his voice is too funny.

"I am. What do you think of the idea?"

"I'm all for it, ye know that, but ye always said a paper didn't matter to ye."

"It doesn't. I love you, and you love me, and that's all that matters."

"Then why the change in plans? Is this about Atlas?"

I shrug. "No...although being reminded that we lead dangerous lives is never a bad thing to keep things in perspective."

"I agree. So, beyond that, why the change?"

"Well, first, it's a woman's prerogative to change her mind. It's kind of what we do."

"No argument."

"Second, the two of us declaring our intentions in front of our family and friends would be nice. We met down at the training rings in July. What do you think about our two-year anniversary being our wedding anniversary? The weather will be warm, and Gran's garden will be in bloom."

He rounds the island and takes my hands, bending to brush his lips over mine. "I think takin' ye as my wife at Lugh's and Lara's place is perfect, but can I make one request? Can we not revisit ye sucker-punchin' me in the knackers as ye did on that day?"

I laugh, picturing him curled up on the ground grabbing his crotch and fuming mad. "Fair. Why risk putting a damper on the honeymoon?"

"Exactly."

"So, your answer is yes then?"

He drops his forehead to rest against mine. "Aye, it is. Consider it official. We're tyin' the knot July nineteenth."

The two of us finish breakfast, reunite with Bruin and Manx, and materialize in Montréal. Instead of meeting at the Montréal City Hall as I thought we would, Garnet has asked us to meet him back at Boucherville National Park, more specifically, where Nikon closed the portal gate yesterday afternoon.

"Good, you're here." Garnet tromps toward us when the four of us arrive. There's a definite growl lacing his voice, but as far as I know, I haven't done anything wrong since last night. "Fi, how is your French?"

"*Ce n'est pas bon*," I say with as much French flair as I can muster. "*Pourquoi?*"

He pegs me with a droll glare.

I shrug. "Seriously, it's not good. Without Dionysus's Rosetta Stone spell, I'm outta luck. I can say please, thank you, where is the bathroom, I've lost my wallet, and threesome."

Jules laughs, stepping through the trees to join us. Rene is with her and despite being a little banged up, looks ready to resume duty. "I think every English-speaking person knows *ménage à trois*."

"It's one of those handy phrases you never know when you'll need." Nikon joins us. I look him over, relieved that our Greek is once again himself and the rainbow effect of Patty's magic mixing is over. "Like *mas cervezas por favor*."

I nod. "Exactly. Or *domo arigato*, Mr. Roboto."

Our police escorts notice Bruin and Manx mulling around on the sidelines. "You remember Bruin from yesterday," I say. "The lynx in snazzy battle armor is Manx, Sloan's animal companion."

"Welcome to Montréal," Jules says before continuing our way. "Good morning, all."

We all share a morning welcome, and I study Rene. "I'm so glad to see you looking better today."

The guy nods. "Much better, thank you. That magical healing of Sloan's is incredible."

Sloan nods. "My pleasure."

"Yes, yes. It's a good morning, Sloan's the bomb, and we're all glad to be here. Yadda-fucking-yadda." Garnet frowns between the five of us. "Can you dispense with the pleasantries so we can get to the unpleasant part of our day?"

To be fair, it's me who always squirrels off-topic.

My poor surly man gets lumped into trouble because of me. I straighten and decide to set a good example. "What do you need, bossman? Are the mayor and Bella all right?"

"Fine. Dionysus is at the bookstore with Mayor Tremblay while she visits her little girl. It's not that."

"Then what is it?"

"This." He waves at where the hobgoblin's portal was yesterday. "It bugged me all night, and I finally figured out why."

"Care to share?"

He nods. "Hobgoblins aren't a magical bunch. They're a warring faction. This wasn't a portal *gate*. It was a portal *rift*."

I glance between him and the others to see if anyone is following the significance of that better than I.

Nope.

Sloan, Nikon, Jules, and Rene all seem lost.

"All right, I'll bite. What's the difference between a portal gate and a portal rift?" I ask.

"Intention," Garnet says. "A gate gets opened on purpose with intention. A rift is simply a magical tear in the fabric between two realms."

"I see the problem." Sloan frowns.

"Then please use more words because I don't pretend to be as smart as you."

Sloan rolls his eyes. "If what Nikon closed was a portal gate, we would assume the hobgoblins were motivated to breach realms and come here fer nefarious purpose."

"That would be wrong?" Jules asks.

"It would be because hobgoblins aren't that magically skilled."

"But since it was a rift?" I prompt for more.

"It increases the chance that the hobgoblins and their groms were here as a by-product of stumblin' upon a rift between worlds."

"Okay, but it's closed now. Beyond the fact that we don't know where the hobgoblins went when they blew us up, the rift is no longer an issue."

Sloan nods and holds up a finger. "That's true, luv, but yer overlookin' a very important distinction."

"Which is what?" Frustration leaks into my response.

"If this had been a portal gate, we could rest assured that though the hobgoblins opened it, Nikon closed it. In that case, yer right, it wouldn't be an issue."

Nikon curses. "Since it was a rift, it was a spontaneous event. We don't know what caused it to open or if it'll happen again."

Garnet shakes his head. "It's safe to assume it opened because of the surge in magical power recently, and I've already got reports that it's happening again. The question is, how do we stop it?"

Nikon groans. "Don't let it be me. Please don't let it be me. I just stopped glowing in the dark."

I squeeze Nikon's arm. "I could do without the splitting apart part, but honestly, you were adorable when you were teal. It's a really good color for you."

Nikon shakes his head. "Not helping, Red."

After Garnet walks us through the aftermath of the grom and hobgoblin invasion, we flash back to the city hall and meet up with Mayor Tremblay. The old building is buzzing with the sounds of construction and the coming and going of cleanup crews.

"Should we even be up here?" I lean to peer out the outer office door toward the atrium.

"We're fine," Mayor Tremblay says. "The fire chief had his team sweep the building and deemed the damage non-structural."

"Chief Côté?" Jules asks.

The mayor nods. "That's right, Leonide Côté. He's downstairs overseeing the cleanup."

Jules glances at me. "Would it be unprofessional if I step away for five minutes and say hello? Chief Côté is my uncle, and I haven't seen him in months. Well, he's not an uncle by birth, but you know, when your parents have a best friend your whole life and you call him your uncle."

I wave away her concern. "I totally get it. Go say hi. We're here for a bit, and I'll catch you up on anything you miss."

"Cool. Thanks."

Garnet follows her out and stops to talk to Nikon privately. The Greek's stiff shoulders and the worry warring across his face break my heart.

I don't want him to have to go through the portal closing process again either.

There must be a better solution.

"Is everything all right?" the mayor asks.

I break out of my reverie and give her my attention. "Sorry. Just worried about a friend."

"It seems that's a pattern with you…extending yourself on behalf of others, I mean."

"That's what we Cumhaills do," Dionysus says, grinning. "I'm an honorary Cumhaill, by the way, so I can weigh in on that."

I wink at him, and he goes back to chat with Sloan.

"He's an interesting fellow." The mayor smiles. "I must say, he's been wonderful with Bella."

"He would be. If you know your Greek mythology, Dionysus

was persecuted for his entire childhood for who and what he was. Now that he's on the other side of it, he's very protective of those who might suffer the same kinds of judgment."

"Well, I appreciate him taking the time to shuttle me to see Bella. Last night was the first time we've stayed apart for more than a few hours since her adoption, and I felt a bit lost."

"How do you feel now?"

"About her and her situation, better. About everything else? There are still people unaccounted for from yesterday's attack, I've got four in the hospital, and Marcel's mother asked me to speak at his service."

"I'm sorry. It's a lot."

"It is, but I'm glad Bella's with Myra and has made a new friend. I'm also thankful that no matter what Gabriel Lauden has in mind, she's not in danger and won't get caught in the crossfire."

"Me too. Like all races and species, not all vampires are monsters, but the good ones are rare."

"Then we need to figure out what Gabriel wants and stop him before he does any more damage."

"Speak the words, and it shall unfold." Garnet's scowl is locked in place as he strides in to join us. He's holding a tablet and turns so we can see the live stream on the screen.

Police Chief Monet is standing behind the podium at a press conference. He looks even more obstinate and judgmental today than he did yesterday.

Mayor Tremblay turns up the volume and Rene and Jules stops to listen. Whatever the man is saying has the three of them looking horrified.

"What is it?" I ask.

Clarissa listens for a few more moments before looking up at us. "He's coming after me."

"How so?" Garnet says.

The news footage of me commanding the knockout of the

protestors is running on a split-screen beside the chief as he speaks to the camera. Then come a series of unflattering mug shots of Garnet from the times Toronto PD arrested him.

"He's trashing us, isn't he?"

Mayor Clarissa nods. "He's speaking out against the recent violence in the city, my choice to bring dangerous outsiders to town, and saying my decisions are biased and reckless because my child is fae."

I scoff. "If Monet has such a bigoted blind spot when it comes to the fae, how can he defend Lauden as a pillar of the community?"

"He's not just defending him." Rene scowls. "He's endorsing him."

"Endorsing him for what?" Garnet asks.

"An interim seat as one of our Councilmen."

Garnet scowls. "Lauden can't take over for a municipal council member without an election and a vote from the people."

"Unless the seat is suddenly vacant," Clarissa says, the color of her skin draining pale as she looks up at us. "My Deputy Mayor, David Olivier, was found dead this morning. The police have ruled it a homicide at the hands of a criminal fae faction. They're implying it might even be your group."

My hamster tumbles in its wheel and gets flung flying. "Fuckety-fuck, that dirty douche canoe."

CHAPTER FOURTEEN

"A criminal fae faction." The words sound incredulous coming out of my mouth. "Seriously? What the hell does that mean? We've done nothing but help. We stopped the riot. We ended the vampire attack. We closed the damn portal. What we need is for the news crews to follow us around and take account of what's going on."

"Don't take it so personally, Fi," Garnet says. "I've been the focus of dozens of witch hunts, and the truth always comes out in the end."

"Still, it affects public perception."

He shakes his head. "I know you well enough to know you don't care about your image. You live by a code. The people who know that believe in you. The people who don't and choose to believe lies aren't worth your time."

Sloan squeezes my shoulders from behind. "He's right, luv. Keep yer focus on the problem. Disparagin' our reputation is a diversion to keep us distracted from Lauden ingratiatin' his way into power."

I prop my hands on my hips and regroup. "If the police found Deputy Mayor Olivier, why wasn't this office notified?"

"I think the answer to that question is obvious, Lady Druid." Garnet's voice is more growl than words. "The motive behind Gabriel Lauden's infiltration of this building yesterday has now been revealed."

Mayor Tremblay blinks and sits heavily in her seat. "Do you think Gabriel came here to abduct and kill David?"

He shakes his head, his ebony waves brushing the shoulders of his suit jacket. "My guess is that you were the primary target, but when you weren't here, and the riot didn't happen, it forced Lauden and his seethe to improvise."

"You're saying he's dead because of me?"

"No, Madam Mayor," Garnet says, his voice gentle. "Never take on responsibility for the violent actions of criminals. This is *not* your fault."

"Yet David is still dead, the chief has still told the city that it's my fault for being lenient with the fae, my daughter has still been outed to the zealots, and I'm still facing Gabriel Lauden being named as my right hand."

I run my fingers through my hair. Eels of discontentment fill my stomach. "We can't let this happen."

"What can we do about it?" The mayor sets the tablet on her desk. "If David is dead, his position will need to be filled. Naming Gabriel the interim deputy mayor is smart. The man is well-loved and respected in this city."

Rene frowns. "What if we prove Lauden is a vampire and that he was behind the attack here?"

Garnet shakes his head. "No. Your chief was right about that. It's too easy to flip him racing in here during the attack to look altruistic and paint him as the innocent victim of slanderous allegations. We only know the truth because Fiona caught him in the act and confronted him."

"Even so," the mayor says. "I don't understand why Thomas would endorse a vampire. His bias and prejudice toward members of the empowered world have been well-documented over the past months."

"Lauden must have compelled him." Garnet shrugs. "It's as simple as a moment staring too long into a vampire's gaze, and now his free will is lost."

"You're not serious."

"Oh, but I *am*. Mental compulsion is only the tip of the iceberg when it comes to the damage vampires can cause. Their ruthless cravings for power likely equal that of their cravings for blood."

Mayor Tremblay sighs. "What do we do?"

"That's the question of the hour." Garnet tilts his head from side to side and the vertebrae in his neck pop. "The chief was very clear in his demand that we not kill anyone within the boundaries of your city. I warned him it was a mistake and now he's a prisoner in his mind."

"Are you saying the only way to free him from a vampire's compulsion is to kill the vampire?"

"It's not the only way, but it is certainly the most effective and straightforward way."

I shrug. "As much as I want to feel bad for your chief, I don't. People in positions of authority need to listen to those who have more information than them, even if it's a hit to the ego. Still, I hate to see his short-sightedness affect your government."

"We'll figure out a way to free him," Garnet says. "I'll speak to the Toronto King of Vampires and see what he'll share with us about negating a compulsion."

"Is that even possible without killing the vampire and severing the bond?" I ask.

Garnet shrugs. "We'll find out. In the meantime, we need to get the rest of the city council and the police force taking vervain. Sloan, see if there's an apothecary nearby run by a green or maybe a white witch."

Sloan pulls out his phone and steps aside.

"Explain please," Mayor Clarissa says.

I field that one. "Vervain is a perennial herb that, when taken regularly, negates the possibility of a vampire compelling you and usurping your will. It's perfectly safe. We all take it."

"And the green or white witch?"

"Before we start your government and police force taking it, we need to ensure the source is pure and the person supplying it is trustworthy. Green witches are dedicated to nature magic while white witches are devoted to harming none. If we find a local witch who runs an apothecary and can verify their designation, we can source out the vervain we need."

Sloan comes back in and waits for Garnet to give him the go-ahead. "There is a green witch, Emerald Moon, who runs a private greenhouse in Laval. She seems well-respected but won't meet with us without the approval of the Guild of the Laurentians."

Garnet nods. "Fine. I'll put a call in to speak to the local Grand Governor, Bikkali, and get us an audience. We'll have to circle back to that."

"Are we going to investigate the deputy mayor's death?" I ask.

Garnet shakes his head. "There's no point. The vampires will have staged it and the police force, whether compelled or not, will have interpreted it and cleared the scene. If the mayor's office requests a copy, we can see what they've done without wasting our time."

"I can do that," Mayor Tremblay says.

"For now, we'll focus on the vervain, freeing the police chief from his compulsion, and get back to tracking the portal rifts. If I'm right, Montréal will see more because of the massive levels of fae energy."

"Perhaps we could get a bottle of vervain fer the mayor and our two escort officers," Sloan says. "There won't be much point of us bein' here and tryin' to help if everyone is enthralled against us."

"Good point, hotness."

Dionysus moves toward the mayor, a white supplement bottle magically appearing in one hand while a pink umbrella drink appears in the other. "For you, Mayor Clarissa." Then he turns to Rene and another bottle and drink appear. "Policeman Rene."

"How many should we take?" the mayor asks.

"Take three now to get it into yer system," Sloan says, "and one a day goin' forward."

As the two follow our instructions, Jules jogs in from her visit downstairs.

Dionysus delivers his next bottle of vervain, but Jules doesn't take it. She sidesteps his offering looking stricken. "We've got an attack in Old Montréal. By the descriptions coming over the wire, it sounds like our hobgoblins from yesterday."

Garnet nods. "Then by all means. Let's pay a visit to Old Montréal."

Nikon portals our group to the location Jules says is the hardest hit by the hobgoblin attack. Whether it's a good or a bad sign, when we get there, all seems quiet. Badly damaged…but quiet all the same.

Jules frowns, glancing up and down a long line of historic buildings. The streets and sidewalks are absent of all signs of people other than the scattered and abandoned belongings left behind during a mad evacuation.

"Old Montréal is tourist central at this time of year. Even with the chaotic changes in the world, the flood of travelers has continued."

"So where are all the people?" Nikon asks.

I glance toward Manx. "Can you give us a hint on that one, buddy? What do you smell?"

"Fear, mostly." Manx lifts his head, the long black tufts of hair extended from his ears twitching in the breeze. "Yes, fear, but also the scent of hobgoblins."

Bruin, ghost out and see what you can find. If there are hobgoblins still around, let us know where as soon as possible. It's like a creepy ghost town here.

On it, Red.

My bear flutters in my chest, and when I release him, he surges off in a gust of wind.

Old Montréal is a historical area with a remarkable concentration of buildings dating from the seventeenth, eighteenth, and nineteenth centuries. It has a real Parisian-style quarter feeling, much like New Orleans.

As we ease up the street, I take in the devastation. "Wow, they went on a real smash and grab."

It's true.

The glass windows of dozens of shops are smashed, the contents of the displays stolen, and the destruction of the historic ambiance left to spill out onto the sidewalks.

"Fucking hobgoblins." Garnet scowls at the aftermath of the looting. "Anything shiny draws them, and if it's valuable, they'll claim it without consideration."

"Definitely the pillage and plunder sort of brutes," Dionysus says. "Don't get me wrong, I like shiny things too, but I wouldn't bash someone's skull in to get it."

"So, what are we looking at now?" Jules asks. "Are they still around or have they moved on?"

Garnet scans the street again, lifting his face toward the sky and inhaling a large breath. "The scents are dispersing on the wind. My guess is they came, they conquered, and retreated to their home base to rifle through their loot and celebrate their success in conquering this new world."

I chuff. "Yeah, a world that doesn't train to dominate or arm itself to defend against physical assault. That's quite a win to be proud of."

"I suppose it could have been worse." Rene assesses the damage. "At least we don't have dead bodies and bloody people running for their lives today."

Garnett shakes his head. "No, but if I'm right, when you take the statements of witnesses, there will be accounts of the hobgoblins taking slaves."

Jules turns, her gaze filled with a fire I admire. "Slaves? Please tell me you're kidding. You're being dramatic, right? You don't mean they've taken tourists to enslave them."

"That's exactly what I mean. One of the biggest mistakes a human population can make is to equate the ideals of their society with that of the empowered community. The two are not the same."

"But snatching people off the street to force into slavery is brutal and barbaric," Jules says.

"No argument, but that doesn't mean I'm wrong."

Jules and Rene share a worried gaze, and Rene steps back, pulls his police radio out of his pocket, and calls it in.

"This is a nightmare," Jules says.

I shrug. "For us, this is a Tuesday."

Garnet chuckles and scans the street. "Moving forward, the first thing we do is track down the hobgoblin horde to wherever they've set up camp. Then we need to free the hostages and force anyone who shouldn't be here back to the fae realm."

"Do you think that's possible?" Jules asks.

"In a best-case scenario outlook? Yes. In reality? We'll have to wait and see."

I read the hurt and anger in her and understand exactly what she's feeling. It's devastating to see a place you call your home invaded and threatened by beings you barely understand.

I move closer to her and lower my voice. "If you want to stay and help sort out the damage done here, that's fine, but we need to keep moving. The longer we take to track them, the farther the hobgoblins get, and the harder it'll be to rescue those taken."

Jules shakes her head. "No. I'm good. Rene can handle things here and catch up. I'm with you. If they're holding citizens of my city prisoner, I want to be there."

"All righty, I'll call Bruin back, and we'll get going."

It's no surprise that after tracking the hobgoblin migration through the streets of Montréal, we end up back at Boucherville National Park. Hobgoblins in the fae realm make their homes in forested areas, caves, and enclosed valleys where they have defensible positions.

The hobgoblins of Toronto made an abandoned subway platform their home and utilized the track system to come and go.

At least they did until Bruin took them out.

"Bruin, great work on getting us here, buddy. See what intel you can find about what we're dealing with and report back."

"On it, Red."

When he ghosts off, Jules and I hustle over to catch up with Sloan and Garnet. The two of them have their heads together, and history has proven that's usually when I need to listen.

They are geniuses in their fields and when they collaborate, I learn a lot.

"—and that's when we entice them to return from whence they came," Garnet says, finishing whatever he said before I arrived.

"Do you think they'll retreat to the fae realm without an inordinate amount of bloodshed?" I ask.

Sloan nods and grins. "I had an idea about that. Something Garnet said earlier got me thinkin' outside the box."

"That's always dangerous. Your wheelhouse is definitely inside the box."

Sloan chuckles. "That might be so, but it keeps things from blowin' up in our faces. Yer an idea menace."

"Hey, now. If I'm going to do something, I might as well knock it out of the park."

"Your idea?" Garnet pulls us back on track.

"Right. So, I was thinkin' about yer comment about hobgoblins plunderin' fer all things shiny and valuable."

"I'm with you." Garnet crosses his muscled arms. "Go on."

"Over the past year, I've had many donations and estate bequeathments to STOA."

Jules looks confused, so I add a sidebar to catch her up. "Sloan is the curator of the Shrine of Toronto's Objects and Antiquities or STOA."

"Technically, a stoa is a covered porch in ancient Greece." Nikon rolls his eyes.

I wave that away. "It is a Greek word, and we had a theme, so we went with it. The point is, people donate weapons, antiques, and enchanted items for him to secure and use when needed."

When Jules nods, Sloan carries on. "Right, so I assess the value of things on several scales, magical significance, enchantment strength, possible danger to the public, and so on. Many things get slotted away, but many other items are pilin' up."

I clue in then, knowing where he's going with this. "We could gather a bunch of shiny treasures and sweeten the pot to get them to leave."

Sloan nods. "If stayin' here becomes more trouble than it's worth, we make it worth their while to go home. Maybe we can get it done with minimal bloodshed."

Garnet nods. "All right. It's a decent idea. Dionysus, escort Sloan back. I don't want him draining his power right before battle. Also, if you can round up Calum, Dillan, Aiden, and Tad, that would be even better."

"I'll text them and have them report in," I say, pulling out my phone and accessing the WhatsApp chat. "Oh, and if you have a chance, can you grab my battle crown off the bedpost?"

"You have a battle crown hanging on your bedpost?" Jules asks, her eyes wide.

"Sure, doesn't everyone?"

Jules laughs and rakes her fingers through her hair. "Who are the men you mentioned?"

"A friend and three of my brothers." I finish my message and hit send.

"*Three* of your brothers? You have more?"

"Five. Remember? I told you they were all cops."

"*Tabarnak*, yeah, right. Sorry. The past two days have been a blur."

"No worries."

"But five brothers. Shit. I have two brothers and a sister, and that's more than enough at times."

I laugh. "At times for me too, but mostly we all get along and enjoy each other. Now that we're druids fighting for justice together, it's even more fun."

She chuckles. "I can't imagine. I think me and my siblings might kill each other if we were paranormal crime fighters together."

"There are those moments too. In a few minutes, you'll see why." The responding notifications come back, and I wink at Dionysus. "The boys will meet you at our house."

"Okeedokee. BRB." He lays a hand on Sloan's shoulder, and the two snap out.

The familiar *whoosh* of air that accompanies the return of my bear encircles me. Then Bruin materializes right in front of us. "Found them. They've dug in at a golf course about two miles north of here on the farthest section of the islands."

I relay that information to those who don't speak mythical spirit bear.

Jules knows exactly where I mean. "Grosbois. It's a much less populated island."

"What about any civilian hostages?" Rene asks.

"I counted six women in the clubhouse and three men getting bossed around and terrorized outside. It seemed to me they were supposed to be feeding the grom, but I'm not sure if they were to be the meal or not."

"Yikes, well let's hope they're not." I take a moment to repeat that to everyone too.

"It's strange that they chose something as modern and civilized as a golf course clubhouse," Garnet says.

"I suppose if there's not a lot of forest or caves to lay claim to, the golf course clubhouse will have to do."

He tilts his head from side to side as he considers that. "This works in our favor. Hobgoblins are a warring and strategic race. They won't like being in a place where they're exposed to attack. If they had found someplace wooded and overgrown, we might not have had the same chance at evicting them."

"Then we consider that our handicap. Let's tee up and take our swing." I waggle my eyebrows at Jules, Rene, and Nikon. "See what I did there?"

Nikon groans. "You duffed that one, Fi."

"Can I get a mulligan?"

Garnet looks at Jules and Rene and shakes his head. "It's best to ignore them until they stop."

Dionysus returns ten minutes later with Sloan, my brothers, and Evangeline. The boys are all dressed in their druid garb and ready to rumble.

Jules takes one look at them and blinks at me. "What's with your family and the badass sexy gene?"

I burst out laughing. "I don't think that's a thing."

She swallows, taking in Calum with his bow and arrow. "Oh, it's a thing. Is Robin Hood available?"

"Gay and married, sorry."

She laughs. "Now you see exactly how my love life goes."

The two of us are still chuckling as we join the others. "Everyone, this is Jules and Rene, our Montréal liaisons. Jules and Rene, this is Calum, Dillan, Aiden, and Evangeline. Where's Tad?"

Calum shakes his head. "He needed to pop back to Ireland to deal with something."

Sloan hands me my battle vest and my crown. I strap into my vest and set my crown on my head.

With that out of the way, Garnet recaps what Bruin found and calls up the Google Earth image of the golf course north of our position. "If you snap us in here, behind this stand of trees, I think that will be close enough for Dillan and Bruin to do their thing."

Rene looks at me for clarification. "My brother with the cloak, Dillan, can pull up his hood and have magical access to intel about his surroundings. Combine that with Bruin being a mythical bear able to take spirit form, and we usually have strong intel going into battle."

Garnet finishes with the recap for the boys and Evangeline, and then we're good to go.

"All right, assholes." Dillan grins. "Let's do this."

CHAPTER FIFTEEN

"How fare thee, my queen?" Sloan smiles at the Fianna crown on my head. "Another day, another battle."

I adjust the heavy headpiece and position it so it's secure. Pushing onto my toes, I kiss him. "Watch your back, hotness. If the hobgoblins aren't impressed with what's in your Santa sack, *poof* the hell out of there. Your idea is great but if they double-cross you or counter by trying to take it, just let them have it."

"I love that ye have so much faith in me." The sarcasm is thick in his deep voice.

"You know I have faith in *you*. It's the hobgoblins I don't trust. I think after my past encounters with them, I'm entitled to my opinion."

"Aye, ye are." He brushes his lips over mine and smiles. "It'll be fine. When the battle begins, I'll transport in, find the one in charge, and make my pitch."

"I hate that you're in the line of fire. It's giving me spousal anxiety."

"Believe it or not, I know exactly how that feels. Ye may have given me a moment or two of anxiety as well."

I roll my eyes and give him another quick kiss. "Don't get

dead."

"I have no intention of it. I've got a big date coming up. July nineteenth. Mark it on yer calendar."

I laugh and look around. "Focus on the now, or there might not be a then."

He's about to respond when my shield flares and I turn and call my armor. "Here we go, people."

From that moment, the opposition moves in hard and fast, and Manx, Aiden, Garnet, Eva, Calum, and our Montréal escorts take position around the clearing and dig in. I hear the whimper and yelp of a couple of grom on my right and understand their fear.

Bruin has materialized, standing on his back legs. Wearing his battle armor, he's a sight to behold.

A black sphere the size of a baseball streams through the trees at us, and I choke up on Birga and swing. It's a line drive up the middle of the second fairway, and if I'm not mistaken, I'm in good shape to putt that sucker into the cup.

Until it explodes.

In a violent blast of dirt and grass, it creates a divot the size of a moon crater.

I grin at my enchanted spear. "You rock, Birga girl. Now, how about we quench your thirst?"

The moment I mention her spilling blood, I feel her magical energy soar. At first, I worried about having a necromancer weapon, but honestly, she's amazing.

As angry hobgoblins charge in on us, her wickedly sharp marble spear tip greets them. She's rare and powerful and one of my most treasured gifts from Fionn.

Along with my iron crown.

I adjust the battle crown and relish the power surge as my fighting force comes online. For a year and a half, I thought this iron headpiece was just a showpiece. I'd tried to make it show me what it was capable of and got nothing and nowhere.

Then Fionn trained me on how to use it.

Fighting alongside my family and friends, I take in the data uploaded into my mind. The crown acts as a scanner of stamina and strength, informing me about their well-being and areas of weakness.

With that information, my armor activated, and Birga in hand, I begin to cut a swath through the enemy.

The plan is for Garnet, the Cumhaills, and the local cops to fight forward as the primary distraction.

Dionysus and Nikon will use that distraction to free and flash out the ten captives we know about while searching for any we don't.

At the same time, Sloan and Manx will seek out the hobgoblin in charge to make a deal with his bag of treasures.

Our party engages, and all the cogs of our plan seem to sync up nicely.

Evangeline is a phenom. I could watch her swinging her scythe forever and never tire. She's so incredibly graceful while at the same time brutal and swift.

As the first head lops and sails through the air, it hits me that we may have forgotten to inform her about not killing anyone while we're in Montréal.

Oops.

Eva is especially fond of decapitating bad guys. It's her reaper training…and the fact that her scythe is wicked cool and deadly.

Aiden grunts and I get a flash of his pain through my connection with the crown. I spin to help my brother and find him, sword in hand, pushing back two foes.

His injury registers. He took a hard strike to his left ribcage, but nothing broke. He's good to continue.

I rush to back him up as four arrows whistle past my ear. Two to their heads and two to their throats and they drop like rocks.

Okay, I guess we're totally tossing the do not kill order out the window.

I spin to where Calum is standing on the roof of the golf cart garage and smile. Kevin's right…he truly is our Robin Hood.

As the fight continues, he goes back to nocking arrows, and another volley flies in.

Dillan is back from intel gathering, and if I didn't sense him through the bond created with my crown, I wouldn't have noticed his arrival.

His cloak of concealment is pieced with enchanted layers of green, brown, and copper fabrics, and when the light catches it, it looks almost like a living forest.

His hood is up—no surprise there—and he is wielding his dual daggers. Closing in to fight at Eva's side, he's mincing, stabbing, and slicing through a barrage of furious grom.

Bruin materializes beside him, and the two of them tag-team and go at it.

"They must've gotten the captives free," I shout to Jules and Rene, pointing. "Dionysus is back."

"What is he doing?" Rene frowns at the God of Wine and Fertility cavorting around.

Dionysus spins off one attacker, rolls to the ground, chops the next man's ankles, and launches up to jump on the back of the next. He raises one hand in the air as if he's riding a bronco out of the chute, then he sinks his blade and dismounts like he's an Olympic gymnast.

I chuckle. "He's being himself."

That's all that matters.

Red! Sloan's in trouble. Around the back of the clubhouse on the putting green. He's overrun by grom.

My heart races as I feel his fear for Sloan across our bond. "*Dionysus!* Back of the clubhouse. Help Sloan."

The world spins as I throw all my strength and focus into racing around the clubhouse. Sloan's in trouble. I hear Bruin's call for help replaying in my mind and fight to stay in the moment.

Bruin won't let anything happen to him.

Dionysus won't either.

Or Manx.

The heavy *thump, thump, thump* of my boot pounding the cart path's asphalt thunders in my ears. Fuckety-fuck, I wish I could portal.

I round the corner of the building, and three hobgoblins rush in from my right. I duck a dagger blade and swing Birga to keep them at a distance.

One drops low and sweeps my foot. I'm too busy defending and too distracted to evade the hit.

I go down hard, landing on my back and cracking my skull onto the pavement. Thankfully, my armor is up so my brain only sloshes around inside my noggin.

When the first one drops to dagger me, I grip Birga above the spearhead and swipe left across his stomach.

The liquid gush of his intestines spilling out onto me is one of the grossest sounds ever, but I don't have time to dwell.

Evading the grappling hands of the other two hobgoblins, I grip the closest one's face. "*Frostbite.*"

He growls in a wordless rage as the skin of his face freezes beneath my touch. When he recoils, he rips and cracks his brittle flesh. His buddy roars at me when he sees bits of his friend's face stuck to my hand.

I flick the hobgoblin cheek chunks into the grass. "How about you?"

When he lunges, I'm ready.

"*Bestial Strength.*" Rolling back, I accept the force of impact and launch him over my shoulders in a children's helicopter ride gone wild.

The one with half a face kicks me in the ribs. Despite the violent force, with my armor up, I barely feel the impact.

The shuffle of footsteps closes in, and I prepare myself for another assault.

Only the attack doesn't come.

The one I'm facing flies backward with the force of a hurricane and crashes into a tree. The sound of bones crunching to dust is nasty, but I've heard it enough times to know that opponent won't be getting up.

Ever.

A moment later, Bruin is there, standing over me. "Are you okay, Red?"

"Yeah, I'm good, buddy, thanks." Rolling to my knees, I take a moment until the world stops spinning, then I grab my crown from the ground and push up to my feet. "How's Sloan?"

I search the putting green, and the massive amount of blood makes my stomach churn. The entire area is strewn with dead grom, but their blood is a weird, gloopy, dark green, not the scarlet seeping into the grass.

"Whose blood is that?" I ask.

Bruin drops his chin. "I'm sorry, Red. It was bad when I found them. I got to him as fast as I could, but there were so many of those mangey asshole groms, it took time."

"Where is he?" I ask.

"I'm not sure. Dionysus grabbed him and snapped him out of here in the blink."

I search the furry mounds of downed beasts and my heart stops. "Manx."

Rushing to a stack of carcasses, I shove two groms out of the way to get to Sloan's companion.

"Manx, are you okay?"

His eyes open and he shakes his head. "I blacked out when two of them landed on me. If you get me free, I'll be fine."

A flick of Bruin's mighty paws relocates the dead grom, and Manx is free to get up. "What about Sloan? Where's our boy?"

"Not here." My face is strangely numb. "Dionysus took him somewhere to get him help. All we need to do is find Nikon and have him portal us home so we can check on him."

"Where is Nikon?" Manx asks.

"I don't know," Bruin says.

"He's with Garnet on the side lawn." Dillan jogs over to join us. He looks a bit rough but whole. "The Greek is working on opening the portal and sending the hobgoblins packing."

"I need him to help me find Sloan. He's hurt." I gesture at the blood soaking into the manicured grass of the putting green. Seeing it makes me dizzy, and the world blurs behind the moisture stinging my eyes. "Sloan is *not* a red shirt."

Dillan shakes his head. "No. Of course he's not, baby girl. I never should've made that earlier crack about red shirts on our team. Ignore me. I'm an asshole. You know that."

"I need Nikon to help me find him, D. I need to find him." I strike off toward the side of the golf club, but my feet don't seem to remember how to get the job done.

I only make it five or six feet before I pitch forward, and darkness overwhelms me.

"Here she comes." Calum's voice rings inside my head, and I try to follow it.

I blink awake, my eyes fluttering against the brilliance of sunlight shining on my face. "What happened?"

Dillan leans over me and blocks the sun. "You faceplanted and checked out. Bad form in the middle of a battle. If a wayward hobgoblin got a big idea, you could've been seriously hurt."

The idea of being seriously hurt brings it all rushing back. "Sloan. Where is he?"

"Dionysus took him," Bruin says, nudging me with his nose. "I told ye that, ye saw the blood, and down ye went."

Right. That sounds vaguely familiar.

"Okay, so who can get me to him?"

Calum says, hauling me to my feet. "Nikon's your best bet, but he's in the process of controlling a portal to the fae realm to deport a hobgoblin horde."

I check my balance when I'm upright, and I'm good. "Okay, naptime is over. What about Eva? Can she take me to my guy?"

Dillan shakes his head. "No. Eva's helping Nikon. After him splitting in two last time even with Patty's help, she thought she better assist."

"Right. That's a good idea." I feel the power of the portal energy surging around the side of the clubhouse and strike off. "Maybe we can help hurry things along. The sooner this is wrapped up, the sooner I get to Sloan."

My whole body is shaking, and I'm not sure if that's because I passed out or because I don't know what's going on with Sloan, but I don't understand why Dionysus would take him and be gone.

Check that. I *do* know, and that's what's scaring me.

The only reason he'd race off and leave me behind is if there were no time to waste.

Thinking about that sends another round of the quakes through me, and I pause to grip a stone retaining wall rounding the corner. Doubling over, I groan. My stomach gives my blueberry pancakes the old heave-ho.

"Seriously, Fi," Calum says, gripping my hair. "What the actual fuck? Are you okay?"

With my arms braced in the soil, I breathe through the nausea. "Yeah, I'm fine. I cracked my head pretty bad during the battle. I must have a slight concussion or something."

"Or you're preggers," Dillan says.

I glare at him and shake my head. "No. That's not possible."

He chuckles. "Are you saying you and Sloan are holding out? If you are, I'm calling bullshit."

Calum chuckles. "Fi is obstinate not abstinent."

I send a surge of power through my connection with the earth and churn my mess to fertilize the soil. "Har-har. You boys are hilarious. No. I'm not pregnant. I'll pee on a stick when we get home to prove it."

Dillan scowls. "That's a phrase no sister should ever say to her brother."

"Then don't stir up rumors. The level of the ambient magic here has been making me nauseous since yesterday, and I really did crack my head. Add that to not knowing what's going on with Sloan, and my body's a bit overwhelmed, that's all."

"All right, baby girl." Calum hugs me against his side. "Let's check on Nikon's progress so we can track down Dionysus."

I nod and brush the soil off my palms. "Yes, let's."

By the time we get around the building, Aiden, Rene, Jules, and Garnet are frog-marching the last of the groms and hobgoblins through Nikon's portal.

"Good riddance," Rene says as the last one passes through. "Can this day please be over?"

"From your lips," I say, stepping in to join them.

Garnet eyes me up and down, his scowl deepening. "You look like shit."

"What every female yearns to hear. Thank you."

"Fi fainted and fertilized the petunias with her pancakes," Dillan says.

"Are you pregnant?" Garnet asks. "Fi, if you're expecting, you can't be joining battles like this."

I hold up my hands, my head seriously starting to pound out a brutal rhythm. "Please stop. I'm not pregnant. Sloan's hurt. I saw the aftermath of his injuries, and it hit hard. Can I please steal Nikon to find out where Dionysus took him?"

Garnet grips my shoulders and steps in close. Lowering his face, he brushes his nose against my brow and inhales. "I don't smell the change in your scent a new life would cause."

"Because I'm not pregnant," I repeat. "But I am about to lose my shit."

"I'm here." Nikon jogs over to join us. "But I'm not going to be much use to you, I'm afraid. In fact, after my portal work, *I* might faint and puke into the flowerbed next."

"Are you pregnant too, Greek?" Dillan asks.

I ignore them and head straight for Eva. "Sloan's hurt. Can you please take me to him?"

"Of course, sweetie." She reaches toward me. "Take my hands and focus on being with him."

I do as Eva suggests. With our hands linked, I close my eyes and focus on my need to see my guy.

Eva's Angel of the Choir magical signature is very different than Nikon's, Dionysus', or even Sloan's. When she connects with her power, it's like grasping the sun's rays.

Except nothing happens.

Her portal doesn't initiate, and we don't go to Sloan.

I open one eye a crack. "Is there a problem?"

Eva frowns. "Yes. I can't find him."

My heart stops in my chest, and I fight to breathe. "Is he dead?"

"That's not it. I was born a reaper, and even though I've changed my designation, I can still sense souls whether living or dead. I simply can't find him."

"What could that mean?" I ask.

"I don't know. I'm sorry, Fi, I have no idea."

"Maybe it's like when Death took Fi up to the Choir of Angels," Dillan suggests, casting me an encouraging smile. "Maybe Dionysus took him somewhere other than to Wallace for healing."

That brings me back to what I said a few minutes ago. I meet the gazes of my friends and family, and the truth is in their eyes as well. The only reason he'd do that is if it was really bad.

Really, really bad.

CHAPTER SIXTEEN

There are certain moments in life when you feel like the world is holding its breath around you and you know that somehow, this precise snapshot in time will stay with you forever. This is one of those moments.

With Sloan missing and seriously hurt I'm afraid to move. Maybe if I stay frozen and wait for my life to catch up with me, everything will be all right.

Sloan would never leave me...especially now.

Yeah no. We've got a wedding to plan and a promise to keep. There's no way he'd move on now.

As the seconds drain away, anxiety builds in the bodies around me. I can't look at their faces. I can't meet their gazes, or my heart will crack wider.

My poor little ticker is already threatening to break, but I'm hanging in there, waiting, my faith in hotness so absolute that I refuse to believe in any outcome other than him coming back to me.

Movement at the side of the house catches my attention, and there he is.

Breathtaking, brilliant, and beautifully alive.

I leave my family and friends in the dust and run. Do my feet touch the ground? I don't know. Is everyone witnessing me fall apart? I don't care.

When I connect with him, I hold on tight, thankful he's solid because I can't feel my legs.

"Hush now, *a ghra*. I'm here," he whispers quietly so only I can hear. "Easy, luv. I've got ye."

Thank the goddess for that.

After soaking up as much strength as I can from him, I ease back and look him over. "Are you all right?"

"Fine."

"How? What happened? Where's Dionysus?"

Sloan's expression falls, and he squeezes both my hands. "Come sit with me, and I'll try to explain."

The agony of foreboding returns and I grimace. "I'm not going to like this, am I?"

"No, luv. Yer not."

I follow Sloan, led by the warmth of his hand tugging me toward the outdoor patio off the pro shop. Dillan and Calum hustle to get there first and start turning chairs upright so we can all sit and take a breather.

When we're seated and gathered, Sloan takes my hands in his. "By now ye know I was set upon by a pack of grom and never got the chance to bribe the leader to return home."

I knew about the grom but not the last part, but honestly, I don't care. "Why didn't you *poof* out?"

"I tried. Somethin' about the unstable portal energy here was givin' me trouble."

"What about Dionysus?"

"When Dionysus found me, my injuries were severe. Too severe fer my father and his staff to counter."

The dizziness from earlier is taking another run at me, and I blink to stave off a second round of flower fertilization. "And so, he saved you. How?"

"He took me to the Fates and bartered fer my life to be spared. When I woke, I stood before Clotho, Lachesis, and Atropos."

That tangles up in my mind, and I try to make sense of it. "He had the Greek Fates spare you? He can't. That violates everything his pantheon laws demand from him. He can't alter the course of human lives beyond that of the efforts of any ordinary empowered man."

"Aye, and that's the rub of it."

The sadness in his expression kills me. "What did he barter?"

"I don't know exactly, but whatever it was, he told me it might be some time before we see him next."

Tears sting my eyes, and I fight to swallow. "What did he do?"

"I wish I could tell ye, luv. I don't know. I'm sorry."

I wave away his apology. "No. It's not your fault. He did what he had to do so I didn't lose you, and I won't pretend I'm not glad about that, but…"

"At what cost?" Calum asks.

"Exactly. Dionysus matters too…so much."

"Of course, he does." Nikon squats beside me. He lifts a fabric handkerchief and wipes my cheek. "You know how big his heart is. If he saw a way to save Sloan, he'd take it without regret."

"Right, but how can I be happy now? I don't know what bartering for a change in our lives will cost him."

Nikon finishes with the cleanup and cups my jaw. "When this Montréal business is over, we'll go to Rhodes, and I'll have my cousin take us back to visit the temples. Maybe we can find out what happened."

Garnet grunts. "Or maybe, instead of jumping back in time and hitting the panic button, you should give it a minute and wait to see how things play out. As Fi reminded me, Dionysus might act like a child, but he is older than us, has survived worse than any of us, and is completely capable of taking care of himself."

I know that's what I said, but it doesn't make things any easier. "Fine. For now, we'll send some good vibes into the world so he knows we're thinking about him. If that doesn't help, we'll flip back in time and try to connect with the Fates or with their mother."

Nikon nods. "Themis likes you, and she has always loved Dionysus. I'm sure between the four of them, they'll take care of him."

That makes me feel a little better.

I draw a deep breath and scan the tired and bloody faces of the people around me. "Back to today's problem. We can worry about tomorrow's problem tomorrow. Aiden needs healing, Nikon needs to rest, and Montréal needs us to figure out what the King of the Vampire Seethes is plotting."

"What will we do about the bodies?" Rene asks, gesturing toward the front of the building.

"What bodies?" Garnet asks, feigning confusion. "I don't see any bodies, do you?"

I glance around and chuckle. The grounds look like a slaughterhouse tornado has hit them, but there is no hobgoblin fallen or dead grom lying around. Either the hobgoblins claimed their dead and toted them home, or Garnet got rid of the evidence while I wasn't looking.

Or maybe Eva used her reaper skills and escorted them to their final resting place.

However it happened, they're gone.

I chuckle. "How could there be bodies when the chief told us not to kill anyone while we were in Montréal?"

"Exactly right." Garnet grins.

"Having seen what you come up against, I'm certainly not going to say a thing," Jules says.

"Me either," Rene agrees. "They're gone, and the tear between realms is closed. That's all that matters."

"Sadly, it's not." Garnet waves at the remnants of the bloody carnage. "What happened here today is only the first such occasion. We need to figure out a way to track the opening of portal rifts so Nikon can close them."

Nikon chuffs. "If we can find anyone else with an affinity for portal magic, that would be great too."

Garnet nods. "I promise, I'll put out a call and try to find others. In the meantime, you're our go-to guy, Greek."

Nikon forces a grin. "Oh, goody. Lucky me."

With the hobgoblin fiasco over, Nikon snaps back to Toronto and takes my brothers and Eva with him. I try to send Sloan home to rest, but he assures me he's been magically brought back to full power and restored strength, so recuperation is unnecessary.

Manx is sticking close to his side, and I doubt he'll ever let us go anywhere without him now.

Which is also fine. I love having Manx with us.

"Good, you're back," Mayor Tremblay says as she buzzes us into her office. She stands and glances up, and her reaction of horror is almost comical. "Oh my! What happened? You look...."

I raise my fingers to keep her from having to come up with an adjective to describe us. "Yes, we're aware. We came to check in. If there's a lull in the vampire plot, we're going to *poof* home for a few hours to shower, change, and eat."

"There hasn't been any trouble from the vampires since the press conference. What happened to you?"

Garnet takes a moment to fill her in on the highlights of the looting in Old Montréal and how we found and rescued the local citizens and tourists taken prisoner.

"And the blood?"

"The hobgoblins have a form of domesticated wolf they command." Garnet downplays the whole thing. "They are a vicious breed, but we survived mostly unscathed."

I'm not sure if Clarissa buys the understatement of facts, but she does us the courtesy of not pushing for more details. "Yes, please take some time to eat and clean up. I'm sure we can manage."

My phone buzzes in my pocket and I excuse myself and step away. I don't recognize the number, but it's coming in on the line forwarded to the Toronto liaison, so I swipe green and answer it. "Fiona Cumhaill."

"Fiona, it's Diesel. Are you available?"

I've only had a couple of conversations with the guy, but even so, I can tell there's something off. "Hey, Diesel. What's up?"

In the background of the call, the shouts of men and the cries of women are ringing out. "I walked in on something, and it's bigger than me. We're about to have major bloodshed. Can you and a few others come?"

Another confrontation is the last thing I want or need. I'm tired, emotionally and physically drained, and I have given all my fucks for one day.

I have zero fucks left to give.

"Fi? Can you?"

I draw a deep breath and shake off the urge to bail. "Yeah, of course. Where are you? We're coming."

He explains that he's in the parking lot of a country bar I've been to many times. "I know exactly where you are. Two minutes. We're on our way."

I hang up and slide my phone into my pocket. "Showers have to wait I'm afraid. There's trouble on the home front."

"Where?" Garnet asks as our group closes in.

"The parking lot of the Rock 'N' Horse Saloon on Adelaide. Diesel needs backup." I take Sloan's hand and Manx presses in close. "Do you remember where it is?"

Sloan nods. "I do. I'm good."

Garnet nods at Mayor Tremblay. "Tonight, I think you should stay with Myra, me, and the girls at the compound. I'll put a member of my team on your house and will bring you back first thing, but until we know what Lauden is up to, you're safer not being where he expects to find you."

"That's fine. I trust your judgment."

He nods. "Let me take care of this, and I'll be back to get you, but if you need me sooner, call. Don't try to take vampires on by yourself."

"She won't be by herself," Rene says. "We'll stay with her until you get back."

Mayor Tremblay waves us off. "Go ahead. And good luck."

Sloan *poofs* us back to Toronto, and I curse when I see what's happening. It's an empowered issue, but it's one-sided. A couple of brutes have some shifters cornered, and it looks like they're about to lose control of their animal sides.

I check out the primary brute. He is tall, has silver wings, and is suffering from a severe case of verbal diarrhea. The problem becomes clear in an instant. "It's those Green Guardian dickwads again. And look who's causing the trouble."

Sloan frowns. "Do ye know them?"

"The idiot with the silver wings, yeah. That's Bivin, the guy I astounded because I turned down his awesomeness for Team Trouble."

The fight is ratcheting up fast, and the three of us run to get into the mix.

"*Bestial Strength. Tough as Bark.*"

As my calls to magic take hold, Diesel sees us and joins in from where he's standing in the wings. "Thanks for coming."

Garnet and I position back-to-back. He's facing four Moon Called about to lose their shit, and I take on the vigilante assholes supposedly keeping the peace.

"All right, simmer down, boys." I raise my palms like a traffic cop and try to hold their attention. "Whatever you pictured happening isn't happening. You need to clear out."

Bivin's gaze narrows on me and challenge flares in his eyes.

"Not a chance. You don't get to swoop in here and steal our thunder. Besides, it looks like you've already had your fun today."

I glance down at the blood and death coating me and shake my head. "See, you thinking that this is us having fun is exactly why you didn't make the squad. Now, off you go."

"What the fuck have you done here?" Garnet snaps, turning my way. Two of the three lunkheads Bivin has teamed up with have the good sense to flinch. "Why can't they flash out?"

Bivin grins. "Green Guardians 101, big man. You don't let your opponent escape. Then they only go make trouble somewhere else."

"There was no trouble until these assholes pushed in on our females and we couldn't flash them out," one of the shifters snaps. "We know better than to stoop so low as to fight in a parking lot, but they penned us in."

I turn, horrified. "You blocked their portal? How?"

Diesel points across the Green Guardians. "The guy with the tats and tail has something in his pocket. I heard them boasting about it before it all went south."

Bivin gives Diesel the finger. "What the fuck is wrong with you? Macho alpha boys like this think they own the city. Why would you help them? Look at you. You're a giant among giants. You don't need to roll over for this bitch."

I stretch my neck and draw a breath, letting that one wash over me. "Look, Biv-boy, call me a bitch again, and I'm going to slam you so hard into the ground your balls will tickle your throat. Policing the city doesn't mean you get to cause trouble you can solve. We're a calming force…a support team to ensure no one gets hurt and everyone gets heard."

"Yeah, kumbaya, I remember."

"I'm at the end of my last nerve, boys." Garnet holds his hand out. "Give me the portal jamming device and get the fuck gone."

"No way," the guy with the tail snaps. "I don't answer to—"

Garnet's roar rings through the parking lot as his fist sails through the air. The mouthpiece with the tats and the tail discovers his head can only spin a one-eighty before it forces his body to follow.

He hits the asphalt hard, and Garnet follows by gripping the front of his shirt and yanking him up for a close and personal convo. "If you don't think you answer to me in this town, you haven't been paying attention, dipshit. Now, give me the fucking device before I rip your head from your shoulders and bowl your friends over with it."

Before Dipshit with Tats and Tail has a chance to respond, Bivin and his boys make their move.

I palm thrust Bivin in the chest, following through with enough force to knock him flying backward. He catches himself with the flutter of his silver wings. Then he corrects his stance and attacks again—this time, though, he's coming straight for me.

I consider fighting force with force, but after the afternoon we've already had, I go for a hands-off response.

"*Whirlwind.*" I stand tall and reach for the heavens. The calm air gathers into a breeze, then straight into a gale. Squinting at the hair whipping my face, I thrust my hands forward and knock Bivin the Green Guardian backward ass over end until he disappears into the night.

Just to make sure he gets the message, I call lightning into the funnel of air and let it snap into the distance to give him a shock both physically and figuratively.

"Call me a bitch again, asshole. I dare you."

CHAPTER SEVENTEEN

The next morning, I lay awake in bed, listening to Manx's soft snore and staring up at the intricate carvings in the roof panel of King Henry.

This week has been tough.

Dionysus is gone. Sloan almost died. Atlas did die. Liam is heartbroken over Kady. Emmet still misses Ciara. I still miss Emmet...

If the hits on the private front aren't bad enough, there are the ones we've taken on the professional side of things. Being named a menace in Montréal, Lauden getting rewarded for murdering Deputy Mayor Olivier, and having no idea how to spare Nikon from being the go-to guy for portal rifts.

My phone buzzes silently beside my pillow, and I roll over to unplug it to read the display screen. "Hey, Da. Is everything okay?"

"Right as rain, *mo chroi*. What's the craic?"

I draw a deep breath and try to exhale my anxieties. Nope. I fail miserably. "No craic here lately, I'm afraid."

"No? Weel, then I think ye should get out of yer bed, pull on some clothes, and come have breakfast with yer family. Oh, and if he's awake, call Liam and bring him along. His mam would love to see him."

"That sounds nice, Da, but there's a lot going on. Maybe once everything settles down."

"Nonsense, baby girl. When life's too busy and pressin' in on ye, that's exactly when ye need to take a breath and step back. It's only breakfast, and ye gotta eat whether yer here or there, amirite?"

I chuckle. "You usually are."

"Good of ye to notice. Now, up ye get. I'll get started on the griddle and see ye here in twenty."

"I'll have to check on a ride first. Tad is in Ireland, Dionysus isn't here, and Sloan can't afford to use up his wayfarer energy. If Nikon's free, I'll ask him and let you know."

He chuckles on the other end of the line. "I think if ye check, the Greek is havin' a coffee with Sloan downstairs and waitin' to bring ye here."

"Of course, he is." I shift to kick my feet out of the slit in the drapes. "Who was the snitch who told you I needed to have a family breakfast?"

"Och, I'll not give up the names of my informants. What kind of cop do ye take me fer?"

I pad across the bedroom to the clean basket of clothes. "The best kind, naturally."

"I always said yer the smart one of the lot. Those brothers of yers are eejits most of the time."

I laugh at his ribbing.

He's not serious. My brothers are sharp as tacks, and we all know it. I pick a few things and head into the ensuite. "All right, I'm up. I'll see you in a few."

"I'm countin' the minutes, *mo chroí*."

I toss my stuff onto the bathroom counter and smile at myself in the mirror. "Thanks, Da, for having your spies and checking up on me."

"Of course, *mo chroi*. Ye may be out of sight, but yer never out of mind."

When the call ends, I set the phone down and reach into the shower. After opening the faucet, I wait for the water temperature to adjust and decide to pay it forward and let someone know I'm thinking of them.

Going back to my phone, I search through my contacts and hit send. It rings a few times and goes to message. "Hey, Kady, it's me. It's…"

I check the time and curse. "Sorry. It's way too early to call you if you worked last night. Listen. I just wanted to say how sorry I am about the way things played out. Liam wanted to tell you a hundred times, but the empowered world is dangerous, and we swore him to secrecy for your protection."

I think about how scared I was when the hobgoblins kidnapped us. Liam ended up with a bullet in the chest. "He hated every minute of excluding you. If you can, work toward forgiving him."

I've known Kady for almost a decade and couldn't think of a better girl for my bestie. "Liam is amazing, which you know, and if anyone deserves a second chance to fix things that weren't his fault—it's him."

I run out of steam and figure I'll take the hint. "Okay, I'm done. And listen, now that everything's out in the open, we'd love to have you come over. There's so much for you to learn about."

I chuckle and decide to appeal to her adventurous spirit. "Did you know I have two dragons and a forest full of faeries living in my backyard? Oh, and a grizzly bear companion, and well, so much. Forgive him, Kady. He loves you and is lost. 'Kay, that's my pitch. I hope you're okay."

I end the call and set my phone down. "She'll forgive him. She has to. Happily ever afters is how we roll."

Twenty minutes later, Nikon snaps Liam and the Toronto Cumhaills thirty-two hundred miles to Ireland to meet up with our elders for a quick family breakfast. After three decades of estrangement, my father and his father patched up their relationship. Since then, we've become a bigger, happier family.

"There they be," Granda says, throwing his arms to the side to welcome us. "We're glad to have ye, kids."

I step into my grandfather's warm embrace and then move on to Gran, Da, and Shannon. "We're glad to be here." It's true. My world is already righting itself simply from being in their presence. "You're right, Da. I needed this."

"Of course, ye did." Da waves toward the living room. "Now come along. Fill yer plates, and we'll take them to the other room. I know yer busy with vampire business and such, but a girl's got to eat."

I breathe deep and smile at the familiar scents of Da's lumberjack breakfast. "Wow. You're pulling out all the stops. What's the occasion?"

I grab a plate off the dining room table and grip the handle of the first ladle.

"Does a man need an occasion to cook breakfast for his family?" Da asks.

"Nope." I stack a half-dozen slices of bacon on top of two pancakes. "Just making sure I didn't forget a birthday or an anniversary or anything."

"Nothing like that, although there is something I'd like to talk to ye about."

The tone in Da's voice brings my gaze up off the buffet spread to meet his gaze. "What is it? What aren't you telling me?"

"See, Da?" Calum grabs a plate as he, Kevin, and their foster daughter Bizzy join us. "I told you she'd think the worst and panic."

Da waves away my concern and shakes his head. "That's the

strain of bein' all things to all people. Somewhere in here, my sassy little spitfire still lurks."

I blink. "What do you mean by that? I'm me."

"Are you though?" Dillan arches a brow as he joins the food line. "Over the past year and a half, you've had to take a crash course in mature druid leader. We miss our silly, sassy sister."

I pause with my fork halfway to my mouth. "What the hell are you talking about? I'm still your sister. I'm still me."

Dad takes a long sip of his juice and raises it in a toast. "If ye say so, still, I think my announcement might alleviate a little of yer worry."

"Are you moving home?" I ask before my filter kicks in.

"Och, no. The opposite, actually."

What's the opposite of moving home? He already moved away from home. "I'm confused."

Da chuckles. "Yer granda and I have been talkin' and makin' some plans. In light of me movin' back here and the change of the world demandin' yer presence, I've decided to reclaim my duty to act as the Keeper of the Druid Shrine if, and when, the time comes fer that position to be filled."

I look from Da to Granda and back again. "Hubba-wha? What are you saying?"

"I'm sayin' yer off the hook. Ye needn't worry or feel pressured that yer obligations will force ye to leave yer life and move to Ireland anytime soon."

I'm stunned. "Are you sure?"

"Positive. It's been good fer my soul to circle back to the life I left behind. The position was mine to embrace, and the only reason ye agreed to it was to save yer Granda's life. Ye needn't be held to it."

I'm blown away. "Okay, yeah, great. Thanks."

I see the disappointment in Gran's and Granda's expressions and clarify. "Don't get me wrong. I wasn't wholly upset about becoming Granda's successor. I love it here and think the work you do is very important."

Granda waves that away. "Ye needn't explain. I know yer city is in yer bones and blood."

"It is, but I love Ireland too. I like having both homes. When the stress and strain of the city become too much, I have the Irish countryside or even Emmet's Island to fall back on. Conversely, when the slow and steady of this life wears on me, I love the energy and pulse of the city."

"Then it's good that ye keep both options open, luv," Gran says, "although we'd like to see ye a wee bit more than we do."

"I'd like that too. In fact, Sloan and I have a little announcement of our own."

"See, you *are* preggers," Dillan says. "I knew it."

I see the fireworks going off in Gran's eyes, and I shake my head. "No! Dillan, you need to shut your mouth and stop saying that. No, that's not it."

While Gran is visibly crestfallen, I think Da is recovering from the onset of a heart attack.

"No. That isn't what I was going to say, and now you ruined it, you jerk."

Dillan shrugs, not looking the least bit repentant. "My bad."

"Ignore yer brother, Fi," Da says. "What did ye want to tell us? Yer news isn't ruined, I promise."

I meet the expectant gaze of my grandparents, Da, and Shannon, and decide not to let Dillan ruin my mood. "I asked Sloan to marry me, and he said yes. And if it's okay with you all, we'd like to have a private ceremony by the training rings."

"Where ye first were introduced," Gran says on an intake of breath.

"Where she sacked the boy and left him wheezin' in the grass." Granda chuckles.

"We've already discussed that particular reflex not being included in the ceremony." I wink at Sloan.

"Aye, we have. So, if yer up fer hostin' our nuptials, we'd love to make it official."

The squeals of delight from Gran, Shannon, and Eva reset my world, and I exhale a heavy breath.

Everything will work out in the end.

It always does.

After breakfast in Ireland, we return to Toronto to grab our belongings before continuing to Montréal. The family time-out did me good. I'm ready to face the world of vampires, portal rifts, and compelled police out to get us. I check my phone, and there is no reply from Xavier, but there is one from Benjamin asking me to give him a call.

Opening his message, I tap his contact info and connect. He picks up on the second ring. "Thank you for calling me back. Can we meet up?"

"Of course. Shall we come to you?"

"No. Not here."

"Okay…where and when?"

"Laurel is suggesting the place where you and she used to hang out to get up to no good after field hockey."

The evasion is weird, but hey, vampires can be weird. Letting that go, I chuckle at the reminder of what our sixteen-year-old selves thought was wild and unruly. "Perfect. When?"

"How soon can you get there?"

"We're on our way." I end the call and shrug when Sloan pegs me with a quizzical gaze. "I have no idea why we're playing cloak and dagger, but we're already dealing with vampire drama, so I won't borrow trouble."

"A sound point." Sloan takes my hand and laces our fingers together. "Where are we goin'?"

"To the treehouse in the woods. No need to *poof*. We can walk across the road."

Sloan grins. "That's a novel idea."

"Right? It seems so normal."

The two of us head toward the back door, and I lean over the railing to call into the basement. "We're meeting Laurel and Benjamin in the woods. Do you guys want to come or sit out?"

"Och, no. We're comin'," Manx says.

Bruin grunts. "Ye can't even be trusted to go across the road to the trees without gettin' yerself into trouble. And that was before the natural world went wild."

I laugh as Manx bounds up the stairs, but there's not much I can say in my defense. They're right.

"I love you too, boys."

Sloan, Manx, and I slide out the back door and start across the back lawn when Bruin materializes beside us. He rarely uses the door in his animal form because he doesn't fit well and doesn't want to break the house.

"Where are we off to on this fine morning?" Dart asks, emerging from the grove.

My blue dragon has grown a lot in the year and a half of his life, but not as much as he's grown in the past four months. Sloan thinks it's a combination of the veil being down and the time we spend on the island with the other dragons.

The overgrowth of amped power is real.

When he first hatched, he could sit in the palm of my hand. Now he has almost grown into his adult size, which is the size of a short bus and twice that with the length of his tail.

I change my course and redirect from the gate to hug him and pat the center horn on his snout. "A quick visit to our childhood fort and back to Montréal to face the vampire horde."

"Can Saxa and I come?"

I hear the gentle plead in his voice and I kick myself. Da has always given me a hard time about me thinking I can do everything on my own.

Yes, I am independent, but I've been leaving behind all the incredible creatures in my life who are not only gifted but incredible assets in a tough spot.

"Yes, you can come. How long do you think it will take you to fly to Montréal?"

"How long does it take an airplane to fly Toronto to Montréal?" Sloan asks.

"An hour and fifteen minutes," I say.

"We can do it in half that," Saxa says, stretching out in the warm glow of the morning sun. Saxa is a full-size, sunshine yellow, ancient dragon. She grew up in Merlin's lair in the time of Arthur and the Round Table. She's seen a lot in her centuries and knew my blue boy was a keeper early on.

Smart dragon.

Flexing her wings out to greet the morning breeze, she limbers up. "It'll be good to get a flight in and stretch our wings."

All right, we'll sacrifice half an hour, so my dragon boy is looped into the events of my life.

I'll make that work.

"Just remember Montréal is a city and dragons aren't outed yet. You'll have to remain glamored and try not to be seen."

"Isn't there a nearby mountain range where we can spend some time in the wilds?" Dart asks.

"Yes, to the north of the city."

"Excellent. We can be nearby if you need us but stay out of the streetlights and traffic jams if you don't."

"Fair enough. But first, the treehouse to meet Laurel and Benjamin."

Sloan, Manx, and I make the trip across the road while Bruin moves in his spirit form and Dart and Saxa fly overhead glamored to stay unseen. Once deep in the trees, my bear and the dragons are free to be themselves.

The Don Valley River system is where my brothers and I spent most of our childhood. In hindsight, our druid heritage has always weighed heavily on our love of spending time in the great outdoors.

We just didn't realize it.

Our father's determination to leave that part of his life behind him meant we didn't know about our heritage until it came knocking on our door.

The rest, as they say, is history.

"Hey, Fi, thanks for meeting us." Laurel rises off the board swing when we arrive. A cute, ponytailed, pretty blonde, Laurel looks like she did in high school.

We lost touch when I believed a fire killed her eight years ago. Turns out her vampire boyfriend Benjamin saved her, and she's been living as his companion and private feeding source since then.

Well, she was…until a rival vampire murdered her and she got stuck as a ghost in Benjamin's life.

I'm so thankful Merlin and Sloan were able to craft a spell to bring her back to the land of the living.

"Hey, girlfriend. How's life treating you these days?"

I know the answer before she says anything. It's written all over her face. "It's been wonderful. To be seen and heard again is great, but to be back together with Benjamin and the family is even better."

The win is a balm to my soul. "I'm glad. Both of you look much better than the last time I saw you."

Benjamin nods. "That's why we're here. We owe you so much, and both you and Garnet asked about how to break a compulsion from a powerful vampire."

I shrug. "A lot of good it did us. Xavier said there was nothing beyond what we already know."

"What do you know?"

"If it's an event-specific compulsion, like the riot in the park the other day, we can pull the plug and knock them out until after the event has passed. The compulsion will cancel itself out."

"That won't work for anyone compelled for something like an alliance or to forget something," Benjamin says.

"Right. Which is what we're dealing with in Montréal. Gabriel Lauden is compelling the police chief and likely half the police force and city council, but there's nothing we can do about it."

"Almost nothing." Benjamin eases his hand into his jacket to pull out a dagger. "If the king of a bloodline is daggered—or any ancient and powerful vampire for that matter—it will free anyone compelled by him or any of his heirs from the compulsion."

It takes a moment for the significance of that to sink in. "Him or any of his heirs?"

"That's right."

"Wow. That's huge."

Sloan steps in to accept the dagger. It's slender, bejeweled, and the blade has a subtle oil slick sheen when he holds it in the light to examine it. "Through the heart, I assume?"

Benjamin nods. "From the chest or back. It doesn't matter which."

"Why didn't Xavier mention this?" I ask.

"Because this is one of our most guarded secrets. Most vampires don't even know about it. Letting this dagger out of our sight is a huge leap of faith. This is a one-of-a-kind dark object, and it can be used on Xavier or any of us as easily as Gabriel Lauden."

"I told them you won't let them down," Laurel says, looking worried. "Please don't let them down, Fi."

"Of course, I'll do my best not to."

Laurel nods. "Good. Just dagger your vamp, set everyone free, and get them on vervain. Then, when that's all taken care of, pull the dagger and return it to us."

"And be prepared to defend against Lauden's second-in-command."

"Vincent," I say, remembering what Xavier texted me. "Yeah, so far I haven't seen any sign of the right-hand man."

"Consider yourself lucky." Benjamin pegs us with a serious look and frowns. "Don't lose track of this dagger, Fiona, please."

"I won't. I swear we'll guard it with our lives. When the job is over, we'll bring it straight back to you."

Benjamin still looks worried, but there's nothing more for me to say that could reassure him. "Remember, if Lauden sees you coming with this blade, he'll know what you're trying to do. The gloves will come off, and you'll have the fight of your life on your hands. Daggering a vampire takes stealth, strategy, and most importantly, surprise."

I nod. "I understand. Thank you both for your faith in us. We won't let you down."

Benjamin looks ill. "I hope not, Fi. The lives of the people I care about are in your hands."

CHAPTER EIGHTEEN

With the vampire dagger tucked safely into the side sheath of my weapons vest, Bruin returns to his place within me. Sloan speaks quietly with Saxa, making sure she's okay with him riding Dart for this trip. They shared some intense time in the dragon cave after the Culling. Saxa offered to union bond with him, both because it was her wish and to help bring Sloan out of a spell that held him in stasis.

He comes over with Manx, and we get into position on Dart's back. My dragon saddle is secured around the first spike on my blue boy's back. I take my position while Sloan passes to go to the second spike.

Sloan picked up a branch from the forest floor. Now he takes a moment to manipulate it with his powers and creates a harness to attach to Manx's battle armor.

In truth, once we're mounted and airborne, I cast a bubble around us anyway, but I understand Sloan's need to make sure Manx is secure.

The forty minutes we spend soaring through the skies is a rude awakening. It has been too long since I've ridden with Dart.

Yes, Sloan's wayfarer skill makes immediate travel appealing, but there's something to say about taking a moment between stressful events to breathe and ponder.

Maybe that's the balance I've been missing.

It's not only that too much is coming at me. I negate the time between one crisis and another because everything is urgent and immediate.

Mind blown.

This was an inspired idea, buddy, I say to Dart through our bond. *I'm sorry I haven't engaged as much as I should be with you.*

It's not a problem. You spread yourself thin, and a lot of people are vying for your attention. We've got time.

Luckily, you've had Saxa to keep you company.

There is that too.

Connected as we are, I feel the rush of affection and happiness as he considers that. *I'm happy for you, buddy. She's lovely and obviously smart enough to realize you are fabulous.*

She's pretty fabulous herself.

I glance at the yellow dragon gleaming in the sun and can't help but smile. *No argument. She's lovely.*

We talk a little more, passing the time as we glide over Lake Ontario until it narrows and becomes the St. Lawrence River. Twisting back, I check that Sloan and Manx are enjoying their ride.

The two of them seem as happy as I am.

This.

Me, Sloan, and our boys out in the sunlight, breathing in the ambient energy of our new world.

This is what we need more of.

I take a mental snapshot of this moment to play back when I need to be reminded of what's important. Why does the dark and crazy overshadow the bliss?

It shouldn't, especially now that the world has even more magic.

I close my eyes and fill my lungs with the power of ambient prana. From now on, I want to be proactive and not reactive.

Onward and upward.

Oh, except we're going down.

There's a park at the back of Montréal City Hall. You can land and let us off, or Sloan can poof us down.

It's likely better if he portals you down, Dart says. *Even if people can't see us, we displace a lot of air with our wings when we land.*

Good point. Have fun, you two. I'll reach out if we need you.

Be safe. Call us if you have any trouble with the vampires.

Will do. Releasing the handle of my saddle, I walk back to the second spike. "We're here. Dart thinks it's best we portal from here to avoid stirring up the locals."

Sloan releases the branch harness holding Manx secure and pats his side. When his lynx companion stands on his hind paws and presses his front paws against Sloan's chest, I step in to complete the circuit.

The familiar signature of Sloan's energy tingles over my skin, and a moment later, we're standing in the outer office of Mayor Clarissa Tremblay.

Before we break apart and let our day intrude, I kiss the top of Manx's head and move to Sloan. "I love you boys."

"We love ye right back." Sloan accepts the quick brush of our lips and smiles. "What makes ye say so right at this moment?"

"I was thinking I need to be more proactive with what I take on and cherish the quiet moments that matter more."

"Och, that's the wisdom of the ages, luv. I think we could all stand to do that."

"Okay then, let's vow to do better."

Manx licks my cheek and jumps down on all fours. "I'd like to visit Lugh and Lara more."

I understand that. My grandparents practically raised Sloan, and he and Manx spent a great deal of time there. "Done. We should make a new family ritual that takes us there. Maybe we move Sunday dinners to Ireland."

Sloan nods. "That's a splendid idea, but let's not forget Emmet and Brendan aren't to leave the island. We need to include them as well. Maybe it's Sunday dinners in the golden palace."

Manx flicks his ear. "If Lugh and Lara come, I don't care where it is. I just miss them."

Sloan chuckles. "Is it Lara ye miss or the homemade treats she makes ye?"

"Is it wrong if I say both?"

I chuckle. "No. There's no wrong answer, puss. We can definitely—"

"Good, you're here." Garnet opens the door to the inner office and waves us inside. "Come, we'll fill you in on the run."

It seems my moment of reflection and my resolve not to be reactive is over. Sloan, Manx, and I follow Garnet inside the mayor's office. After we say good morning to Rene, Jules, and Mayor Clarissa, we turn to Garnet. "Fill us in? Is everything all right? Is Bella okay?"

The cloud of worry blanketing Mayor Tremblay's expression lifts and she lights up. "Bella is fine. She's wonderful. She's having the time of her life petting lions and riding unicorns. She's learning about the changes in how she looks and is handling everything in stride."

"Excellent. I'm glad she's taken so well to Imari and Myra. I thought she might."

"She has. I think the biggest problem will be convincing her to come home."

I imagine that will be tough. It's hard to give up a life of sunbathing in an oasis and riding unicorns. Then again, when I was that age, I would've given anything to spend time with my mother.

Life giveth and taketh away.

Pushing that gem down, I focus on what's happening here and now. "If it isn't Bella you need to update us about, there must be news on the Gabriel Lauden front."

Clarissa nods. "The swearing-in is moving forward as planned, and there isn't a damn thing I can do to stop it. Between Gabriel, the chief, and the other cabinet members, I have no opening to object."

"You did say Gabriel Lauden is a shrewd businessman. He earned that reputation by being good at what he does to ensure he gets what he wants."

"I didn't realize where that cold-blooded instinct came from. The man I've sat with and spent time with during board meetings was quite warm and charismatic."

"I'm not surprised in the slightest. Vampires can be quite compelling," I chuckle and wave that away. "Compelling, sorry. I didn't mean that, but yeah, they compel people to like them."

"When is the swearin'-in ceremony?" Sloan asks.

The mayor lifts her wrist and checks her watch. "Eleven a.m., so, in twenty minutes."

"Where is it bein' held?"

"Downstairs in the council chamber."

"We should head down," Garnet says.

"Head down to put a stop to it?" I ask.

Garnet shakes his head. "I'm afraid not. We have no play...at least not yet."

"So, we're letting it happen?" Glancing between them, I have no idea how they're so calm. "Are we permitting Gabriel Lauden to get his claws into the government of Montréal, or do you have a plan?"

Garnet pegs me with a look. "I have at least three plans to fall back on at all times. Right now, the one that makes the most sense is to allow Gabriel to assume the role of deputy mayor."

"How does that make sense?"

"While all eyes are upon him, we can't afford to move. He's the boy of the hour and tarnishing his image will make Clarissa look bad, not him."

"Agreed but allowing him into office is a gamble. What's his plan?"

"Maybe he wants a foot in the door, or maybe he wants to run the show. There's no way to know for sure. At least not until the novelty of his appointment dies down, and he shows his hand."

What if showing his hand is killing Clarissa?

I can't voice that aloud, but surely Garnet has considered it. That could very well be his end goal. If he can do that, with ruling the municipal government and Police Chief Monet under his control, he's got Montréal nailed down.

It's smart, considering the vampires are losing ground in the empowered world.

I think about the dagger Benjamin gave us. I'm not sure it didn't come from Xavier.

I've learned enough about vampire politics to recognize he couldn't give me a dagger like that directly. The vampires in his family might trust him enough not to riot, but the other seethes he runs would lose their minds.

Especially because it's me.

Funny enough, there are a lot of empowered folks who don't like me. Go figure.

I consider telling Garnet about the dagger but bite my tongue. Something about the way Benjamin pleaded with me to guard the weapon and the secret of its existence has me keeping that info to myself.

If he's there when I plunge the blade and he asks me about it, I'll tell him. Until then, I'll keep the vampires' private business private.

"Okay, so we go downstairs and force a smile on our face while Gabriel Lauden becomes the Deputy Mayor of Montréal, then we see where that takes us."

Garnet nods. "That's my take on things, yes."

"It makes me sick," Clarissa says, her cheeks flushed. "David was a wonderful man and a dedicated leader of this community. To know that Gabriel thought of him as nothing more than an obstacle to be removed is barbaric. He killed a good man to step over his body and take his job."

Garnet folds his arms across his muscled chest and lowers his chin. "I understand your reaction. You're right. If this were about justice, we'd go downstairs, rip his head off, and be done with it."

"Isn't it about justice?" she asks.

"Not entirely, no. This is about you and Montréal's faith in their leadership."

Now that we've gone through things, I understand where Garnet is coming from. "So, you're saying that to keep things from blowing up, we first need to allow them to settle down. At least from the viewpoint of the citizens."

"Exactly right."

A knock on the outer door has Rene crossing the room to admit a petite woman wearing a polka-dot dress. "Madam Mayor, they're waiting for you downstairs."

"Of course, Lynne. Thank you. We're on our way."

CHAPTER NINETEEN

The council chamber inside Montréal City Hall is as impressive as the rest of the old building. With its arched stained-glass windows soaring twenty-five feet toward the ornate, hand-carved ceiling and the rich wood finish of the tables, chairs, and elaborate wood paneling, it's not only elegant but inspiring.

The swearing-in ceremony doesn't last long and is uneventful. Given who's involved, that could be good or bad. Sure, Lauden isn't trying anything, but why?

When the deed is done, Mayor Tremblay plays her part as the congenial hostess and invites everyone in attendance to a reception room.

The staff sets out cake and refreshments.

Cue the glowing smiles and congratulations.

"Who's the Italian dreamboat rocking the black-on-black in the corner?" I ask Garnet, tilting my head toward a guy who hasn't taken his eyes off Lauden in the last half-hour. "Bodyguard? Rival? Secret lover?"

"I can't speak to their sexual attachments, but yes, bodyguard. That's Lauden's second-in-command, Vincent Bianchi."

I pass an appraising glance over him and chuff. "That's the thing with vampires. Appearances are deceiving. He looks more like a NASCAR driver than a second-in-command."

"No argument. Another reason we can never assume to know anyone in the empowered world."

I watch Gabriel work the room, and I agree. Very deceiving. If I hadn't had a one-on-one with him, I'd think he was legit. "Do you think he genuinely wants to be part of Montréal's governing body? Maybe he loves his city like we do and wants the seat on the council, so the government reflects members of the empowered world and non-magicals."

Garnet chuffs. "If that were the case, he would've run for office and not murdered an innocent to assume his seat."

"Good point."

Garnet's phone buzzes inside the breast pocket of his suit jacket, and he reaches in to retrieve it. Accepting the call, he points toward the corridor and steps away.

The rest of us stay to keep an eye on the mayor.

Rene and Sloan move with the mayor as she works the room. Jules, Manx, and I stay at the door.

"How long is your team committed to staying here?" Jules eyes the pieces of cake set out to claim.

I step over and grab two pieces and two forks. "Here. Today is officially a cheat day."

She chuckles and accepts a piece. "Thanks. It wasn't that. I was trying to remain professional."

I chuckle and fork in a bite of bakery bliss. "Professional is overrated. Go for authentic. It's way better."

"I'll remember that." She takes another bite, scanning the room. "So, your plans? How long are you here?"

"I can't imagine we'll be here too much longer. Montréal is mostly managing what's being thrown at it."

"Other than the hobgoblins, the rift between realms, a

vampire enthralling our chief of police, and the same vampire named the deputy mayor after murdering his predecessor."

"Right. Other than that." We both chuckle at the outrageousness of the week we've had. "Seriously, though, if Lauden plans to play the long game, we'll have to leave it to you to manage. Toronto's having growing pains of its own, and so are many other places. We'll always be around for backup support, but soon this will be your show."

"I think you overestimate our readiness."

"You might be underprepared right now, but what we want to do is to build empowered response teams in the cities we visit. Then, as things happen, you have designated people to handle them."

She sets her empty plate on the serving tray of a woman passing by. "What people? Who would be crazy enough to do what you do on a daily basis?"

"We hope Rene will take up the mantle. He's got the experience, he knows the city, and he's dedicated to both sides of the equation."

"Both sides? What do you mean by that?"

There's no way in hell I'll be the one to out him to his partner, so I go a different route. "Just that his sense of justice and fair play makes him a great candidate. He can empathize and advocate for fae and human alike."

She arches a brow and chuckles. "That's the first time you've lied to me since you got here. Let's not make a habit of that."

Huh, and here I thought I was getting better at blurring the lines between fact and fiction.

Before I think of a better explanation, she leans in. "You know about him, don't you?"

"Do you? By the way he responded when we first broached the situation, I'm surprised you know."

She shrugs. "When you spend extended blocks of time with

someone, and you're an observant type, you don't need to be told."

I grin, wondering if she has any idea about her fae genes? Sloan says her latent levels are off the charts, yet she doesn't seem to have any idea.

If she's so observant, it's funny she's clueless about her change coming.

"Yes, well, Rene turned us down and didn't want to hear about it. Mind you, that was three days ago before the riot. Now, who knows. Maybe his take on things has changed after seeing how important it is to have a champion for the city."

Garnet returns and scans the room. He lifts his chin toward Sloan, Rene, and the mayor.

As quickly as political politeness will allow, the mayor makes her way over, and the guys follow. "What is it? What's happened?"

Garnet glances at Sloan and gives him the universal signal of buttoning his lips. It's not the first time he's used that signal, and Sloan casts a veil of privacy.

A wise course with vampires in the room.

When my ears pop and his magic tickles my skin, Garnet drops his chin and leans in. "I just heard back from Bakkali, the leader of the Guild of the Laurentians. He's willing to meet us, but he's not a patient man. Is there any chance you are finished with the swearing-in and can get away?"

Clarissa nods. "To advance our position to get rid of Gabriel, anything. I'll let Lynne know we're leaving."

Sloan and I follow Clarissa when she speaks to Lynne, and we take our leave.

"Where is the Batcave for the Guild of the Laurentians?" I ask, readying for the meeting ahead.

He chuckles. "Doesn't matter. He's meeting us at the Notre-Dame Basilica."

The moment Garnet flashes us in front of the famous Montréal cathedral, I know Sloan is in love. Hell, I'm not even into old buildings, and I'm crushing hard. "Wow. It's incredible."

"Notre-Dame Basilica is a gem in Montréal's crown, to be sure," Clarissa says.

It sure is.

I have a feeling Sloan and I will be coming back here very soon to spend some time exploring.

"This fountain is cool too." I glance up toward the bronze of the musketeer planting the flag above. "Who's the swashbuckler?"

"That is Paul Chomedey de Maisonneuve, the founder of Montréal, and the four statues at the base of the monument are four famous contributors to the city's establishment."

Noice. It's not too often the bigwigs spread out the credit to those who helped make it happen.

"Let's not keep the man waiting." Garnet gestures toward the church and leads the way up the front steps and inside the center of three arched, wooden doors.

The inside of the historic cathedral is even more magnificent than the outside.

My jaw drops. "So pretty."

"It's a masterpiece," Sloan agrees.

"Thank you for appreciating it." A tall, blond man strides toward us from the back of the church. A braid falls from each of his temples, and the scruff of a clipped beard covers his chiseled jaw.

Wow. I don't know if I've come across a Viking of myth and legend before, but it wouldn't surprise me if the man standing before us is a true Norse raider.

He meets my gaze and flashes me a knowing smile. "The interior of this cathedral is considered among the most dramatic in the world. The deep blue vaults with their golden stars…the azures, reds, purples, silver, and golds of the sanctuary are incredible, aren't they?"

"Without question," Sloan says, his awe as obvious as mine.

"Was there a reason you wanted to meet here, Bakkali?" Garnet asks.

"Of course. This is my city, and this is my favorite place within it. What kind of ambassador would I be if I didn't ensure you got to experience it?"

Sloan's gaze is still scanning the surfaces, taking in the hundreds of intricate wood carvings. "I see why it holds such power over ye."

"Do you?" Bakkali says, curiosity coloring his tone. "Then by all means, enlighten me. Why do you think this place enchants me?"

Sloan blinks back to the present and realizes he's been speaking out loud. "Och, I expect it's the timelessness of the interior. To anyone comin' in today, it might speak of beauty and history, but to ye, it would speak of a life of long ago. I expect yer connected to the memories rooted in a time and place very different than this one."

Bakkali nods. "The insights of an empath and the wisdom of a scholar. I'm impressed, Grant. I'm used to you surrounding yourself with knuckle-dragging brutes. Your Irishman is a pleasant surprise. The ladies are an upgrade as well."

Garnet doesn't look amused but also doesn't rise to the bait. Hey, Bakkali is the man here, and we need his endorsement to get the green witch on board.

We're certainly not going to make waves.

"Thank you for coming as well, Madam Mayor." Bakkali shifts his attention to Clarissa and offers her a warm smile. "Although you may not have known I exist. Throughout the centuries, I have always considered myself and the mayors of Montréal as co-custodians of this great city."

"Centuries," Clarissa repeats. "No, I had no idea. Well, I thank you for your part in keeping our streets safe and our people happy."

He bows his head, his braids hanging free beneath his chin. "It has been my life's honor."

"Further, I believe Mr. Grant mentioned I wish to establish a rapport with a green witch to secure vervain. May I count on your endorsement of trust?"

"May I ask why you need it?"

"It seems Police Chief Monet and members of our force have fallen victim to vampire compulsion. I wish to end that and keep it from happening to others."

Bakkali's mouth curls up at the side. "I see. Thus, the recent endorsement of Gabriel Lauden as your deputy mayor."

"Exactly."

"You're not so naïve to believe Gabriel desired the post of *deputy* mayor, are you, Lady Clarissa?"

She shakes her head. "During a recent siege of city hall, Mr. Grant and his team whisked me out of harm's way. Unfortunately, Deputy Mayor Olivier suffered for it."

"My condolences," Bakkali says. "It is difficult to lose a team member but even more difficult when you feel at fault in some way."

"Mayor Tremblay isn't at fault in *any* way," Garnet snaps, correcting him.

Bakkali offers him a crooked smile. "Of course not. I said *feel* at fault. There's no rationalizing the violence of villainous acts. Mr. Olivier was an unfortunate victim of circumstance."

The tightening of the mayor's expression speaks to her disapproval. "Gabriel Lauden cannot be allowed to profit from his criminal disregard for life. I must protect my people going forward. You understand that, yes?"

Bakkali tilts his head left to right as he considers that. "I do, but to supply vervain to not only you and the sixty-four council members and forty-six hundred officers and another sixteen hundred police volunteers is an incredible burden of demand. And what about judges, lawyers, and care workers?"

Mayor Clarissa's expression drops. "I see what you're saying. Where do we draw the line? How do we determine who is valued enough to need protection and who isn't?"

"Exactly. In a perfect world, no one would have to worry about being coerced or enthralled to do the bidding of another, but in the empowered world, the truth is that not all can be saved."

Mayor Clarissa looks at Garnet and frowns. "What are our options?"

He shrugs. "The most straightforward answer is still to end Lauden. If we do, his hold on your people will end."

"But that does nothing to protect us from the next vampire who comes along with aspirations of grandeur," she says.

"No. It doesn't," Bakkali says, obviously not impressed with Garnet's suggestion. "The hard truth is when we tear the vilest of weeds from the garden, the vacancy of the soil allows for the next weed to sprout in its place and grow. There is no end to it."

Clarissa frowns. "Well, if killing him doesn't solve the problem, then I can't justify it."

"I think that's a mistake," Garnet says, a growl in his voice. "Gabriel Lauden will come for you. It might not be today or tomorrow, but men like him don't accept second position."

"Speaking as one who knows," Bakkali says, pegging Garnet with a look.

I'm not sure what has passed between these two, but I get the feeling they don't see eye to eye about much.

Clarissa studies the two men and comes to the same conclusion. "For now, I'll establish an attainable supply of vervain and search for another way to safeguard against vampires moving forward. I won't sign off on Lauden's execution as an offensive play. If I did, that would drag me down to his level."

"You can't afford to make empowered decisions based on human morals, Madam Mayor," Garnet says.

"You may be right, Mr. Grant, but I have to live with myself and treat people of the empowered world how I'd have them treat my daughter in the same situation."

Bakkali seems pleased with Clarissa's answer and nods. "A wise choice, Madam Mayor. Yes, I will join you and speak to Emerald Moon on your behalf. While she won't be able to supply everyone with the protection they need, she will be able to help you and your team, I'm sure."

CHAPTER TWENTY

Sloan boosts Garnet's portaling strength to flash our group north of the island of Montréal to the island of Jesus and the countryside of Laval. Smaller than Montréal, the Ile de Jesus is much less developed and home to fertile, rural land.

When we materialize at the property line outside the private greenhouses of Emerald Moon, I know exactly why we didn't make it closer.

I hold my palms up toward the vast stretch of farmland before us, and the hair on the nape of my neck stands on end. "Wow, the warding on this place is epic."

Bakkali winks at me. "Em is a smart girl. She knows what she offers to people, and she knows who and what won't want her products on the market."

"Does she think vampires will come for her?" Mayor Tremblay asks.

"Vampires, wendigo, wizards, rival witches, the list goes on. When your magical designation puts you in a position to either enhance or negate another race's power, there is an inherent risk."

"That's why she wanted you to be part of this conversation." I scan the farmland, the rows of greenhouses, and the little market store set up by the road. "Is that where we're going?"

Bakkali nods. "It is."

As we walk the short distance from the laneway to the parking lot bordering the public storefront, I study the spattering of trees in the distance, the barn across the road, and the fields of lavender in between.

"What is it, luv?" Sloan follows my gaze.

"I don't know. Something doesn't feel right."

"Is yer shield weighin' in?"

"No. Nothing yet."

"Yet," he repeats, arching a brow at me. "That's not disconcertin' at all."

A cheerful windchime tinkles at the corner of the building, and we open the door to enter Emerald Moon's apothecary shop.

The inside smells of dried flowers and patchouli, the space a mind-bendy contradiction. From the outside, the building is maybe ten feet by twelve. On the inside, it's probably three thousand square feet.

"A great use of feng shui. Is the expanded space the furniture placement or the use of smoke and mirrors?" I chuckle.

"It's like stepping into the Weasley's tent when they go to the quidditch match," Jules says.

Sloan takes in the floor-to-ceiling shelves and all the bottles, containers, and bundles of dried herbs and flowers hanging from the ceiling. "Emerald Moon practices spatial magic. Perhaps we should ask if she might speak to Nikon."

"Nikon? About what?"

"There are more elements of spatial magic to master beyond portals and transportin'. Spatial magic can also involve manipulatin' the perception of space and light and developin' pockets on other planes. It would be prudent to find out what Nikon might learn from her. Ms. Moon is obviously adept at her craft."

"Nice of you to say." A busty woman with painted-on jeans

and long, straight, ebony hair steps out from behind a swinging cabinet.

After she gauges us, she swings the large hutch back to sit against the wall. I wonder about the room she's coming from. A panic room maybe? A witch's private casting space? One of those creepy corridors behind the wall so she can look out the eyes of paintings and spy on people?

Emerald Moon slides her attention up and down Sloan like a contestant in an eye-fucking contest. "I'm also adept at a great many things that have nothing to do with magic if you're interested."

This happens often enough that as annoying as it is, I try not to get upset. Sloan can't help the attention, and he doesn't encourage it. He does, however, have a dozen turndowns he falls back on. It's a little game I play with myself to guess which one he'll choose.

"An offer well-received, Ms. Moon, but we're here solely fer the purpose of securin' the mayor and her team from the undue influence of vampire compulsion."

She takes in the crowd, nods at Bakkali, and smiles. "Ah, so you're the man who belongs to the sultry voice on the phone yesterday. I admit, I may have called our conversation back up last night when I spent some quality time with myself. Your accent is delicious."

I take a step forward at the same time Sloan gestures for her to join Garnet, Mayor Tremblay, and Bakkali. "I believe yer Grand Governor is here to give ye that endorsement of trust ye needed before helpin' us. We'll leave ye to it then."

Stepping back, Sloan grips my elbow and escorts me over to check out the dried herbs. "Would ye look at all these variants of wormwood? Who would've thought it possible? Certainly not me. Do ye think I should pick up a few bundles while we're here, luv? Goddess knows my little apothecary room downstairs could use an infusion."

I look up at him and scowl. "You don't seriously think you can distract me from that witch with talk of wormwood, do you?"

"I thought it worth a shot."

"Not even close."

He waggles his brows at me and lays on the charm. "Still, there's been no bloodshed, so are ye maybe not as angry as I thought ye'd be after her ribald slight?"

"I'm not pleased, that's for sure, but hey, I know where we stand, and she isn't on the playing board. Even so, who talks like that? Seriously, does being vulgar with a man you just met work?"

"Not with me, no."

Good answer. "Point to you, Mackenzie."

I let him pull me into a side hug, and he lowers his head to whisper beside my ear. "I much prefer the thrill of the chase. That's how ye snared me, ye know? There was nothin' about me ye found worth yer while. Ye made me prove I was more than a pleasin' package and earn yer favor. That is much more fetchin' to a man like me."

I chuckle and glance at where Garnet, Clarissa, and Bakkali are doing their vervain business with the witch bitch. "Fetching, eh?"

"Mhmm. Besides, I'd never want a—"

My shield flares and the door bursts open.

I will my armor to activate, shielding my face as wooden splinters explode through the air and shoot at us like dozens of wooden darts.

Bestial Strength. I call the power I need to hold my own against the attackers coming inside because I know before I get a good look at them what this is.

"A vampire attack," Sloan shouts.

Of course, it is. Lauden anticipated we'd seek out a supply of vervain. I call Birga to my hand and release my bear. "Bruin and Manx, protect the mayor. She matters most."

On it, Red.

"Count on it," Manx says, calling his armor forward and racing off.

The chaos of a dozen vampires invading the store is considerable. "How can they come in here? Was Emerald stupid enough to invite them over the threshold?"

Sloan raises a hand, calling a thick strangling vine down from the hanging grid on the ceiling. "The store is open to the public, not a private residence. Vampire trespassin' laws don't apply."

"Well, bully for them."

Two guys spot us as they rush through the door and alter course to intercept.

Sloan's magic flares, and the vine he called wraps around the chest and arms of the first to charge him.

The guy who comes for me looks more like a used car salesman than a vampire raider.

I shall call him Carl.

Wow, Carl may not look the part, but he's stinking fast. When he advances, I call Birga and swing. His evasion is so fast I miss it.

I grunt as his boot connects with my gut and knocks me flying. The force crashes me right through the wall's board and batten onto the grass in front of the little store.

The ground is spongy and cushions my fall.

I use the momentum to roll back and get ready for the follow-through. Carl might not look like much, but he's a decent fighter. The two of us lock in, and honestly, it feels good to vent a little witch frustration. I may even think it's karma that her store is getting trashed.

"You came a long way to start a fight, Carl. Is Lauden so worried we'll get the mayor set up to foil your plans that you tracked us down?"

Carl isn't the talkative sort.

He does like to fight, though.

He comes at me fast, and I misjudge his attack. I swing high, and he goes low. The sheer force of him taking out my ankles has me faceplanting in the dirt.

Okay, serves me right.

I always mock men for underestimating me. I suppose I deserved this. Carl the Car Salesman is a worthy opponent.

Pushing back to my feet, I recall Birga and get serious. "Well played, dude. Respect."

He doesn't seem to care for my accolades. He scrunches his face, his fangs drop into sharp points, and his eyes glow red.

Okeedokee. Carl's bringing it.

The next advance, I stay in the moment, tracking the blur and waiting for him to telegraph his intentions. My focus allows me to evade his right hook.

I'm thankful to escape that assault since he's bared his claws and I'm not keen on receiving the Wolverine treatment.

My evasion pisses him off. His pupils dilate, and he comes at me hard and fast.

Pinwheeling my spear in my hands, I shift my footwork and prepare for impact.

A loud *crash* inside the apothecary shop ratchets up my need to get back to the others. The fact that Sloan hasn't come out to join me means there's more going on in there than I realize.

By now, Garnet will have flashed Mayor Clarissa out. Once she's safe, he'll be back to crack heads.

Gaining some distance from Carl's offense, I stretch my neck from side to side and breathe to the depths of my lungs. The ambient magic in the air refuels my energy and sings in my cells.

"Dayam. It's like a hit of NOS, isn't it? Power just hanging in the air around us...oh, right, sorry. You don't get any of that. You're undead. Sucks to be you."

Carl takes a fourth run at me, and this time, instead of waiting for him to engage his attack as I have been, I change things up and go on the offensive. A quick spin, a slice of Birga's spear tip through the air, and his head rolls off and lodges under the boxwood.

Carl's headless corpse drops to its knees and flops forward on Emerald Moon's front walkway. The toxic ooze of vampire blood seeps out and slicks the cheery beige flagstone.

"That's going to stain. Sorry, not sorry."

The sass is barely off my tongue when two vans pull into the parking lot. Their side doors slide open, and more vampires start hemorrhaging out of the vehicle like undead clowns out of a Volkswagen.

Well, crappers. I may have celebrated too early.

Bruin, we've got serious reinforcements rolling in.

Do you want me out there instead of protecting the mayor?

Is she still here?

Yes. Garnet doesn't seem to be able to flash out.

Crap on a cracker. What's with blocking Moon Called portaling this week? Is it Moon Called specific? *Can Sloan get her out?*

I don't know. He's busy fighting.

Try to free him up and see if he can poof Clarissa free of this.

On it.

"I recognize you." A tall, brown-haired surfer dude vamp grins and points his knife at me. It's a butterfly knife, and with every twist and swirl of his wrist, he flips it open to expose the blade and closed.

Open and closed.

I shake my head, taking inventory of what's coming at us. "Sorry, you're not ringing any bells for me. Maybe you have me confused with someone else."

"I'll ring your bells, little girl. You ruined all our fun at the protest."

"Oh, the protest. Right, yep, that was me. Call me crazy, but I don't support vampires compelling innocents for mass riots."

As they advance, I spin Birga in my palm, shifting my footing to get the store at my back and the vampires in front. When I'm in position, I press my thumb against the Team Trouble pendant I wear, calling for our reinforcements.

I wait for a few beats, but when nothing happens, I wonder if Garnet's portaling ability isn't the only thing these asshats are blocking. Maybe our backup can't portal in either.

Okay, not good. *Very* not good.

I reach across my union bond with my dragon and try that. *Dart. If you can hear me, I would much appreciate a dragon intervention.*

I act cocky at times, but I also understand the difference between confidence and idiocy. Me against fifteen vampires is just that—cray-cray.

The beauty of my union bond with Dart is that he can sense and track me down if he's in range.

I hope he is.

While I wait to find out, it's time for Plan P.

Raising my hands to the heavens, I connect with the potential prana power around me. The world is buzzing with it and feeding my magic.

Utilizing it is easier than ever before.

I call a whirlwind to encircle me, which holds the vampires back for the moment. It won't work for long, though. Vamps are often more brawn than brain.

Soon they'll charge the windstorm and where will I be? Back to one against fifteen. Hard pass. Calling more energy to my aid, it responds fast and furious.

I yelp as my fingers burn, and I realize my problem isn't about not having enough power to defend myself. It's about having too much power.

What if I can't control it?

What if I can't slow it down?

A long rumble overhead brings my focus to the magenta

cloud gathering above. It's stunning, like a summer sunset when the entire sky is streaked like nature's Cosmopolitan.

Only it's midday, and those aren't cranberry swirls.

Power vibrates in my cells, and I grit my teeth. It's not the first time I've felt like the spinning rooster on the top of a weathervane. That doesn't mean I'm anxious for a repeat of what happened last time.

Lesson learned. Don't call lightning when you're on a yacht in the middle of the sea. A gigantic hole in the hull of the ship is a bad thing.

Another rumble above brings my focus to the current dilemma. The cranberry swirls above are really rocking.

Awesomesauce. The environmental energy building to heed my call is humbling.

"See what's happening here, boys? Back away before you get fried." I fake as much calm as I can manage. Inside, I'm starting to freak out.

I'm no longer calling energy to build in my palms.

The prana has identified me as a conduit and has a mind of its own. Fae magic is powerful, yes, but it's also chaotic and a bit asshole-ish.

Yikes. My muscles quake with the influx of energy and a steady stream of fireworks shoot out of my palms like I'm a freaking Roman candle.

The vampires are getting antsy about being held at bay. I see them searching my defenses for holes, looking for a way inside the apothecary shop.

Garnet's roar precedes a thundering crash inside. I can imagine the kind of damage happening in there.

Forget bull in a china shop.

He's a lion in a witch's apothecary.

Surfer Dude makes his play and rushes me. Thankfully, I was about to overload. I use the attack as an opportunity to get level again.

"*Lightning Strike.*" The bolt of lightning builds fast, and I focus to harness it. The rod of primal power cracks free of the swirling pink mass above and strikes surfer dude right on the top of his curly mop-top.

I expect it to end there, but the bolt breaks free of my intention. Instead of shooting straight down and grounding, it side arcs to hit one, two, then three vampires on each side.

Surfer Dude falls to the ground smoking, his skin hissing with the release of steam. The collateral damage vampires drop to the ground too. I'm not sure if they're fully fried or just roasted.

The other vampires stop their advance to reconsider.

Look at that. They aren't totally stupid.

"Holy schmoly." I shake out my hands. "That got away on me a bit, but I think I stuck the landing. Seven down with one lightning strike. Impressive right?"

The remaining vampires are locked in a holding pattern. Maybe they're intimidated, leery of approaching the Lady Druid powerhouse, or maybe I'm the Lady Druid maniac. Either way, it works in my favor.

They're afraid of me.

"Give her another minute, boys," one of the vamps calls, chuckling. "The little sparkplug is about to burn out."

Or maybe they're *not* afraid of me.

Rude. What's worse than him not being wowed and wary is that he might be right.

Prana power rumbles and rolls, swirling and spinning in magenta swipes across a champagne sky. Its power snaps in the air, and the *cracks* of energy are deafening.

Incoming! We're almost there, Fi.

Dart's voice enters my mind and with it comes a rush of control. I don't know how he's doing it, but he's breaking the connection the prana storm has on me and is returning me to the driver's seat.

Dragons are ancient creatures powered by source prana. We

found out when Dart's mother was being drained by witches last year. I'm thankful he has a greater understanding of how to wield that power than I do.

Better?

Much. Thank you.

With the power now locked in check, my control is both stretched and enhanced. My focus has grown and is no longer overloaded.

Laughter bubbles up from inside me, and I giggle.

"She's a loon," one of the vampires says.

"No, I'm not. I leveled up and laughed because you haven't clued in about how screwed you are. Welcome to the new world, motherfuckers. May I introduce you to Saxa and Dart?"

As if the world is their stage, Dart and Saxa drop their glamors and swoop low. Pumping their wings hard, their mouths open and long streams of fire pierce the air.

They lay two runways of flame. Saxa's strip follows the line of the road and blocks the vans. Dart does the same thing, his fire strip igniting a bunch of the vampires themselves.

The chaos of vampires lighting up allows me to move in and end them.

"*A ghra*, are ye all right?"

I glance back at Sloan standing in the gaping hole in the side of the building, looking worried. I capture my hair and hold it out of my face. "Fine. Come on, Dart and Saxa did the hard part. Big finish."

Birga and I launch into the fray and start putting our attackers out of their misery. Sloan grabs a chunk of the wooden boards that blew apart from the building and uses his powers to hone one side to a razor edge.

"A couple who slays together stays together," I say.

Sloan grunts. "Yer ridiculous."

"It's true, I swear. There are t-shirts."

Dart and Saxa make another two passes and fly off. *Sorry, Fi.*

We need to get out of this part of the sky. The air here is getting too volatile for us to navigate.

I wave at the sky and shield my eyes from the wind whipping my hair into them. *Thank you, guys. Mad love going out to the dragon rescue squad.*

Mad love coming right back at you.

When they're gone, and we've won the battle, I see what Dart meant about the sky's volatility. My whirlwind of hot pink power didn't dissipate when I disconnected from it. The opposite, actually. It seems like I've created a massive prana cyclone.

Oops.

"Hey, hotness. Have you got any idea what the protocol is when caught in a runaway prana storm?"

"Find a prana storm cellar?"

I chuckle. "Good one, but somehow I don't think that's going to cut it."

"All right then, what do you think we should do?"

After assessing the growing storm and its current trajectory to take us out, there's only one answer. "Run."

CHAPTER TWENTY-ONE

Across the road from Emerald Moon's farm, the neighbor's barn succumbs to the might of the magical storm. The cracking of the wood and the creaking of the wind dismantling the steel siding are incredible. I harnessed the power and gave the prana-filled air purpose, but since then, it seems to have gained momentum and a mind of its own.

My bad.

As the cyclone of raw fae power tightens into three distinct funnels, I shield my face, and Sloan grabs my arm. Tugging me back toward the witch's shop, I bend, chunks of board and rocks flying past us as we run.

The violence of the biggest funnel creeps onto the road and edges toward us. It eats the leftover fire and picks up the bodies of first one vampire, then another.

As it sucks them into the sky, we watch them swirl past twice before they're lost. Then go the—

"Head!" I duck as a vamp noggin almost coconuts me and bowls me over. When it passes, I turn to see the cyclone pick up another dozen. "Shitters, those are going to be brutal to track down and clean up."

The storm has built beyond our control.

Two power poles crash down and crush the vans.

"We need to get the hell gone," I say.

"Yer storm is heading straight at the store. Everyone we're supposed to be protecting is in there."

"Shit. If we destroy her farm and shop, she's not going to want to help us with the vervain, is she?"

Sloan blinks at me. "Likely not, no."

"What's happening out here—oh, *tabarnak*," Jules says, her horrified gaze locked on the incoming funnels of death.

I wave her back inside. "Ask Emerald if she's got a storm cellar."

"That's one hell of a storm."

"Go big or go home, baby."

Nikon snaps in beside me with Dillan and Calum. "Sorry we're late, we—" he freezes as he takes in the state of our surroundings. "What the serious fuck? Fi, what did you do?"

"*Me?* Rude. Why would you automatically jump to the conclusion that this is my fault?"

Nikon frowns. "Irish, who caused this fiasco?"

Sloan looks at me. "He's not wrong, luv."

"Et tu, Brute?"

Sloan chuckles. "Gettin' theatrical, are we?"

"That thy unkindness lays upon my heart. Wound me not with thine eye, but with thy tongue."

Sloan bites his bottom lip. "Let's circle back to quotin' Shakespeare later."

I know that look. "You have the strangest turn-ons."

Dillan hunches forward. He's shielding his eyes and squinting at the storm. "Is Fi's vortex of death swirling around dismembered heads?"

I shrug. "Maybe."

Sloan waves that away. "The important thing right now is that we evac the people inside and get them to safety."

"You boys work on that. Nikon needs to help me stop this storm from leveling this farm."

Nikon looks at me like I've flown over the cuckoo's nest and I'm never coming back. "Fi, you realize that's a raw prana hurricane, yeah? And this farm is directly in its path of destruction."

"Yes, I do."

"You think I'm going to fix it?"

"Yes, I do. If you open one portal here and one portal over there over the water, you could spare this farm."

"*Two* portals? To move a cluster of *three* magical hurricanes? What the fuck, Fi? I can barely close one, and you want two?"

Okay, so he doesn't seem as optimistic as I was hoping. "Two very small portals, Greek. We're not talking about a big distance like between the realms. I think the two of us can do it. I'll give you the juice, and you guide the storm."

He rolls his eyes and I know if anyone other than me suggested this, there's no way he'd consider it. But it is me, and he's good like that. "Okay, but I can't die, and if you do, I'll be really fucking pissed."

"I'm with you on that. So, let's not die."

"How do ye think yer goin' to juice him up enough to get it done, *a ghra?*" Sloan asks.

"I need you to remove the filter on the ambient power. If I absorb everything I can, I can transfer it to Nikon for the dual portal maneuver."

Sloan scowls. "This is reckless. Let the feckin' farm rot. We'll find another solution fer the vervain."

I shake my head. "It's not only that. I caused this. I have to try to fix it."

Sloan curses a blue streak, and I know he's really mad because it's mostly in thick ancient Irish and he only does that when he's really getting profane.

"Do ye truly think ye can do it?"

I meet his frantic gaze and offer him as much confidence as I can muster. "Yes, I do."

He mutters a few unflattering things about stubborn redheads, lunacy, and hero complexes. In the end, he reverses the anti-ambient aura he put around me and lets the full weight of the Montréal prana power hit me.

"Okay, how do you want to do this?" Nikon asks.

I stand behind him and grip his hips. Instead of trying to shout over the wind whipping at us, I speak to him on the private communication channel he leaves open for me. *Just two pockets of space. The storm flows into one and out the other. Easy-peasy.*

Lemon squeezy.

Connected as we are, I feel his doubts, and I focus my energy to boost him. *We've got this, Greek. We've been a great team since the first day we met. We're the Marauders of Mischief, right? Believe, and we shall achieve.*

He snorts. *Okay, stop the pep talk, Tony Robbins. I'm trying to focus over here.*

I do as he asks and close my eyes and my mouth. The drugging high of the ambient power is closing in, but I'm fighting it with all I've got.

While Nikon focuses, so do I.

We can do this, Greek. I know we can.

CHAPTER TWENTY-TWO

By the time Nikon and I finish the portal displacement of the prana hurricanes, the two of us are ready to drop. And we do…right on the spongy grass outside Emerald Moon's apothecary. The drunken rush of prana power isn't as overwhelming now as it was the first time but catching my breath has given me a great buzz.

"I can't decide if I love or hate you at this moment, Red." Nikon closes his eyes.

I chuckle, and my head lolls to the side. It weighs a ton, and I'm quite sure I could use it as a ten-pound bowling ball if it detached. "They say there's a fine line between the two. I'm going with you loving me. I've screwed up way bigger before and I'm hard not to love."

"A couple more ideas like this and it'll be easier."

Sloan blocks the sun, leans over us, and smiles at me. "Yer in good spirits."

I giggle and pull another deep breath into my lungs. "Me likey. The air here is a good time."

He arches a brow. "I'll give ye another five minutes to enjoy yerself. Then I'm cuttin' ye off."

"Buzzkill."

"Uh-huh. Fer now, I'll tell everyone inside the coast is clear. Or at least find out if anyone is still inside."

"Gird your loins, hotness." I hold up a pointed finger. "Don't let that witch suckerfish onto you in a show of 'oh, you saved the day' gratitude."

He chuckles. "My loins are well girded, luv, and yer the two who saved the day. But I hear what yer sayin' and I'll take yer warnin' under advisement."

"You do that."

He steps into the store, and for some reason, I find it hilarious that he goes over to use the door when a massive section of the wall has been blown out.

"Hey, Fi?" Nikon says.

"Yeah?"

"Did you really think I could do that or were you hoping I could and shining me on?"

I meet his gaze and sober. "I would never risk your life on a half-assed idea, Greek. I don't care if you're immortal. A piece of me dies every time you do. No. You sit in the first position at the Guild Governor's table because you are that powerful."

"Yet, in over a thousand years, I've never done anything notable."

"I think you're like Emmet that way. You're strong in the ways of the Source, but you haven't grasped what that means yet. In my mind, you're just coming into your stride."

"If that's true, I'm a *really* late bloomer."

"Nah. You just needed the right catalyst."

"Right, of course. All I needed was for a Fi-induced prana hurricane to threaten to level the Quebec countryside. Why didn't I think of that?"

"Don't worry. That's what I'm here for." We lay there for a bit longer, catching our breath and enjoying the world swirling around us in a prana-induced haze.

"Thank you for always believing in me, Red."

I log roll across the grass until I can squeeze his hand. "Honestly, I didn't know the details of how you'd do the whole dual portal thing, but I knew we could do it. If that guy on *Shang-Chi* can do it, you certainly can."

Nikon barks a laugh. "Tell me you didn't just risk both our lives banking on me pulling off a move you saw in a Disney movie."

I arch an eyebrow. "I would if I could, but I can't. But you know what they say, art imitates life."

He frowns. "I think the saying is life imitates art."

"Is it?" I think about that, but I've got nothing. "I think it works either way."

Nikon's busts up. "Oh, you slay me, Fi."

His laughter takes hold and gets me laughing too.

It's more than him thinking I'm a nut. It's the drunken bliss of the ambient energy here and the cathartic relief of surviving what we did.

We laugh and celebrate living through yet another magical mayhem event.

It takes a while for our mirth to die down but eventually, Nikon rolls to his feet and pushes off the grass. He offers me a hand to help me up and smiles. "You're right. It's definitely love."

I rise to my feet and hug him. "It goes both ways, Greek. I heart you hard. Now, let's go find Sloan and make sure the witch bitch hasn't got her claws in him."

With the excitement of Lauden's vampire attack over, Garnet figures out what blocked his ability to flash out. It wasn't the vampires. Emerald Moon's warding was the culprit all along.

Although I'm pretty sure his lion would rip her head off if he had the choice, we are envoys at the moment. It would do the mayor no favors to kill the witch we need to safeguard her team.

Instead, he steps outside and flashes away.

"Are you certain he's all right?" Mayor Clarissa asks when Nikon snaps us, Rene, and Jules back to her office at city hall. Sloan has taken a quick detour to return Bakkali to the Notre-Dame Basilica.

Left to his own devices and his passion for ancient architecture, Sloan might never return.

"He'll be fine. His lion is very dominant, and the witch took a measure of control from him. It will take a moment to get his animal side calmed down enough to be around people without growling and baring his teeth."

She rounds her desk and slumps into her office chair. "Your world is so hard to imagine. Garnet is a strong, powerful man, and I witnessed him turn into a lion right before my eyes. Then there's the bear protector who you carry within you. You and your Greek friend opened a portal in the path of three hurricane funnels and transported them to another portal over the lake... And dragons?"

I shrug. "Technically, the existence of dragons isn't public knowledge, so I need you to keep that one between us. But yes, when you say it like that, it's pretty incredible."

She leans back in her chair and stares up at the ceiling. "And this is the world my daughter belongs to."

"Partly, but Bella also belongs to the world she shares with you. The home you share, the park the two of you walk in, the restaurants you eat in. Those are as real to her as having a friend who can turn into a bear and has a pet unicorn."

That seems to give her some comfort. "Have you or Myra learned anything more about her birthmark?"

"Honestly, I don't know anything about the crescent fae or what that means. Once all this settles down, I'll look into it. I promise, Myra and I will put our heads together to see what we can figure out."

"I appreciate that. Thank you, Fi—" The mayor stops talking and by the way her gaze locks over my shoulder, I throw my fatigue off and get to my feet to block her from whoever it is.

Gabriel Lauden.

"*Tough as Bark.*" I call my armor forward and flex my palm to welcome Birga. Adjusting my stance, I ensure I'm positioned to protect the mayor. "What happened, Lauden? You didn't hear back from your kill squad and decided to get your hands dirty by taking a run at the mayor yourself?"

His brow comes down, and he makes a face. "Kill squad? Little girl, if I intend to do anyone harm, I don't need a kill squad, but I didn't, so it's a moot point."

"Well, that's good to hear because you're down about twenty-five men after your attack on us in Laval."

I give the man credit. He's unflappable. "I don't have any idea what you're babbling on about. How about you run along and let the grown-ups speak?"

"Yeah, I'm sure this is all coming out of left field. You're innocent, right?"

He tugs at the cuffs of his shirt, pulling them to extend beyond the sleeve of his suit jacket. "Innocent of what? I have no idea what you're talking about."

Mayor Clarissa steps past me. I move to take a step, but Nikon grabs my wrist and speaks into my mind. *Give them a moment, Red. The mayor got to where she is by taking on challenges and fighting her own battles. You can't be here babysitting her forever. This guy is her counterpart. She'll need to deal with him.*

Yeah, I hate that idea.

Although, he's right. I'm not Clarissa's bodyguard.

Clarissa walks straight up to Lauden and stops directly in front of him. Back straight and chin high, she gives him a stare down to be proud of. "David Olivier was a principled, decent man who didn't deserve to be killed."

"Agreed. I'm sorry for—"

The slap of her hand across his cheek rings out, and I catch myself before I chuckle. *Dayam, Clarissa. That took balls.*

Gabriel Lauden takes the hit, and though he looks shocked by her assault, he doesn't vamp out or retaliate. "It seems I've caught you at a bad time. Perhaps I'll come back when you are in a better frame of mind, and we can have a private conversation."

"Think again, bloodsucker," Garnet says, rejoining the party. "If you think waiting for us to leave will give you a straight shot at the mayor's position, you're highly overestimating your place in the hierarchy."

Gabriel turns toward Garnet and, if it's possible, grows more imposing. "Back off, Grant. This isn't your city, and you're not welcome here."

"They're here at my request," Clarissa says. "And considering how many times they've saved my life from you and your vampire hoodlums, I'll take them staying over you any day of the week."

He turns back to look at the mayor and shakes his head. "What vampire hoodlums?"

"The ones who came after me on Monday and killed Marcel. The ones who killed David to vacate his seat. The ones who came after me today and tried to kill me in Laval. You disappoint me, Gabriel. I always knew you were driven and ambitious, but I never pictured you as a monster."

"If you're calling me a monster because I was mugged in the streets and woke up a vampire, I understand your repulsion. But if you think I had anything to do with acts of violence against you or your deputy mayor, I'm offended."

She laughs. "Offended? I had to have Marcel's blood steamed out of the carpets. I had to call David's wife to console her about her husband getting murdered in the city he devoted himself to. I am offended. How could you have such disregard for the lives of—"

"What the hell is going on?" Chief Monet shouts, storming in with Vincent hot on his heels.

If looks could kill, Mayor Clarissa would be up on charges for murder one. "Just letting your personal pick for the council know where I stand, Monet. Not that my opinions concern you in the slightest."

"When are you going to get it? Everything in this city concerns me." The balding loudmouth turns a cold stare at Lauden. "Especially manipulative bloodsuckers caught murdering our elected leaders."

Lauden growls and his eyes flip blood red. "If one more person calls me a bloodsucker and accuses me of murder, I might forget I'm a gentleman."

"A gentleman," Monet says, handing a police file to Clarissa. "I don't think Deputy Mayor Olivier thought having his throat punctured and his body drained dry was very gentlemanly."

The chief looks back toward the door and waves in six cops. "Gabriel Lauden, you're under arrest for the murder of David Olivier."

"That's ridiculous," Gabriel shouts, taking a step to the side to keep the building group of enemies in front of him. "I didn't kill Olivier. Whatever you're fabricating won't hold up, Monet. This is asinine."

Clarissa's gaze stays locked on the contents of the police file, and I go over to look.

Ugh, the crime scene photos are gruesome.

"Is it asinine that they found one of your cufflinks with the body?" Clarissa pulls one of the glossy photos free to hold up for him to see. "Don't try to deny those are yours, Gabriel. Your initials are engraved in them, and I've seen you wear them dozens of times."

Gabriel glances at the photo and rushes forward.

I step into his path. "Easy."

"I only want to see the file. Out of my way, kid."

Garnet growls, and now he's pushing in from the other side. "Step the fuck back and give the woman some space."

I take the file from Clarissa's hands and hand it to Lauden, easing her back toward Nikon. *If he goes vamptastic on us, snap her out of here, Greek.*

In a heartbeat.

Movement in the outer office draws my attention to half a dozen latecomers. Dammit. I'm so done with these assholes.

Bruin. I need you to ghost around the outer office and see what's going on. If Lauden throws down his gloves, don't allow the men in the next room access to back him up.

Got it.

Focusing on the flutter in my chest, I release my spirit bear and smile as his gentle stirring of air brushes my cheek before he *whooshes* off.

"Stop growling at me, Grant," Lauden snaps, frowning at the evidence gathered against him.

"You should've let me put him down days ago," Garnet says, his purple eyes gold with the power of his lion coming to the fore. "I told you the bloodshed would be on your hands, Monet."

The police chief doesn't look like he cares. "My city, my rules. I don't take orders from fae freaks or vigilante criminals. The two of you can put on your fancy suits and pretend you are decent men, but you're not."

My shield is buzzing, but the sensations are all wrong. Why is the police chief picking a fight with Garnet and Lauden? If he's under Lauden's compulsion, why is he bringing the evidence of his guilt in Olivier's case to everyone's attention?

"Enough of this," Monet snaps. "I said arrest him. Vampire or not, criminals go to jail."

The cops move forward, the guy in front holding a pair of

wrist shackles. By the lack of fear in their expressions, I wonder if they understand the danger they're in.

Or maybe they can't. Not if they're compelled.

Lauden sees the shackles and must know what they do because his eyes flick back to blood red. He closes the file and drops it on the floor. "I don't know what kind of a game you people are playing, but it won't work."

"I think that's our line, Gabriel," Clarissa says.

Lauden scowls, his gaze whipping around the room. "Vincent. Tell them where I was the night before last. That police file says Olivier was killed between ten and midnight. What were we doing then? Tell them."

Vincent looks torn. "Night before last, sir? I, uh…I couldn't say."

Either Vincent is lying, or it's Lauden. It's too close to call and no way to know.

The cops move in, and Lauden launches.

The room breaks into a battle and there's a free-for-all. Sloan, Rene, and Jules push back the cops, Nikon pulls Clarissa into the corner and stands in front of her, Police Chief Monet shouts orders, and Garnet and Lauden go at it.

All the while, my shield warns me of something, and my instincts twist up.

What am I missing?

Bruin roars in the outer office.

I curse and call on *Bestial Strength*. "We've got more vampires moving in. Manx, you're in the outer office with Bruin."

"Aye, I'm there." Manx races out the door and I turn back to Monet. "Maybe you should step into the sitting room with the mayor, Chief."

"I'm not going anywhere." Monet glowers at the battle between Lauden and Garnet and curses. "Fine. You win, Grant. End this. Take him out. Gabriel Lauden is not to leave this office."

Garnet roars, his lion pleased to be freed from his cage. He grips Lauden by the shoulders and throws him across the room. The King of the Montréal seethes takes out part of the wall before dropping to the floor.

Being undead, Lauden won't get hurt by a tussle, no matter how rough. If his head is attached, he'll get up.

A problem soon to be rectified if Garnet has anything to do with it.

The violent scramble takes over the room, and soon adrenaline brings out all kinds of poor judgment. The six cops are pushing in on Lauden as Garnet fights to take him down.

"Can't you see it's not time to arrest the man?" Rene shouts, grabbing the arm of one of the uniform cops.

"No. They can't." I release Birga to return to her resting place in the tattoo on my forearm and rush to help. "The cops were compelled to arrest him. Even if it gets them killed while they're trying, they won't stop. They can't."

Sloan, Rene, and Jules join me in the struggle to keep them safe.

"What do we do?" Jules grunts as she blocks the strike of a baton with her forearm. "Because, *ouch*, we can't take them out. We're on the same side."

"But we can take them out." I nod at Sloan. "How about Boucherville? It's far enough that you should be good."

Sloan grabs Rene's arm plus one of the officers and *poofs* out. A moment later, he returns for two more. Then, two more. And last, Jules and the one she was pushing back.

When they're gone, the room feels remarkably less chaotic. Nikon has relocated Clarissa to the sitting room, and the two are watching from the doorway.

As much as I'd prefer for her not to be here, Nikon's right. This is her fight, not ours.

That leaves Vincent and Chief Monet watching the battle, me guarding the door to ensure no unwanted vamps get in past Bruin, and Gabriel and Garnet in the fight to the death.

I feel the weight of carrying the vampire dagger in my weapons vest both literally and figuratively. If I could get close enough to Gabriel to plunge it, I could immobilize him and release everyone from these idiotic compulsions.

They could all be free: Police Chief Monet, the arresting officers, the members of the council I'm sure are compromised, as well as the countless others.

I reach under my left arm and grip the leather hilt.

How am I going to get into the middle of that battle?

Shifting my footing, I skirt the edge of the room, looking for my opening. My shield is still burning a warning. It's so annoying when it gets like this.

Why can't it tell me what's wrong?

The reflection of Vincent's expression in the mirror is what does it. His maker and boss is battling against almost certain decapitation and final death, and he has a triumphant gleam of delight in his gaze and a sly smile curling his mouth.

Hubba-wha?

It all slides into place, and the bigger picture opens in my mind. On instinct more than thought—because who are we kidding, that's my wheelhouse—I change my intention and spin.

The dagger sinks into Vincent's chest with a hard thrust, and I follow through, forcing him back until he hits the wall.

When his look of utter confusion registers, a sickening panic twists my insides.

Oh, crap. Maybe I'm wrong.

CHAPTER TWENTY-THREE

Standing over the fallen body of Lauden's vampire second-in-command, Vincent, my confidence is shattered. I was so sure. Have I misread the cues and totally screwed up? Did I just dagger an innocent guy? If I pull the dagger free, will he recover?

The effect of the dagger is severe.

To my horror, the vampire appearing to be a healthy guy in his late thirties desiccates into a shriveled, ghostly apple doll of his former self. His skin pocks, his fangs protrude, and black spidering veins snake out from his scarlet eyes.

Shit. What have I done?

Chief Monet drops to his knees beside me, and I snap out of my panic with a new crisis to focus on. "Chief? Are you all right? What's wrong?"

He shakes his head and looks up at me. "What happened? How did I...? Wait, no...I remember."

I stare into the clear, blue eyes of the man before me, and the reality is obvious.

The compulsion is broken.

Considering that Garnet and Gabriel are still going at it, I must've been right the first time. It *was* Vincent.

"Greek, call Sloan and see if the cops have settled?"

I grab an overturned chair and bring it over so the chief can get off the ground. By the time I have him settled, Nikon is calling to me from the doorway of the sitting room. "You called it, Red. The cops are deprogrammed and coming around."

A horrendous crash behind me has me twisting to see the fight. "Garnet, stop!"

Sloan *poofs* back with Rene, and I wave him over. "Hotness, I need you here." I point at Vincent and the dagger. "Don't lose track of that."

"I swear it."

Leaving the enchanted weapon in Sloan's care, I rush to intervene before Garnet kills an innocent man.

Well, honestly, Gabriel Lauden is the King of the Montréal seethes. I doubt very much that he's innocent, but he's innocent of what Vincent framed him for.

"Garnet, stop! Lauden, enough!"

Shouting gets me nowhere, so I hit them with a bolt of faery fire. Garnet, the man, is all but lost to his lion when he turns to roar at me.

"I'm sorry, Puss," I say, hoping to get through the fog of the fight. "I figured it out. It was Vincent. All of it. It's been Vincent the whole time."

It takes a few repeats before he releases his hold, and the two men break apart.

Thank you, baby Groot. I kneel on the floor between the two of them. They are covered in blood and sweat, panting for every ounce of oxygen they can pull into their lungs.

"Think about it. Why would the chief pin the murder on Gabriel, then give you permission to kill him? He was compelled. If that compulsion came from Lauden, there's no reason to implicate himself and play the part of a martyr.

"Vincent orchestrated all of it—the attacks, the killings, the appointment to office—in an attempt to build tension and mistrust. Then, when everything boiled over, he gave you the go-ahead to end him."

"Because he couldn't end me himself," Gabriel says, coughing to one side. "No child of the night can end their sire without ending themself."

I didn't know that, but yeah, that works with my theory. "He needed us to do it. He set you up, so we thought you were vying for the power and control of the city, then turned the tables to have us take you off the board."

"If you hadn't figured it out, I'd be dead, and he'd have Monet, the force, and the governing cabinet under his control."

I nod. "Exactly. If Garnet killed you, he would've assumed control of the seethes, and no one would've realized it was a total double-cross."

"So, Gabriel isn't the one who killed Marcel and David or who has been after me?" Clarissa asks, coming out to join us.

Gabriel shakes his head and staggers to his feet. "No, Clarissa. I give you my word. I would never. We're friends. I thought you knew that."

"Then why did you break into my office and come after me when we foiled the riot outside?"

"I saw a group of vampires rush the building and I wanted to ensure your safety."

"*Your* vampires," she says.

He tilts his head from side to side. "In the sense that I am their king, yes, but they weren't from my bloodline, and I didn't know them."

"You didn't try to stop them," Garnet snaps.

He shrugs. "There has been a great deal of turmoil in the hierarchy of my people since the veil dropped. I don't try to police every action of every one of my charges. That would be ludicrous. I did, however, meet with the head of the family behind it."

I chuff. "Let me guess. That was where you were with Vincent two nights ago when Deputy Mayor Olivier was killed."

He nods. "That's right."

"An alibi Vincent could deny, and at the same time the other vampires knew right where you were so you couldn't interfere with their plans."

"It seems so." He adjusts the shreds of his fancy suit and runs his fingers through his hair to straighten things. "I apologize that vampire politics spilled over into your lives. Rest assured I will address and deal with it."

Clarissa presses her hand against her throat. "Oh, Gabriel, I'm sorry too. With everything that was happening, I believed the worst about you."

"From the sound of it, that was exactly what Vincent wanted you to believe."

"You took the appointment to office because you genuinely want to be the deputy mayor and work with me?"

Lauden releases a long exhale and settles. "Of course. I love this city, and when the chief of police wanted to endorse me, I thought being your second-in-command would be an opportunity to have a say in the decisions and ensure representation for the empowered community. I was rather pleased about it…at least until now."

Clarissa shakes her head and steps forward, offering him her hand. "Let's start again. Gabriel, I look forward to working with you. Thank you for stepping in during a difficult time. I'm sure David would be pleased to know his position is in good hands."

Gabriel takes her hand and covers it with his other hand. "Thank you, Clarissa. I'm impressed and surprised you can look beyond my status in the empowered community and welcome me."

"These are strange times, to be sure, but I have my reasons for wanting to stabilize the relations between magical and non-magical citizens of Montréal."

"Would you care to enlighten me?"

Clarissa steps back and shakes her head. "In time, perhaps. For right now, let's work on building a working relationship."

"I'd like that...very much."

Gabriel finishes making his peace with Clarissa and joins Sloan, Garnet, and me where we're standing above Vincent. I pulled the dagger a few minutes ago and tucked it away for safekeeping.

The dagger's devastation is quick, but the recovery isn't. He still looks like something you'd see in a sci-fi movie after the aliens suck all the vitality out of some poor sap.

"May I ask how he ended up in this state, Miss Cumhaill?" Gabriel points.

I shrug. "You can ask, but a girl's gotta have her secrets. Otherwise, the mystery will be gone."

He arches a brow, but thankfully, he's in no position to try to dominate me. This entire fiasco lands squarely in his camp, and he knows it.

"What will you do with him?" I study his expression.

"Don't worry about that. He'll get dealt with as any of my enemies would. No need to give you nightmares."

I chuckle. "I don't suppose that's possible. I've seen a great many horrors and still sleep like a baby."

"A baby who snores like a buzzsaw maybe," Sloan says behind me.

He's not wrong.

"He will be ended though, yes?" Garnet asks, his voice graveled and growly. "He murdered two people, and there would've been many others if Fiona hadn't pulled the plug on that riot."

Gabriel nods. "I'm relieved you did, and yes, Vincent will suffer a final death."

"Good," Mayor Clarissa says. "That may not be a politically

correct opinion, but I don't care. Two very dear friends of mine are lost forever."

"While I can't reverse that outcome," Gabriel says, "I can help you ensure something like this doesn't happen again."

Garnet rolls his eyes. "Yeah, well, we'll see. I'll be keeping tabs on Montréal. Until the key players are on vervain, and we feel confident this power play is truly over, I'll be breathing down your neck."

"Knock yourself out, Lion, but you'll be wasting your time. I've never wanted anything but for Montréal to thrive."

Red, we've got vamps in the outer office again.

I glance at where Bruin's furry brown ass is taking up the open doorway and blocking all entry into the office. "That's fine, buddy. Let them in. These should be from Lauden's seethe."

Gabriel follows my gesture to the door, and when Bruin moves and the vampires enter, he nods. "Drake, put Vincent in the trunk of the car. The rest of you remove the bodies from the outer office and use the van to deliver them to Armond. Then, come back with a steam cleaner and get to work. The mayor doesn't appreciate blood in her carpets."

They do as instructed without a word.

Gabriel gives us all a final nod and leaves.

Nikon snaps in a moment later with a very excited little girl. Isabella closes the distance between her and her mommy and hugs her tight around the waist. "I missed you, *Maman*."

Clarissa bends over her little girl and hugs her back. "Only half as much as I missed you, *ma belle*."

"Is it time to come home? Did Imari's daddy get the bad guys? She says he always gets them."

I chuckle. "You bet he did. Imari's right, her daddy always gets the bad guys, but sometimes he makes a big mess when he does it."

Bella looks at the devastation of the office, and her eyes grow wide. "Your office is broken?"

Clarissa shakes her head. "My desk is okay, and the couch and your coloring kits are fine. The rest can be fixed. The most important thing is that we're all safe, healthy, and happy."

Bella nods. "Can we go home now?"

Clarissa looks at Garnet for the answer. "Yes, sweetie. Why don't I take you and mommy home right now?"

Sloan, Manx, and I enjoy a glamored dragon ride back to Toronto, and honestly, I don't know when I've ever been happier to be home. We land in the back yard, and as much as I want to go inside, lock the doors, and isolate for a week, a promise made is a promise kept.

Pulling out my phone, I text Benjamin and invite him to meet us at his convenience.

His reply *pings* back almost instantly. *Can you come to us? We're having a moment.*

"A moment? What does that mean?" Sloan asks.

"I don't know and really don't care. The way I look at it, the sooner we return the dagger, the sooner we have a long, hot shower, get nakey, and lounge in bed for a week."

"Sold." Sloan grabs my hand, and the power of his wayfarer gift washes over us.

The two of us take form inside the first horse stall of the old carriage house of Casa Loma. When I first became acquainted with the empowered community in Toronto, I was stunned to find out that the King of the Vampire Seethes for Toronto lives with his bloodline family in the secret U-boat bunker under a historic Toronto landmark.

"Great, you're here." Benjamin jogs into the stall to join us. "I hate to be rude and show you the door, but yes, it's incredibly important I get this dagger back, and yes, it's a very bad time, and I need you to leave."

I feel the tension he's giving off, and since Benjamin has always been a bit of a dullard, I take the not-so-subtle hint. "No offense taken. Here's your dagger back with my thanks. It saved the day. We'll catch up another time when things settle down."

"Thank you for understanding."

I spin the dagger as I extend it to him and hand it over hilt-first. "Good luck with whatever you're dealing with. If you need backup, I'm here for you."

"Thank you. Much appreciated."

Sloan *poofs* us to the back door of our house, and I blink at him. "Okay, I said I didn't care, but now I'm curious. What the hell was that about?"

"No idea." He sits on the bench against the window on the back wall, bends forward to unlace his boots, and pulls them off. "I'm sure we'll find out in time, but fer tonight, I believe ye mentioned a hot shower and gettin' naked fer a few days in King Henry?"

I groan, toe off my shoes, and unstrap the sides of my vest. "Doesn't it sound decadent?"

"It does." He waits while I finish hanging up my vest. Then I release my bear. He materializes in the back hall with us and opens his mouth in a wide yawn.

"I'm with you, Bear. Consider Sloan and me off the clock. Entertain yourselves as you wish."

"A well-deserved respite, Red. Enjoy yer downtime and don't worry about a thing. Manx and I are very self-sufficient."

"Thank the goddess for that." Lifting my arms, I wrap them around Sloan's neck and rest my head against his chest. "*Poof* me upstairs, Mackenzie. Let's get this winding down started."

With that, the two of us check out of our lives.

CHAPTER TWENTY-FOUR

"Can a loft be sad that its person is gone?" Bending in the middle of the living room, I pick up two samurai swords off the floor and walk them over to the fireplace mantle in Dionysus's bachelor apartment. "It feels lonely here without him."

Sloan comes back from checking the other rooms and hugs me. "I'm sure the moment he's able to return, he'll be back. He loves ye and the life he's built with us. Him bein' gone is only about payin' a debt owed."

"I know. I just miss him."

"We all do," Nikon says, coming out of the VR room. "I hung the garlands and sent up a few prayers. He'll know we're thinking of him."

I ease the swords back into their cradles, then pick up the *Encanto* skateboard and put it over by the foyer door. "I watered his Chia Pet collection and lit the big ivory pillar candle."

"Do ye think Mother Nature might intervene on his behalf?" Sloan asks. "It's a different pantheon of magic."

"It is, but anyone who spends quality time with him loves him. If they were creation buddies back in the early days, she might put in a good word."

"Maybe we should reach out to Hel and the Norse gods too."

I nod. "That's a good idea."

"I spoke to Eros already," Nikon says. "He's going to do what he can. If not free him from whatever obligation has taken him from us, then at least put in a good word and hopefully let him know we're working on how to get him home."

"Contessa McSparkles is going to stay with Imari at the compound for now but asked that we let her know if and when we hear from him."

Nikon sets a scrambled Rubik's Cube on the top of a pyramid of other solved cubes and nods. "He'll be back. If not because he's satisfied his agreement, then maybe because he's driving them crazy."

I laugh. "Yeah, there's that."

Sloan kisses my temple. "Shall we go downstairs? The others are likely waitin' on us to begin the duty assignments."

I take another long look around the loft, and my heart aches for my sweet god of good times. "Come home as soon as you can, Tarzan. We love you."

"Welcome back to the land of the living," Andromeda says a moment later, one floor below. "How are things in the life of you? A week away. Kudos to you."

I lean against the door jamb of her office and sigh. "Other than missing Dionysus like crazy, no complaints. We spent a couple of days of private time and a couple of days in Ireland checking in with Sloan's father, my brothers, and my dad and grandparents."

"Excellent. You gotta take care of yourself if you're going to be able to take care of everyone else."

"Ain't that the truth."

"The tan's nice. I take it you got some sun?"

I hold out my arms and look at my skin. Having been gifted the pasty-white hue of my heritage, I don't tan. Usually, I burn and peel, but I did manage to get a bit of color with some SPF60.

Mostly, I got freckles.

"Your brother and Dionysus were teasing us about that last week. With all the people around me able to portal, why the hell aren't I spending more time on beaches soaking up the sun?"

"Why indeed. Just make sure Irish covers all your girl bits with lotion. Your Celtic skin can't handle a seaside lifestyle, and certain areas should never get burned."

I laugh. "Consider me warned. How about you? Any self-care moments steaming up your love life? Did you ever hook up with the hottie from the prosecutor's office you told me about?"

"Harper. Yeah, we had a bit of fun, but I'm tired of the suave and sophisticated types. Lately, I've been scoping out a different guy."

"Oh yeah? Do tell."

She flashes me a devilish grin. "It's too soon to spill. I'll keep you posted, though."

"Excellent. You do that."

"Yer new recruits are here, luv," Sloan says, leaning in behind me.

I push off the door frame and stride over to the man and woman coming inside. Without reading their files, there would be no way to know Brady is a hybrid shifter-slash-vampire and Jenna is a Siren. They both look wholly human and have lived with their true selves hidden for their entire lives.

"Hi, guys, welcome. Let me introduce you to everyone. This is Sloan Mackenzie, my fiancé. He's a druid, like me, but has a few nifty gifts the rest of us don't. Over there are my brothers Dillan and Calum, and our friend Tad."

The guys are chatting about Emmet's invitation to host a Beltane celebration on the island next week. Considering it's the one-year anniversary of his handfasting with Ciara and they aren't renewing their vow, it'll be a hard day for him.

We're all going to pitch in and make it festive.

Dillan nods. "From what Em and Brenny said, the work they've done with Sarah has had little result. They hope we can spend some time there for a Drink and Think to brainstorm how to bring the city back to life."

"Hey, guys. Can I interrupt? I want to introduce Brody and Jenna. They're starting with us today." I do a round of intros and notice Diesel stepping off the elevator.

Hurrying over to welcome him, I wait while he goes through the process of scanning in and opens the inner door. "Hey, welcome to the team. I hear it's official."

He nods. "Seems so. Thanks for getting me here. I look forward to helping where I can."

"We're looking forward to having the help."

We start to walk into the room, and he touches my arm to stop our progress. When he steps closer and leans in, I'm momentarily overwhelmed by how massive he is. "Andromeda sent my contract, but I think she might have made an error in my salary. I think there were one too many zeroes in the amount… but you once said I'd get paid way too much, so then, I wasn't sure."

I chuckle. "The first time I looked in my bank account, I almost passed out. What we do puts us in danger every day. Garnet understands that, and he rewards it in the best way possible. He gives us the tools we need to succeed and compensates us generously."

He nods. "I was sorry to hear about Atlas. I only met him the one time here, but he seemed like a good guy."

"Same. I barely knew him, but yeah, he seemed smart and dedicated. Garnet's in touch with his parents and will find out how we can pay our respects if that's something you're interested in."

"Yeah, let me know. I'd like that."

"All right, everyone," Maxwell says, gesturing at the conference table where he and Garnet have the day's assignments set out. "We're ready to begin."

We take our seats.

"How are things looking, Max?" I ask.

"Good, actually. I spoke to Mayor Tremblay in Montréal an hour ago, and she is singing the praises of our team. She sends all of you her deepest thanks and wants us to know that Rene Michaud has agreed to step up and form a fae response team with her. I've sent them the objectives package we came up with and told them we'll be happy to help however we can."

"Excellent. What about Jules? Did she mention if his partner Jules was going to be part of that team?"

Max shakes his head. "She didn't mention anyone else, but that doesn't mean anything. I'm sure we'll get updates as things progress."

"What about Chief Monet? Was him being a specist completely a compulsion thing, or was he already a fae hater before Vincent got to him?"

"From what I gather, it was a mixture of the two."

"I'm sure being compelled and made into a puppet won't improve his position."

"No, but Mayor Tremblay is aware of his prejudice now. With the federal mandates we put in place to protect the rights of fae-born citizens and those awakened, she and her liaison team will ensure no one suffers because of small-mindedness."

"*Noice.*" Calum reaches for the raspberry strudels in the center of the table. "Mark Montréal in the win column."

"One city down, four hundred to go," Dillan says.

I laugh. "We still need to follow up on what the crescent birthmark on Isabella's forehead means."

"Myra's looking into that." Garnet's chair *creaks* as he leans back. "She doesn't want to alarm anyone, but she is concerned."

"Does it have to be a bad omen?" I ask.

"Not bad. Just serious," Garnet corrects. "Historically, the crescent fae are chosen in times of great need. They are guides to the way through a dangerous course."

"She's six years old," I say.

"That's what has Myra most worried."

"So, what do we do?"

He shrugs. "That's what we don't know. Time will tell, I suppose."

I don't love that theory. Isabella is a sweet girl. I don't want her tangled up in some crazy fae destiny she neither understands nor is prepared for.

Time will tell. I draw a deep breath and exhale. "All right, I guess we wait and see. Eyes on the horizon. Max, any chance the world is settling down?"

Max pegs me with a wide smile. "Not yet, but one day when you ask me that, I'll be able to say yes."

"I look forward to that day."

"You and me both."

"What about on the home front?" I ask. "Where are we on the Green Guardian problem?"

Garnet chuffs. "I've got eyes on Bivin and plan to infiltrate their organization. It's one thing to want to patrol streets and act as another set of eyes but an entirely different thing to be species profiling and targeting law-abiding citizens."

"So, you're sending someone undercover?"

"Two people. I trust them to be both discreet and convincing. The fact that the Green Guardians came up with a device that can block portaling is alarming. I had a magi-tech pull the device I confiscated apart, and he says it's a brilliant piece of technology blended with very focused magic intent."

"That pisses you off more, why?"

"Because if it was half-assed, I would assume they're still a bunch of adrenaline-pumping egomaniacs looking for a thrill."

"But they're not."

"No. My guy says the device shows not only innovative thinking but likely a couple of years of research and development."

"Years? That's long before we knew about any of this. That means it's not related to the fall of the veil at all. It was premeditated."

"Exactly."

"Well, shit," Tad says. "The plot thickens."

"Let me worry about that," Garnet says. "For now, we proceed as planned and focus on safeguarding the new world while we try to get that fucking veil back up."

I draw a deep breath and return my attention to Maxwell. "Okay, Max. What have you got for us?"

He opens a file folder and removes a group of photos. "Here's what we know. Two days ago, San Francisco vanished. No bridge, no cable cars, no Alcatraz. At first, the military kept it quiet hoping it would magically reappear."

"It hasn't?"

He shakes his head. "As far as anyone can tell, it's not there anymore."

"Bullshit." Dillan pulls the photos closer so he can have a look. "There's no way an entire city can be there one day and gone the next. It has to be a glamor."

"That's what we thought too, but so far, we have no idea who would have enough power to do something like this or why. What's the end game?"

I have no idea. "I take it we're heading to California?"

Garnet nods. "Yeah. Find that city, Fi, and if it's within your power, put things back the way they were."

I laugh at the craziness of his request. "Yeah, sure, I'm on it. San Francisco here I come."

ENDNOTE

Thank you for reading *Mayhem in Montréal*, book 1 in the Case Files of the Urban Druid. While the story is fresh in your mind, and as a favor to Michael and me, please click HERE and tell other readers what you thought.

A quick star rating and/or one sentence can mean so much to readers deciding whether to try a book, series, or a new-to-them author.

Thank you.

If you want more of Clan Cumhaill, continue with book two of the Case Files of an Urban Druid and claim your copy of *Sorcery in San Francisco*.

AUTHOR NOTES - AUBURN TEMPEST

JUNE 1, 2022

Mayhem in Montréal is literally in the books. It was tough to write a first in series book for one audience and a book sixteen for those of you who have been with us since the beginning.

I hope the final story filled both columns with minimal confusion. If you're still a bit lost, hang in there, I'll work to catch you up. Or, even better, read the first fifteen books if you haven't already and see how we got from there to here.

Start with *A Gilded Cage*.

I'm not sure if you noticed but the first pages of the book included a list of characters and how they fit into the story. There are a couple of pronunciations there as well.

So, where are we?

Chronicles of an Urban Druid is complete. Thank you so much for the amazing reviews and comments about the wrap-up of the series. I was anxious to ensure I hit all the feels. I wanted to both end it on a high note and give us somewhere to go moving forward. I hope that came through to you.

Case Files of an Urban Druid has begun. *Yay!* I'm writing book two and have lots planned there. I think going to different towns around the world will be fun for all of us.

Chronicles of an Urban Elemental is in progress as well. You've now met Jules Gagne the female lead who will kick off the new series. She promises to be a fun character to write. I'm working on book two of that series with character crossovers from Fi and the Fam Jam.

Tons of fun coming your way.

Stay tuned.

If you want to say hi and talk about the books, you can join us on the Chronicles of an Urban Druid Facebook page: https://www.facebook.com/groups/167165864237006

Or feel free to drop us a line: UrbanDruid@lmbpn.com

Slainte Mhath,
Auburn Tempest

AUTHOR NOTES - MICHAEL ANDERLE

JUNE 6, 2022

Thank you for not only reading this book but these author notes as well!

Just a few days ago, Auburn Tempest and I spoke while at the 20Booksto50K™ event held in Madrid. On Saturday, she mentioned she had 9,000 words to go to finish this story and that she knew I was going to be on her case about the words that were due Monday.

Then Sunday, she mentions she is down to 5,000 words.

I sent her a message that I WAS paying attention to her, and I remembered she had words to finish.

Would she get them to me in time? Would Madrid's siren call weave its ugly web around her typing fingers and string them along until she missed the due date?

Well, would it?

The answer is 'no.' She dropped them to me WAY in time (I had little doubt, I admit), and everything is right in the world.

Have you read Chronicles of an Urban Druid?

If you are jonesing for the next Case Files book but HAVE

NOT read about this clan before, check out the Chronicles Books here:

Book One - A Gilded Cage

Where am I?

I am presently in Seville, Spain, for business reasons. The city is fantastic, and a heartfelt thanks to Heidi Heinz for setting up a wonderful tour on the roof of the largest gothic cathedral in the world – Cathedral de Seville. Even if I almost died from the many steep stairs going up and up and up...

I'm not in shape, but pretty sure the medicine I'm on did me in. At least, I'd like to believe it is the medicine and not the fact I could lose 30 pounds and not notice (except for the clothes.)

Of course, as we are about to arrive at the cathedral, I casually mention I have a bit of High-Anxiety. I forgot that acknowledging that little tidbit maybe five minutes before arriving could cause Heidi to stare at me in shock and dread thinking she had set me up for a death-defying tour. I didn't mean that I was insanely scared of heights or anything, and I was fine the whole time I was on the roof.

Well, except for the almost passing out from heat exhaustion because it's insanely hot in Seville.

Oops? Sorry for scaring you, Heidi.

Talk to you in the next story!

Ad Aeternitatem,

Michael Anderle

MORE STORIES with Michael newsletter HERE:
https://michael.beehiiv.com/

BOOKS BY AUBURN TEMPEST

Auburn Tempest - Urban Fantasy Action/Adventure

Chronicles of an Urban Druid

Book 1 – A Gilded Cage

Book 2 – A Sacred Grove

Book 3 – A Family Oath

Book 4 – A Witch's Revenge

Book 5 – A Broken Vow

Book 6 – A Druid Hexed

Book 7 – An Immortal's Pain

Book 8 – A Shaman's Power

Book 9 – A Fated Bond

Book 10 – A Dragon's Dare

Book 11 – A God's Mistake

Book 12 – A Destiny Unlocked

Book 13 – A United Front

Book 14 – A Culling Tide

Book 15 – A Danger Destroyed

Case Files of an Urban Druid

Book 1 – Mayhem in Montréal

Book 2 – Sorcery in San Francisco

Chronicles of an Urban Elemental

Coming soon…

If you enjoy my writing and read sexy/steamy romance, my pen name for the books I write in Paranormal and Fantasy Romance is JL Madore. You can find me on Amazon.

BOOKS BY MICHAEL ANDERLE

Sign up for the LMBPN email list to be notified of new releases and special deals!

https://lmbpn.com/email/

For a complete list of books by Michael Anderle, please visit:

www.lmbpn.com/ma-books/

CONNECT WITH THE AUTHORS

Connect with Auburn

Amazon, Facebook, Newsletter

Web page – www.jlmadore.com

Email – AuburnTempestWrites@gmail.com

Connect with Michael Anderle and sign up for his email list here:

Website: http://lmbpn.com

Email List: http://lmbpn.com/email/

https://www.facebook.com/LMBPNPublishing

https://twitter.com/lmbpn

https://www.instagram.com/lmbpn_publishing/

https://www.bookbub.com/authors/michael-anderle

www.ingramcontent.com/pod-product-compliance
Lightning Source LLC
LaVergne TN
LVHW041755060526
838201LV00046B/1010